Was she losing her mind?

Courtney turned around just as a man entered the room. His expression was neither hostile nor friendly.

"You wanted to see me?"

"Oh, no," Courtney said, finding it difficult to speak. "The housekeeper must have misunderstood. I need to speak to Justin Tanner."

His look held a touch of impatience. "I'm Justin Tanner. What do you want?"

"No," she said. "You can't be Justin. Justin is my husband."

"I can assure you that I've managed to be Justin Tanner for the past thirty-five years. And my wife is dead."

Dear God, Courtney thought, *so this is what it means to be insane.*

JASMINE CRESSWELL

CHASE *the* PAST

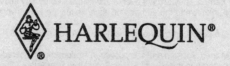

HARLEQUIN®

TORONTO • NEW YORK • LONDON
AMSTERDAM • PARIS • SYDNEY • HAMBURG
STOCKHOLM • ATHENS • TOKYO • MILAN • MADRID
PRAGUE • WARSAW • BUDAPEST • AUCKLAND

ISBN 0-373-47053-3

CHASE THE PAST

Copyright © 1987 by Jasmine Cresswell

This edition published by arrangement with Harlequin Books S.A.

® and TM are trademarks of the publisher. Trademarks indicated with
® are registered in the United States Patent and Trademark Office, the
Canadian Trade Marks Office and in other countries.

www.eHarlequin.com

Printed in U.S.A.

ABOUT THE AUTHOR

Jasmine Cresswell was born in England, and early in her career worked for the foreign office. Later she was assigned to the British Embassy in Rio de Janeiro, where she met her husband, another expatriate Briton. Jasmine believes that writing is the only profession she can take with her anywhere in the world, and she has lived in nine different places in three countries. Currently she resides in Denver with her husband and four children.

CAST OF CHARACTERS

Courtney Long—The truth was locked in her subconscious.

Justin Tanner—He had to find out who had impersonated him.

Amelia Norris—What role had she really played in Courtney's childhood?

Jane Grislechy—She might know too much for her own good.

Harvey Nicholson—He was determined to put the past to rest.

Pauline Powers—Could she give Courtney the right answers?

Prologue

The May sun shone with mocking brilliance on the crowd of mourners gathered at the grave side in Queens. Dry-eyed, grief stricken beyond tears, Justin Tanner watched the priest scatter a symbolic handful of dust over his wife's coffin. He gritted his teeth, willing himself not to scream.

Beneath the singsong murmur of the final prayers, he could hear his mother-in-law sobbing. For the past three days he'd been wishing that he could cry, but that minor release still seemed denied him. Grief tore at him until he was swamped by pain, unbearable in its intensity. Why did it have to be Linda? Sweet, gentle Linda, who in her entire twenty-nine years had brought only laughter and love into the lives of everyone who knew her. It was unfair that she had been forced to suffer.... It was unbearable that she had died.

His sister-in-law, Helen, touched him on the arm, and he realized the funeral service was over. Over. He would never see Linda again, not even submerged beneath those hideous life-support machines that had dominated their last few weeks together. The realization was too painful to tolerate, and he thrust the hurt deep into a corner of his soul. Numbness gradually crept along his limbs, wiping out the pain. Oh, God, the blessed relief of feeling nothing! Please God, he prayed silently, let me never feel anything again.

He commanded his feet to walk away from the flower-

smothered grave. When he stopped walking, he realized he
had arrived at the entrance to the cemetery. The entire Padechowski family—Linda's parents, her grandmother, her
brothers, her sisters and their husbands—had arranged themselves in a supportive group around him. With detached envy
he realized that every one of them was crying: noisy, gut-
wrenching, *healthy* tears, which would eventually allow them
to accept Linda's death as a natural, inevitable end to living.

His mother-in-law turned and hugged him. She grieved for
her daughter's death, but Justin knew that she derived comfort from her faith and from her unshakable conviction that
Linda was now safe in the hands of her Maker. Not for the
first time, Justin found himself regretting his New England
heritage of cool rationality and intellectualized religion. If
only the aching dryness in his throat would go away, so he
could yell out his anger at the injustice of it all.

Justin's father, looking every inch the successful Boston
banker, came up and shook Justin's hand. His mother, elegant
as usual, followed behind. They said, rather helplessly, that
they were very sorry. Justin made some polite response, sigh-
ing with relief when his father announced that he needed to
get back to Boston, unless Justin wanted him to stay.

Justin assured him that he didn't. "Good man." His father
clapped him awkwardly on the shoulder. "The British have
the right idea, my boy. What's finished is finished. Stiff upper
lip, chin up and all that. Life must go on."

"Certainly, Father. What else?"

In a rare display of emotion, Mrs. Tanner squeezed her
son's hand. "Take care, Justin, my dear. We'll be thinking
of you."

She caught up with her husband, and they moved with
stately dignity toward one of the waiting limousines. Their
place in the line was taken by the next in an unending stream
of Padechowski relatives. After the relatives came the friends.
Surely there had to be a hundred of Linda's colleagues wait-

ing to offer their condolences. Justin wasn't really surprised. Linda's effervescent warmth had always attracted people into the magic circle of her friendship. Her loyalty had invariably kept them there.

Justin glanced down the line of waiting mourners. It didn't seem to be any shorter. The director of the soap opera on which Linda had played a nurse-with-a-heart-of-gold was now approaching. What the devil was his name? Harvey. Harvey Nicholson, that was it. Linda had always said he was a terrific director who ought to be making feature films, not fiddling around with daytime television. Justin had accepted her professional judgment, although personally he didn't much like the man.

Harvey's expression was lugubrious as he clasped Justin's hand. "A terrible thing. A terrible loss for us all. Linda was a great actress and a wonderful human being."

Harvey always spoke in clichés, Justin thought. Still, at funerals, how else could you speak?

"Thank you for coming," Justin said. "I appreciate your taking the time." The man didn't move on, and Justin sought for something else to say. "I wasn't expecting to see you, Harvey. Somebody on the show told me you were out of town. Taking an extended vacation."

"I was in Mexico," Harvey murmured. "But naturally I came back to pay my last respects to Linda."

"Glad you could make it." God, he sounded like the host at a cocktail party. With a surge of panic, Justin realized that his numbness was starting to wear off. The blazing sun, unusually strong this early in the year, beat down mercilessly. He was drowning, choking in the heat.

He turned blindly toward his parents-in-law, knowing that twenty or thirty people still waited to speak to him. "I have to go," he said, bending down to kiss his mother-in-law. "I'm sorry, Mom and Dad. I'll be in Aspen if you need me. Call anytime."

He left the cemetery almost at a run.

HARVEY NICHOLSON WATCHED him go, his handsome features shadowed with sympathy. "He'll soon get his act together up in the mountains," he remarked to the Padechowskis. "Personally I've always found Aspen a wonderful pace for solving my problems."

Mr. Padechowski murmured some response, then turned to greet the next group of mourners.

Harvey was frowning as he left the cemetery. Linda's funeral had brought home to him the wonderful, *clean* finality of death, although, of course, he was sorry that dear little Linda happened to be the person getting buried today. If there were any justice in the world, it would have been Ferne's daughter who contracted the fatal illness, not Linda. Linda had been an innocuous little thing, all cheery laughter and not too many brains. Ferne's daughter was a different kettle of fish altogether, too damn bright for her own good.

He strolled toward his waiting car at a suitably sedate pace, but the sweat collected in two rivulets along the side of his jaw. Yes, there was no denying that death would have been the neatest solution to his problem. Should he have taken the ultimate step with Ferne's daughter? Acknowledged her letter, perhaps, and then simply disposed of her in the nearest empty building lot? An inelegant solution, but wonderfully *final*.

In retrospect he was beginning to think that he had allowed the softness of his heart to get the better of his common sense. The trouble was, the wretched girl looked too much like her mother. When she stared up at him with those huge, violet eyes, he sometimes found his heart racing with the rhythms of a passion that he thought had been dead for the past twenty-two years.

The studio chauffeur swung open the door of the Mercedes, and Harvey sank gratefully into the air-conditioned comfort of his car. This funeral was playing tricks with his nerves. Really, there was nothing in the world that could go wrong with his plans. He'd covered all the potential problems with his usual masterly attention to detail.

He glanced down at his watch. Twelve-thirty. They'd had her for a week now, almost to the hour. He wondered if she was still in one of the high-risk confinement areas, or if they'd moved her out into one of the semiprivate rooms. The rooms were perfectly comfortable. He'd checked them out personally, just to reassure himself. Perhaps, in a few years or so, they might even let her out. Anyway, the decision was out of his hands now. Best not to dwell on it. She wasn't mad, of course, but she deserved to be locked up. She was a whore at heart, just like her mother. Just like his mother. Hadn't his father taught him years ago that all women were whores?

Harvey pressed an immaculate handkerchief to his brow, pursing his lips in distaste when it came away damp with sweat. He dropped the offending handkerchief onto the floor, then leaned forward. "Take me to Rockefeller Center, please. I've decided to have lunch there."

"Yes, sir."

He'd have Dover sole and a good French Chablis, Harvey decided, closing his eyes in pleasurable anticipation. Slavs were so appallingly emotional. Ethnic gatherings were not his favorite scene. The view from the Rainbow Room Grill was spectacular, and he deserved a reward after putting himself through the exhausting misery of a Polish funeral.

If he had to go to a funeral, pity it hadn't been for Ferne's daughter.

Chapter One

An aide wheeled the bedtime snacks into the patients' lounge at eleven minutes past ten, six minutes behind schedule. Courtney had counted out every second of the delay, and her body was dewed with sweat from the effort of keeping her face expressionless and her eyes fixed quietly on the flickering TV screen.

"Evening, everybody," the aide said. "How are we all doing tonight?"

With quick, efficient movements she flipped out a side of the cart to form a serving tray, seemingly unperturbed when her remarks were greeted by a stony silence.

She'd worked around crazy people long enough to know that some nights you could wait forever and still not get a word out of any of them. Other nights you couldn't stop them talking. On the whole she was just as happy when they were in one of their silent moods. It usually meant that she got through her rounds that much quicker.

She unscrewed the cap from the gallon jug of apple juice. "Ready when you are, Nurse," the aide called out cheerfully.

Courtney forced her gaze back to the television and gradually uncurled her fingers, placing her hands on her knees in a careful parody of relaxation. Only one more hour and it would be lights-out. Only two more hours and it would be time to try her escape.

She shut her eyes quickly, afraid of what they might reveal. Dear God, she hadn't even meant to think the word *escape*. It was far too dangerous. The staff members at the Walnut Park Mental Health Institute—known to the locals simply as the Nuthouse—were trained to spot unusual tension in their patients, and tonight of all nights, she had to avoid giving them any cause to watch her more closely than usual.

Courtney concentrated on making her body limp and her mind a blank. Starting at her big toes, she moved mentally up her body, carefully visualizing her muscle structure and willing the wire-taut muscles to unwind. It was a technique she had used before all her big races, and sometimes even here she managed to make it work.

On the periphery of her consciousness, she was aware that the night nurse was already walking briskly around the room, dispensing the inevitable pre-bedtime medication. Courtney shifted her chair, moving out of the nurse's line of vision. Nurse Buxton's heavy horn-rimmed glasses concealed eyes that were uncomfortably perceptive, and her nose for troublemakers was perilously acute. She had already come over once and asked Courtney how she was feeling. Courtney, clamping down hard on the terror swelling inside her, had replied that she was feeling wonderful.

For a moment Courtney considered postponing her escape until another night, a night when fluttery little Nurse Matlock was on duty, perhaps. After twenty-one weeks shut up with Colorado's looniest, one day more or less no longer seemed all that significant. Her priorities had certainly changed since that mind-blowing morning when she had first woken up and found herself locked in a windowless room with only a mattress for furniture. That morning she had wanted nothing except to be let out. She had pounded on the walls, screaming hysterically for Justin, begging for her freedom. What she had gotten was an overworked psychiatric nurse and a hefty shot of phenobarbital.

Now, after five months of imprisonment, she wanted more than simple freedom; she wanted answers to a hundred questions. Most of all she wanted to know what had happened to Justin, and why he had never been to visit her.

No, she couldn't wait any longer to make her escape. Unless she went tonight, she didn't have a hope in hell of getting away with the petty-cash box she had stolen from the head nurse's office. And without money she wouldn't have a chance of making it all the way from Denver to Aspen. At best she might have three hours before the night staff realized she was missing. Three hours before every police patrol car in the state would be looking for her. No, she definitely needed money, which meant that Nurse Buxton or not, she would never have a better chance to escape than tonight.

Courtney glanced down and saw that her hands had once again curled into two tight fists. She forced herself to open them. Her mental discipline seemed to be increasingly shaky, and her gaze turned toward the snack trolley. Nurse Buxton handed a paper cup of pills and an accompanying cup of water to young Bill Di Maggio. The nurse conducted a few minutes of one-sided conversation, then moved on to the next patient. The aide trotted along in her wake, collecting the empty pill cups and rewarding the patients with chocolate-chip cookies and plastic mugs of chilled apple cider. There was no glass or china on the tray, of course, in case one of the inmates should suddenly be overcome with an urge to do violence either to himself or to one of the other patients.

The trolley had just reached Courtney's side when Mrs. Anthony—stage name Adrienna Antonio—stood up in the center of the room, carefully balanced a cushion on top of her head and launched into the opening chords of an operatic aria. It was the "Jewel Song" from Gounod's *Faust*, Courtney realized. Mrs. Anthony, despite her obvious preoccupation with keeping the cushion balanced on her head, was singing it brilliantly.

Most of the patients glanced, uninterested, toward the singer, then continued to munch on their chocolate-chip cookies. Freddy Sternham, however, was trying to watch the weather forecast on Channel Four, and he let out a howl of outrage when Mrs. Anthony's soaring notes began to drown out the newscaster's promise of unusually warm weather for mid-October. "Shut up, you crazy old bag! Or I'll shut your mouth for you."

The cushion tumbled from Mrs. Anthony's head, and there was a moment of silence as she bent, with great dignity, to pick it up. As soon as the cushion was in place again, she resumed her impassioned swoop toward high C.

Freddy's chair crashed onto the floor as he jumped up, fists clenched and arms swinging wildly. "Stupid old cow! Didn't you hear what I told you?" he screamed.

An orderly grabbed him before he had taken more than a couple of steps, forcing him back into his chair and scolding him like a recalcitrant child. Nurse Buxton tapped Mrs. Anthony firmly on her shoulder. "It's time to have our cookies and apple cider now. You must stop singing at once, please."

Mrs. Anthony seemed to recognize the cool voice of authority. She stopped her aria in midphrase and sat down obediently in her chair, clutching the cushion. Nurse Buxton returned to Courtney, checked her prescription sheet and handed over the appropriate little package of pills. "Enjoying the television program, Ms Long?" she asked.

Courtney had long since given up telling the hospital staff that she was married and that her married name was Mrs. Tanner. There were some battles, she had found, that it just wasn't possible to win.

She wiped her sweat-slick hand on her slacks and accepted the pills. "I guess it's okay," she mumbled, deliberately avoiding the nurse's eyes. "But they never report any of the good news." She put the pills in her mouth, using her tongue to shove them up high inside her cheek, then drank two or three sips of tepid water. "All gone." She looked up toward the nurse, stretching her lips into the blank, apathetic smile she had been perfecting over the past two weeks, ever since she first started planning her escape.

Nurse Buxton's gaze narrowed, and Courtney realized that somehow her body language had betrayed her, but just at that moment, Mrs. Anthony unleashed a fresh burst of song.

The aide clucked her tongue impatiently. "Let's do her next, Nurse," she said. "Otherwise she'll get this lot all on edge just when you want them to settle down for the night. Lord love us, has that woman ever got a pair of lungs on her."

"All right." Nurse Buxton cast one final, quick glance at Courtney, then walked rapidly toward Walnut Park's most famous inmate. "Mrs. Anthony, you have to behave yourself if you want your juice and cookies."

Courtney pulled a tissue from the pocket of her slacks and raised it to her face. Pretending to blow her nose, she spat out the three pills Nurse Buxton had given her. The blue one was a sleeping pill, she knew, and she thought the others were probably antidepressants of some sort. The state of Colorado required that mental patients should be well cared for. It didn't require that they should know what medication they were being forced to take.

Courtney rolled the tissue into a tight ball, with the pills as a hard center, and quickly pushed it into the pocket of her slacks. In a minute she would make her way to the bathroom and flush the pills down the toilet. During the past two weeks, one way or another she had gotten rid of all the pills the psychiatrists kept prescribing for her. It was amazing how much more coherently her brain seemed to function.

Her heart raced wildly as she smoothed out the creases in her slacks, then clasped her hands neatly together in her lap. Please God, she thought, turning her gaze in the direction of the television screen, let this next half hour be over soon, otherwise I think I really will go mad.

AT LAST THE hospital floor was quiet. Even Mrs. Anthony, Courtney's opera-singing roommate, had finally fallen into a deep, drug-induced sleep. Courtney fought back the urge to spring out of bed and dash for the nearest exit. She estimated that it would be another twenty minutes before Nurse Buxton made her final routine check on all the patients. After that, during the dead hours between midnight and three a.m., the night nurse usually checked on individual rooms only if she was summoned or if she heard some noise that warranted investigation. Courtney was determined that tonight Nurse Buxton would hear nothing unusual from room 10B.

She lay back on her pillows and stared at the window. Through the thin curtains she could see blurred shadows cast by the elegant wrought-iron grille that completely covered the shatterproof glass. Her mouth twisted in an ironic grimace. Nothing as crude as metal bars for Walnut Park, but the fancy scrollwork was every bit as effective.

In the early days of her confinement, she had sometimes filled the long, dark stretches of the night by asking herself how a perfectly normal, twenty-six-year-old ski instructor had managed to end up in a state-approved, maximum-security mental hospital. Unfortunately she had never managed to come up with a satisfactory answer.

She understood the mechanics of the system by now—she even understood how her own obstinate refusal to admit to the "facts" documented in the doctors' files made it impossible for them to campaign for her release. When she first awoke in Walnut Park, she felt as though she had wandered into some surrealistic world where nobody perceived the same reality she did. It took several weeks before she finally stopped screaming that she was perfectly sane and that they had to let her out of this crazy place *right now*. In this calmer state, she realized that somehow the system had made a monumental mistake, and the doctors were no more responsible for the error than she was. Her common sense returned, and she decided to stop protesting everything the professional staff did. What she needed, she realized belatedly, was to work *with* the doctors to secure her release.

The senior psychiatrist listened with great politeness to her carefully reasoned explanation as to why a terrible mistake had been made. Then he placed his fingertips neatly together and peered at her over his glasses. "You remember, Courtney, I've explained this to you before. The state of Colorado requires at least three expert witnesses and a hearing in front of a judge before anybody can be committed to a mental institution against their will. You had your hearing, with a qualified psychologist testifying as to your mental state and with an excellent lawyer to represent you. Judge Brown is extremely conscientious, and he listened carefully to all the evidence before ordering you to be committed to our care. In view of Judge Brown's decision, it would require another legal hearing to get you released."

"That's not really a problem," Courtney said, refusing to give way to depression. "You can get me another court hearing, can't you?" She had even tried to joke. "It probably only means you need to fill out a million forms, give or take a few hundred."

"A new hearing wouldn't do you any good, Courtney, I'm afraid."

"Why not? I'd explain to them how they've made a mistake, and you could tell them that they've made a mistake—"

He interrupted her, his voice kind and rather sad. "The trouble is, Courtney, I might not be able to tell them that."

She drew in her breath sharply. "You mean...you mean you agree with Judge Brown? You think I'm crazy?"

"I don't like to use that word. I don't think it's helpful to either of us. Perhaps we should say that I don't think you're quite ready to face up to the world outside these doors. We hope—''

She cut him off. ''How long before I get another hearing, one where I can testify?''

''When we think you're ready to be released, *we* request the hearing. Your job is to concentrate on getting well.''

''I *am* well. It's the system that's screwed up.''

He took off his glasses and looked at her steadily out of kindly gray eyes. ''My dear, don't you think it's time you stopped worrying about when you'll get out of here, and started thinking about how you can help to make yourself a stronger and healthier person?''

It took two months of black despair before Courtney pulled herself together sufficiently to realize that since the doctors would not help her to leave legally, she had to escape illegally. She knew that she had to get back to Aspen—and to Justin. There was no other way for her to find out what nightmare she had unwittingly wandered into.

There were so many puzzles, so many frightening gaps in her memory. She had been ill, of course; she remembered that distinctly. In fact, she'd been ill almost from the moment she and Justin were married. She'd woken up on the morning of their wedding day with acute stomach cramps, and by the time their plane landed in Mexico City, she'd already thrown up twice.

Her infuriating illness had turned their honeymoon into a full-scale fiasco. Courtney doubted that many new husbands would have been as sweet and understanding as Justin. She told him as much as she lay prostrate in their lovely glass-and-wood bedroom, only hours after their return to Aspen.

''Don't worry about it, darling, it's probably some horrid Mexican bug.'' Justin pushed her long, fair hair out of her eyes, not seeming to care that it was lank and greasy, or that her face was white and unattractively pasty.

"But why do I feel so sick? Justin, I'm *never* ill, I don't understand...."

"I don't understand either, sweetheart. If only I hadn't insisted on going to Acapulco for our wedding trip. I know you'd really have preferred somewhere in Europe."

"I just wish I hadn't ruined it all."

"Darling, you didn't ruin anything. Now stop worrying and concentrate on getting better."

"I expected to spend a lot of time in bed, but not with you playing nursemaid!" She smiled weakly, sipping the cool fruit juice he had brought her. It tasted awful, but she didn't like to tell him so. The illness seemed to have affected her taste buds.

He took the glass and set it carefully on the nightstand. "Courtney, dearest, you have to stop feeling guilty because you picked up a touch of Montezuma's revenge. I'm a grown man, not a college boy, and sex isn't the only thing on my mind. You're my wife, and we have the rest of our lives to make love to each other. What difference do a couple of weeks make one way or the other? When you're better we'll make love, and it will be wonderful, you'll see."

She was comforted by his words, although secretly she felt a little uncomfortable that ten days after the wedding ceremony, their marriage remained unconsummated. Originally she had been touched when he hadn't pressed her to go to bed with him, flattered by his courtly, old-world charm. In retrospect she wished they'd gone to bed together before the wedding. In this day and age, it felt faintly absurd to be married to somebody she'd never made love to.

Her mysterious illness never seemed to get any better. At first she told herself she had nothing more than an upset stomach. After all, everybody knew that Mexican food could wreak havoc with North American digestive systems. But she was really worried when an entire week passed after their return to Aspen and she hardly ever felt well enough to get out of bed. Apart from a few childish bouts with winter coughs and colds and the broken leg that had ended her hopes of a spot on the U.S. Olympic ski team, she had never been sick in her entire life.

Justin was so concerned that he finally called in his personal physician, who diagnosed an upset stomach and recommended lots of bed rest and fluids. Courtney hadn't liked to complain to Justin, who was obviously beside himself with worry over her condition, but she hadn't really found his doctor very competent. He had smelled strongly of whiskey, even though it was the middle of the morning. Still, at least Justin's doctor had been prepared to make house calls. Courtney wasn't sure that she had enough energy to get into a car and drive fifteen or twenty miles to her own doctor's office.

She spent her last few days of freedom confined to bed. The nausea, thank God, had finally gone away, but she felt so weak and exhausted that all she wanted to do was sleep. In the rare moments when she was awake, she often thought that it was only Justin's nursing that kept her from giving up the struggle completely.

When she tried to recall the events of that final morning with Justin, it was as if she was watching an old, faded movie unwinding behind a thick cloud of dust. Every so often a wind would blow the dust away, and she would have a freeze-frame image of startling clarity. These isolated images, however, told her almost nothing she needed to know.

She saw herself lying on the floor of their elegant, sea-green bathroom—with Justin bending over her. For some reason she had been terrified and had shrunken away from him.

Justin had been distraught by her reaction, of course. He had hustled her into his imported white Jaguar, his normally gentle hands rough with urgency. "Darling," he was saying. "We must get you to a doctor."

She saw the the judge's chambers and heard her own voice repeating mindlessly over and over again, "But where's the doctor? Where's the doctor who's going to make me feel well again?''

Then there was nothing, not even the most blurred of images, until she woke up alone in the Walnut Park isolation wing and looked down to find her wrists padded with two thick bandages.

When she asked the nurses what the bandages were for, they stared at her pityingly and didn't answer. It wasn't until hours later that the doctor unwound the bandages and showed her the two neat rows of stitches. Then she realized what had happened. Somebody had slashed her wrists.

''I didn't do it!'' she said to the doctor quickly, and—as she realized later—far too forcefully. ''You must believe me. I've been ill, my stomach's been upset, but I didn't do this!''

He spoke soothingly. Everybody in Walnut Park spoke soothingly except when they were barking out orders. ''Don't upset yourself right now, Ms Long. There'll be lots of time for us to talk about this later.''

''But you don't understand! Somebody else must have done it! We have to find out who's trying to kill me!'' She was still crying and protesting when the doctor pressed a button on his desk and the orderlies came to carry her back to her room.

When she was alone, she wept silently into her pillow, not because the doctor hadn't believed her, but because she wondered—for one black, terrifying moment—if maybe he was telling her the truth.

COURTNEY HEARD THE soft pad of Nurse Buxton's footsteps and rolled over onto her side, turning her head away from the door. The beam of the flashlight flicked briefly over Mrs. Anthony, then danced more slowly over Courtney's bed. Half a lifetime seemed to pass before the light was extinguished and Nurse Buxton's footsteps faded into the distance.

Courtney counted slowly to five thousand, then sat up in

bed and pushed off the covers. She had kept on her bra and panties under her nightgown, so it was only a question of pulling on the gray slacks she had been wearing earlier and adding a navy-blue shirt with a thick matching sweater. The somber colors should fade into the tree-shaded darkness of the hospital grounds. Her sneakers, unfortunately, were new and gleaming white, which meant that they would catch the attention of anybody who chanced to look in her direction. But if she could just get out the main building, there shouldn't be any problem.

Once she had started to study the hospital security systems, Courtney had realized that even at Walnut Park, where the fees were astronomical, funds didn't stretch to paying night watchmen to patrol the boundaries. The twenty acres of grounds were secured by an electronic alarm system, backed up by a few human guards.

She dressed one of her pillows in her discarded nightgown, then arranged it as best she could under the covers of her bed. It might deceive Nurse Buxton on her next routine inspection, although Courtney doubted it.

She opened the door of her nightstand with exquisite care and extracted the stolen cash box. She had already picked the lock—surprisingly easy to do with a bent paper clip—and now she took out the hundred and three dollars of petty cash, stuffing the notes quickly into the front of her bra. Ironic to think that this relatively small sum was so important to her when the bank in New Hampshire was holding a million-dollar trust fund in her name.

Holding her breath, Courtney slid the box onto the shelf and closed the door of the nightstand. It was the first time in her life that she had ever stolen anything, and she was amazed at how little guilt she felt. Desperation performed strange tricks with a person's conscience.

Her stomach was already lurching, and she clutched her arms around her waist, trying to squeeze herself back into a state of calm. *Face it, kid,* she told herself. *You were definitely not cut out for a life of high adventure.*

Courtney took another quick look around the bedroom, then realized she was only delaying the moment when she would have to step out into the corridor. She had no illusions about what would happen if Nurse Buxton caught her trying to escape. A week of solitary confinement would be the best she could hope for. Courtney wasn't certain that she had the mental reserves to emerge unscathed from another week of blank walls and endless silence.

She drew in a deep breath, focusing her concentration as if poised at the top of a hill, about to plunge into the disciplined free-fall of a championship slalom course. Then she exhaled and stepped out into the corridor.

Nurse Buxton was talking on the phone. Courtney heard the low murmur of the nurse's voice and offered up a brief prayer of thanks. Half the lights were kept burning all night, so there was no point in pressing herself against the walls, but she found herself instinctively searching for the pools of shadow between the fluorescent strips. She walked quickly, soundlessly on the balls of her feet. By the time she reached the emergency exit, her blood was drumming so loudly in her ears that she could hear nothing else. Her breath came in huge, gasping pants as though she had expended vast amounts of physical energy. Fear, she realized abstractedly, was an exhausting emotion.

The emergency exit was always kept unlocked, but a sensor system set off an alarm whenever the door opened. Courtney had pulled out the wires just before dinner, taking the chance that nobody would notice. The risk had paid off. She could still see the tiny break in the wire, and there was only darkness where the red electronic eye should have pulsed.

She opened the heavy steel door. Stepping out onto the brilliantly lighted platform of the emergency exit, not pausing to check for passing security guards, she hurtled down the iron stairs with all the agility that years of competitive skiing had given her. Even when she reached the foot of the stairs, she didn't stop to search for pursuers. Either she'd been spotted or she hadn't; there was nothing she could do to change the situation. The door at the foot of the stairs was unlocked, as required by law for emergency exits. She rammed her shoulder against the metal closing bar, half expecting to hear the blare of an alarm as she stepped out into the darkness of the gardens.

Silence. Blessed silence. Avoiding the paths, Courtney ran across the dry autumn grass, following the escape route she had spent two weeks planning. After five minutes each shuddering breath began to hurt more than the last, but she welcomed the physical pain. Pushing her body to the limit had been part of her life from the time she was a teenager, and there was something comforting in the familiar feel of aching lungs and violently protesting muscles.

Ten yards away from the apple tree that would carry her over the hospital wall she altered her pace, preparing her body for the jump. The tree was pruned so that the lowest branch was a good seven feet from the ground. Courtney sprang up, arms stretching. She caught the branch, then hung for a second or so, her body swaying as she gradually regained her balance.

The tree was harder to climb than she'd expected. It was at least fifteen years since she'd shinnied up the trees in Aunt Amelia's orchard, and she'd forgotten how the twigs poked as you clambered upward. She'd also forgotten how hard unripe apples could be when they banged her on the head, and how the whole tree swayed once you got close to the top.

She knew she couldn't avoid making some noise as she swung over the wall, so she paused for a split second to scan the grounds for passing guards. Her breath choked in her lungs when she saw a stolid, uniformed figure not more than fifty yards away from the tree she was climbing. Courtney jerked back against the trunk, swallowing a cry of frustration when her foot dislodged a small apple and sent it tumbling to the ground. The soft thud seemed to her as loud as a burst of cannon fire in the cool silence of the October night.

The security guard looked up from his cigarette and began to walk directly toward the apple tree.

Courtney froze, not breathing, not even thinking. Her life hung suspended in a timeless void until the security guard reached inside his jacket and pulled out a walkie-talkie. She closed her eyes. This was it, then. He had seen her and was summoning reinforcements. They would lock her up in a dark room and throw away the key. Her pathetic attempt to find out what had happened was going to end right here, at the top of an apple tree.

She fought back a faintly hysterical laugh. The absurdity of her situation seemed appropriate. What better place to pick up an escaping lunatic than from the swaying branches of an apple tree?

She opened her eyes, preparing to meet her fate with dignity. The security guard tossed away his cigarette, grinding the stub beneath his heel. He pushed down the antenna on his walkie-talkie and returned it to his inner pocket. Without even a glance in Courtney's direction, he swung around to his left and cut across the grounds toward the main hospital entrance.

Something wet dripped onto the end of her nose. Courtney dashed her knuckles across her face and realized she was crying. She sniffed into the soft woolen sleeve of her sweater, then reached for the branch that hung across the glass-and-barbed-wire top of the wall.

The concrete pavement looked an awfully long way down. Sucking in her cheeks in concentration, Courtney swung as low as she could, then simply let go of the branch. She automatically bent her knees and crouched her body, but she still felt the jar of her landing all the way up her spine, and her left leg collapsed under her. She pushed herself to her feet, scarcely feeling the stab of pain. For once the reminder of her old skiing injury brought not even a touch of regret.

She straightened, scanning the deserted highway and forcing back the yell of triumph. Dear God, she had done it.

She was free!

Chapter Two

Courtney waited until she'd walked at least five miles before she turned into an all-night supermarket. There was only one other customer in the store, but the check-out clerk and the stock boy both looked too bored and sleepy to pay her much attention.

She grabbed a shopping cart and wheeled it quickly along the aisles, selecting a zippered nylon gym bag, a carton of fruit juice and a prepackaged travel kit of assorted toilet articles. The driver on the bus to Aspen would be less likely to notice a passenger who carried some luggage.

"Nice night," the check-out girl said, sliding the carton of juice across the scanner. "Warm for October. Been out jogging, have you?"

"At two o'clock in the morning?" Courtney protested, then kicked herself mentally. If she'd been using even half her brain, she would just have said *yes*.

"Oh, they go jogging at all times in this neighborhood." The clerk stopped to check the price code for the nylon gym bag. "I think they're crazy myself. There's one man comes in here at two-thirty every morning to buy a carton of milk. I'm telling you, he's run so hard he can hardly make it over to the dairy counter. He's a doctor down at the Nuthouse, but if you want to know the truth, I think he's crazier than half the folks he's got for patients. I mean, he says he's jogging to get healthy, and anybody can see he's killing himself. One of these days they'll have to carry him out on a stretcher.'' She shifted her gum to the other side of her mouth with a decisive snap. ''That'll be eleven ninety-five, please.''

Courtney handed over a twenty-dollar bill, then accepted her change and pushed it with trembling fingers into the pocket of her slacks. She would have said something light and carefree to the check-out girl, except she was afraid her face might crack if she tried to speak.

The clerk didn't seem to notice Courtney's silence. ''Have a nice night,'' she said, leaning tiredly against her cash register.

Courtney finally forced her lips to move. ''Thanks. You too.''

Outside, a fit of shakes overcame her. She slumped against the wall a few yards from the entrance, unable to move. Oh, God, what if she'd gone into the store twenty minutes later? What if the doctor had seen her and recognized her as one of his patients?

But the doctor didn't see you, and nobody recognized you, she told herself firmly. She forced herself to move away from the wall and strode briskly across the deserted parking lot. Her lips tightened into a hard, straight line. *You're going to make it, kid. You're going to walk to the terminal and get the bus to Aspen.*

For the rest of her journey across town, she was consumed by an irrational dread of bumping into the Nuthouse's jogging doctor. But the streets remained empty of everything except prowling cats and the occasional delivery truck.

When Courtney finally arrived at the Trailways bus terminal, the only disaster to have overtaken her was the appearance of a huge blister on her left heel. Despite the early hour, there were enough people milling around to prevent her feeling too conspicuous. After a few minutes sitting on a bench and resting her aching legs, she began to feel quite relaxed, until the sight of two patrolling policemen sent her dashing for the privacy of the ladies' room. A junior nurse at Walnut Park had once dropped the information that it was a criminal offense to leave a mental hospital without permission after a judge had declared the patient mentally incompetent. Courtney had little doubt that her escape had already been discovered, which meant that her description would soon be circulated to all the local law-enforcement agencies. It was odd to think of herself as an escaping criminal.

Courtney turned the taps full on, luxuriating in the sensation of hot water pouring over her tree-scratched hands and gritty, sleep-starved eyes. She glanced in the mirror as she dried her face, feeling a rueful sort of relief when she registered the changes that five months of incarceration had wrought in her appearance.

Her once-glowing complexion had disappeared, leaving a face that was pale and much too thin. Her long, thick hair no longer shone with golden streaks, but hung limply around her shoulders, a mousy cloud drained of color and vitality. Her eyelashes were still incredibly long, but stripped of mascara, they were unremarkable. Without their usual fringe of darkened lashes, the subtle, smoky violet of her eyes was transformed into a wishy-washy gray.

Courtney grimaced wryly as she tossed the paper towels into the wastebasket. Her appearance was eminently forgettable, and right now she was grateful for that. Still, Walnut Park hadn't quite stamped out all of her feminine instincts, and somewhere deep inside she felt the burst of a tiny flame of anger. How had this happened to her? How had her life descended to the point where she actually felt glad because she was no longer attractive?

The bus for Aspen left at seven in the morning, with fifteen passengers on board. The mountain scenery was spectacular, but Courtney had seen it many times before, and she gradually abandoned the struggle to keep her eyes open. The wheels of the bus pounded out the message that soon she would be with Justin again. Justin of the hypnotic blue eyes and sleek dark hair. Justin, who had fallen in love with her at first sight. Justin, who hadn't been able to wait to marry her. Justin, who had never visited her in hospital. Because he, too, had lost his freedom? Or because he had betrayed her?

The trouble was, she didn't really know Justin well enough to guess, Courtney reflected drowsily. In retrospect she could see that they'd married with reckless speed. They had been engaged by the end of April, three weeks after their first meeting. Justin had taken her to dinner in one of Aspen's most delightful and intimate restaurants. Gazing deep into her eyes across the candle-lit table, he had taken her hand into his clasp and stroked his thumb gently across her knuckles. "Marry me, Courtney, my darling," he murmured.

For a moment her heart seemed to stop beating, and she felt a strange, suffocating excitement. She'd never been in love before—not really in love—and she hadn't realized that passion could sometimes feel amazingly like fear. The thought flashed into her mind that she and Justin must be one of the very few couples left in America who contemplated marriage before they'd ever gone to bed together.

But she squashed the tiny, niggling doubt. "Oh, yes," she whispered, throwing away twenty-two years of Aunt Amelia's training in caution and self-control. "Oh, yes, Justin. I think we could be very happy together."

"Just like that?" he said. "No worries or questions?"

"None," she said. "As long as you love me."

"How could you ever ask?" He dropped a tiny kiss into the palm of her hand, then closed her fingers around the kiss. Smiling, she ran her hand slowly down the smooth skin of his cheek.

Emotion—surely it was love?—flared deep in his eyes. He smiled ruefully. "You'd think I'd have more sense than to propose in the middle of a crowded restaurant. How in the world am I going to wait until we get back to my house so I can kiss you properly?"

Nervousness bubbled up inside her, or perhaps it was happiness. Her emotions had been in such a state of turmoil since Aunt Amelia died that sometimes she wasn't quite sure what she was feeling. She pushed back her chair, lowering her voice with deliberate provocativeness. "My apartment's closer than your house. We could be at my place in ten minutes."

He tossed a hundred-dollar bill onto the table. "Let's try for five."

Later, curled up together on the sofa in front of a blazing fire in her apartment, she had expected him to make love to her. Instead he had plied her with Irish coffee and witty, entertaining stories.

"You look particularly beautiful tonight," he had murmured. "You don't care that I'm so much older than you?"

"You're not *that* much older. Forty-five is practically the prime of life nowadays."

He looked pleased by her compliment. "But we have to face facts, Courtney. When you're as old as I am today, I'll be over sixty."

She laughed softly. "And I bet you'll be the handsomest sixty-year-old ever to hit the slopes at Aspen."

There was no more discussion of the gap in their ages, only a plea from Justin that their wedding should take place soon. "Tomorrow would be perfect," he murmured suggestively. "Did you know that in Colorado you don't have to wait to get a marriage license? Our honeymoon can't begin too soon for me."

"We ought to wait until at least the day after tomorrow," she said with mock severity. "We don't want people to say we're rushing into things."

"You don't have any family you need to invite to the wedding?"

"No," she said slowly. "Remember, I told you my aunt brought me up? She died a few months ago and there's nobody else. I guess we Longs aren't a very prolific family."

He raised his glass in an elegant toast. "Darling, prolific or not, you Longs are *wonderful*. What more could any man wish for? A beautiful bride and no prospective in-laws. That has to be the perfect recipe for marital happiness."

"What about you, Justin? Don't you have any relatives?"

"Darling, I have at least a million of them. We'll ignore them all, and they can all be equally insulted. They'll have a simply marvelous time making angry phone calls to one another." He pursed his lips into a prim, disapproving line. *"May Beth, do you know what Justin has done this time? He's gotten himself married, in Colorado of all places, and not a single soul from the family invited."*

She laughed. "You should have been an actor, Justin. You impersonate people so well."

He looked at her rather oddly. "I'm much too shy to be an actor," he said, and then they had spent the rest of the night making plans for their honeymoon.

At the time, her rash agreement to Justin's proposal hadn't seemed rash at all. Courtney was sure that fate had thrown them together for a special purpose. Justin usually spent spring in the Bahamas, and Courtney had only recently moved to Colorado, so it was miraculous that they had met at all.

It was Courtney's research into her murky past that brought her and Justin together. On the day of their first meeting, she had been doing some reading in the archives of the local newspaper. She walked out of the building that housed the editorial offices, her nose buried deep in a photocopy of a twenty-two-year-old article about her parents. She was paying no attention to where she was walking, so it wasn't at all surprising that she bumped head-on into the handsome, dark-haired man who was trying to enter the building.

Justin, she learned later, had been on his way to discuss a series of advertisements connected with his real-estate business. Still shaken by the revelations contained in the newspaper article, Courtney had allowed the good-looking stranger to pull her to her feet.

"I'm sorry, miss, I hope you aren't hurt? But you should look where you're walking when you go through a door." He released her arm just long enough to bend down and gather up the scattered pages of the newspaper article.

"You're right. I'm very sorry. I wasn't paying attention." She held out her hand for the photocopies, hoping against hope that he wouldn't notice what she'd been reading.

Her hope was in vain. "This must be interesting stuff to have kept you so engrossed." He glanced down at the banner headlines. She knew, word for word, what he was reading.

Famous Movie Stars Found Dead in Bedroom. Daughter Discovered Unconscious in Driveway. Was Beautiful Ferne Hilton Murdered by Her Husband? Was Little Didi a Witness to the Tragedy?

"It's some research I'm doing." She almost snatched the articles from his hands and stuffed them hurriedly into her bag. "It's boring stuff."

His smile became openly teasing. "You'll get run out of town if you dismiss one of our most famous scandals as boring. Aspen is proud of its movie stars, even when they get themselves murdered."

"Well, it's kind of an old story," she said tightly. "Hardly worth discussing anymore."

"Perhaps not." To her immense relief, he seemed to have no interest in pursuing the subject. "Good heavens, I just noticed your hand. It's bleeding! We'd better get it seen to right away. There's a doctor not too far from here—''

"Honestly, it's nothing. Just a scratch."

"I'm afraid not. Look, you have blood dripping all down your jacket." He insisted on winding his snow-white handkerchief around the cut, tying it in a neat square knot.

"Thank you again," she said when he stepped back to admire his handiwork. "Now I really should be on my way. Do you have a business card, so that I'll know where to return the handkerchief?"

His dazzling blue eyes rested momentarily on her tanned cheeks. "No business card. But if you'll let me buy you lunch, then I'll make you a present of the hankie."

"Oh, no, there's no reason for you to buy me—"

"Please, I insist." He smiled charmingly. "My name's Justin Tanner, and now that we've been officially introduced, I'll ask you again. Will you have lunch with me? Please?"

Normally she would have retreated in the face of such obvious pursuit, but she suddenly craved the warmth of human companionship. "Well, thank you," she said. "That would be very nice. My name's Courtney Long, by the way."

He smiled. "Somehow, I think that's a name I'll never forget."

Later she was able to see that Justin had stampeded her into marriage, pursuing her with single-minded devotion from the moment of that first, unexpected meeting.

But why had he been so determined to marry her? For money? If so, Courtney had no idea how he had discovered she was the owner of a million-dollar trust fund. She was so unused to the idea of being rich that her life-style remained as frugal as Aunt Amelia could have wished. Besides, if all Justin wanted was her money, he must have known that he didn't need to confine her in a mental institution in order to get it. All he'd needed to do was ask....

"Wake up, miss! We're here. Time to go."

She shot upright in her seat. "No! I didn't do anything! I'm not sick. Please don't take me back!"

The bus driver's brow wrinkled in concern. "We're in Aspen, miss. This is the end of the line."

She swallowed hard, forcing her breath to come more slowly. "Yes, of c-course it is. Thanks for waking me."

"You feeling all right? You don't look so hot."

"I'm fine." She forced herself to smile, to pick up her gym bag with appropriate casualness, to speak calmly. The last thing she could afford right now was to draw even more attention to herself. Dear Lord, she should never have allowed herself the luxury of falling asleep! She ignored the iron fist of fear tightening inexorably around her lungs and made herself laugh lightly. "Too many late nights and too much celebrating, that's my problem."

"Celebrating?" The driver seemed more than ready to stand and chat. "You getting married or something?"

She laughed again. "No, not married. Divorced." *Good grief,* she thought in dismay. *Where in the world did my subconscious drag that one up from?*

The bus driver frowned. He was a devoted family man who considered marriage something to be worked at and divorce something to grieve over. But this was Aspen, he reminded himself, and half the people here changed spouses more casually than he changed bedroom slippers. Still, this woman didn't look much older than his daughter, and she was far too young to be so cynical. Celebrating a divorce, indeed! He sniffed reprovingly. "You don't want to go rushing into things so fast," he advised. "My wife and me, we went out together two years before we decided to tie the knot. Nowadays people hardly know each other two minutes, let alone two years, and already they're sending out wedding invitations."

How endearingly quaint, Courtney thought. Most of the

people she knew were too busy hopping from bed to bed to find time to send out wedding invitations. She and Justin, on the other hand, had been too busy getting married to find time to go to bed. Courtney edged toward the bus doors, filled with a sudden impatience to see Justin again, to find out the answers to some of her questions.

"I'm sure you're right," she said, managing to produce a farewell smile. "Next time I plan to look before I leap."

Her words played themselves over in her mind as she called for a cab from a nearby pay phone, then waited impatiently for it to arrive. This time when she saw Justin, things would be different, she promised herself. After the experiences of the past few months, he would find himself confronted by a very different person from the naive, pliable young woman who had followed him so trustingly into marriage.

She was pacing the pavement outside the depot when the cab finally arrived. The driver scowled as he opened the passenger door. "Where to, miss?"

He was young and good-looking and probably doubled during the winter months as a ski instructor. All the better if he wasn't too happy about the nature of his summertime employment, Courtney thought. The grouchier and more bored the driver, the less chance he'd remember their conversation. The bus driver, she had a sinking suspicion, would remember her all too clearly.

"I need to go back toward Snowmass Village," she said. "And turn by the Repertory Theater onto Copper Creek Drive. I want number ten, which is at the very end of the road."

With a grunt he swung out onto Mill Street and headed directly for Snowmass. Courtney's stomach gradually tied itself into a knot of tension so tight it made breathing difficult. What in the world was going to happen when she finally saw Justin?

The cabdriver turned onto the private gravel road that led to Justin's house. He drove for a couple of miles, then stopped at a narrow driveway half-obscured by a thick cluster of blue spruce trees. "Is this the house you're looking for, lady? Says on the gatepost this is number ten."

Courtney closed her eyes, savoring a brief moment of exultation. Despite everything, she'd made it! She was here at Justin's house. And she wasn't going to leave until he came up with a long list of answers.

"Yes, this is it," she told the cabbie, handing over the fare and adding a generous tip. "You don't need to drive up to the door. It's only fifty yards or so, and I don't have anything heavy to carry."

"Whatever you say."

The driver was in reverse by the time she opened the door of the cab, and he had disappeared around a bend in the lane before she was two-thirds of the way along the driveway. Courtney was glad of the silence. She walked along the freshly raked driveway, deliberately focusing on her surroundings rather than the racing of her pulse and the tension in her muscles.

The knot in her stomach was rapidly swelling to unmanageable proportions, but she refused to let the fear overwhelm her. Justin might not even be home, she realized. In that case she would simply park herself on his doorstep until he arrived. She didn't dare to consider the problem of what she would do if he was out of town.

She concentrated on looking at the geraniums, which still bore green leaves although their pink blossoms were nipped by frost. The shrubs were now clothed in the gold and russet of fall rather than the pale green of spring, but the yard still looked beautiful. Up close to the house, the view toward the snow-covered peak of Snowmass Mountain was as stunning as ever. She admired it for no more than a second or two before climbing resolutely up the short flight of brick-and-sandstone steps that led to Justin's front door.

Despite the chill in the air, her palms were so damp she had to wipe them on her slacks before she rang the bell. There was a moment's silence, and then she heard the quiet pad of footsteps on the wooden floor of the hall. Her heart pounded high in her throat. In a minute Justin would open the door. What would she say? Her mouth curved into a painful smile. *Hello, Justin,* might make a reasonably neutral beginning, she supposed.

The door swung open, and Courtney's breathing stopped. She closed her eyes for a split second. When she opened them a middle-aged woman stood framed in the doorway.

A housekeeper? Courtney's grip on her gym bag tightened so convulsively that the straps cut into her palms. She opened her mouth and tried to speak, but no words came out. She cleared her throat and tried again. "Mr. Tanner, please. I would like to speak to Mr. Justin Tanner."

"Of course, miss. Is Mr. Tanner expecting you?"

"I don't think so. But it's rather urgent."

"Well, I don't know, miss. Mr. Tanner usually doesn't like to be interrupted when he's working."

Working? Justin was working? Courtney could feel the sweat gathering in hot rivulets at the base of her spine. If Justin wasn't sick or injured, then why hadn't he come to see her? Why hadn't he arranged for her release from Walnut Park?

"I really do need to see him right away." She tried not to let the desperation sound in her voice. She'd learned during the last few months that people responded more favorably to requests if she didn't sound too frantic. "It's a personal matter. Would you tell him...tell him it's Courtney. I'm sure he'll want to see me."

The housekeeper sighed. "Very well, miss. If you'll wait here in the living room, I'll fetch Mr. Tanner."

"Don't bother to show me in. I know my own way."

The housekeeper frowned, but she made no objections as Courtney entered and walked directly into the living room. "I'll be right back with Mr. Tanner," the housekeeper said, hurrying from the room.

She's afraid I'm going to make off with the family silver, Courtney thought, walking nervously to the giant picture window overlooking a nearby canyon. If she hadn't been so much on edge, she might have found the situation amusing. Suppose she'd taken the risk and introduced herself as Mrs. Justin Tanner? Did the housekeeper even know of her existence?

Courtney heard the sound of sneakered feet walking quickly down the hallway, and she turned around just as the man entered the room. He was tall and tanned, with gray eyes and thick, coarse hair, which might once have been brown but now had been streaked permanently blond by years of exposure to the sun. He wore faded jeans and a loose-fitting sweatshirt which didn't quite conceal the impressive muscles rippling beneath the faded cotton.

He nodded at her, his expression neither hostile nor friendly. "Hello," he said. "Are you Courtney?"

She nodded. "Yes."

He waited for no more than a second, then shrugged. "Is there something you want to talk to me about?"

"Oh, no," she said, finding it more and more difficult to speak. "I need to speak to Mr. Tanner. To Justin Tanner. It's very important."

His look held more than a touch of impatience. "I'm Justin Tanner. What do you want to tell me?"

"No," she said stupidly. "You're not Justin. Of course you're not. You can't be."

"On the contrary, I can assure you I've managed to be Justin Tanner for every one of the last thirty-five years."

"But you can't be," she repeated despairingly. "You must

be a different Justin. Why are you living here in his house?
What have you done with *my* Justin?"

"Look, I think this has gone far enough. You'd better tell
me what this is all about, or I'm going to call the police."

"Oh, no! Please! I won't bother you anymore—"

The housekeeper tapped on the door. "Is everything okay,
Mr. Tanner? Did I do right to let the young woman in?"

Courtney didn't hear the reply because of the roar of blood
pounding in her ears. So this was what it meant to be insane.
She'd run all the way from Walnut Park, only to discover
that she really belonged there.

The mist in front of her eyes made it difficult to see and
impossible to hear, but she sensed that the man—she couldn't
bring herself to call him Justin—had asked her a question.
She had no idea what it was, of course, and no idea how she
should answer. But it didn't really matter. Crazy people often
had difficulty carrying on a normal conversation. In a little
while, she'd probably get quite accustomed to thinking of
herself as crazy.

With the very last dregs of her energy, she pulled her body
erect and clasped her hands tightly in front of her.

"I'm afraid there's been some mistake," she said, with a
dignity her aunt would have been proud of. "I'm most awfully sorry to have bothered you. Good afternoon, Mr. Tanner."

If she allowed herself the luxury of even a single sob, she
knew she would start screaming and never stop. She turned,
praying that she wouldn't collide with any of the furniture,
and walked quietly from the room.

Courtney was probably forty yards from the house when
the mist in front of her eyes turned into an impenetrable wall
of dark gray cotton. She tried to walk forward, discovered
that she couldn't, and collapsed into a neat pile at the side
of the driveway.

Chapter Three

Justin Tanner picked up the cheap nylon gym bag, his mouth tightening impatiently. "I guess I have to take it out to her," he said to the housekeeper. "Otherwise she'll only come back."

"She probably left it on purpose." Mrs. Moynihan didn't attempt to conceal her disapproval. "Strange young woman—and up to no good, that's certain. She was real nervous about something."

"Mmm." Justin's reply was noncommittal. He opened the door and strode along the gravel path, anxious to get back to his computer. He felt no interest in the unknown woman, only irritation because she'd interrupted him at a crucial point in the algebraic equation he'd been working on for the past two days. Since Linda's death five months earlier, he'd found it hard to take much interest in his friends, let alone in total strangers. The symbols on his computer screen had become a refuge, but he didn't care. His work was more intellectually stimulating than people and nowhere near as emotionally demanding. People might die, but an equation was guaranteed to live forever.

Justin was almost at the end of the driveway when he saw the woman lying in a crumpled heap on the grass verge. She looked so thin and frail that his stomach twisted with fright. Heavens, what had happened to her?

He bent down and felt for a pulse. She was breathing and her pulse felt strong enough, although she was deathly pale. The tension in Justin's body relaxed marginally. He scooped her up and turned back toward the house.

She was light, he discovered, far too light for her height. He elbowed his way in through the front door, cursing beneath his breath. Why couldn't she have waited until she got into her car before she collapsed? Come to think of it, where was her car? His house was miles out of town. Surely she hadn't walked?

Mrs. Moynihan looked downright grim as he walked into the house carrying Courtney. "What happened?" she asked.

"She's fainted. She was lying in the driveway. What did you say her name was?"

"Courtney, or at least that's what *she* said. I'll get her some water if you'll take her into the living room." The housekeeper retreated to the kitchen, her back rigid with disapproval.

Justin stretched Courtney out on the sofa, propping her head against one of the pillows. She stirred almost as soon as he put her down, but she didn't open her eyes.

Mrs. Moynihan returned with a glass of ice water and knelt beside the sofa, holding the glass to Courtney's mouth.

"She's coming round, Mr. Tanner, and a good thing, too. If I was you, I'd get rid of her fast. She's probably the sort who'll sue you for having a bumpy driveway. There's a lot of nasty people out there these days."

Courtney's eyelids fluttered open, and she made a vague motion with her hand, pushing away the water.

Mrs. Moynihan set the glass down on a side table and smoothed a lock of limp hair off the girl's forehead. She pursed her lips, not caring that their unwelcome visitor might now be conscious enough to understand what was being said. "Looks to me as if she's on drugs. Crazy, these young things, the way they carry on."

The gentleness of the housekeeper's hands belied the brusqueness of her words, but Justin didn't doubt she meant what she said. In essence he agreed with her, but the pallor of the girl's complexion, emphasized by the deep, bruised shadows beneath her eyes, provoked an unwilling sensation of responsibility. "I think we should call the paramedics, or maybe a doctor. Especially if there's a chance she's high on something."

The word "doctor" seemed to dispel the last of Courtney's faintness. She dragged herself to her feet, swaying visibly. "I'm fine," she protested, her words blatantly denied by her stark white face and shaking hands. She pushed her hair behind her ears in an effort to tidy it, and tugged at the hem of her sweater, adjusting it over the waistband of her slacks. "I'm fine," she repeated, glancing around, somewhat dazed. Her gaze lighted upon the nylon holdall, and she seized it gratefully. "Well, thanks for the—um—water and everything. I'll be on my way."

Justin looked at her coolly. "How are you planning to get back into town?"

"What? Oh, I'll take a cab. I'll be fine in a cab." She turned, her feet not too steady, toward the front door.

"How are you going to find one?" Justin asked. "They aren't exactly lined up outside the door."

"That's no problem," Mrs. Moynihan interjected quickly. "I'll call for one right away. It should be here in fifteen minutes, maybe less at this time of day. The young lady can wait on the porch. It's quite warm in the sun."

"Yes, thank you. That would be great. I'll wait at the end of the driveway. Could you ask the cabdriver to hurry, please?"

She was panicky, Justin realized suddenly, almost incoherent with the need to get away, preventing an even greater display of desperation through sheer force of will. Entirely against his better judgment, he found himself intrigued. She had arrived at his door insisting she must speak to Mr. Justin Tanner. After two minutes of bizarre conversation, she'd run from the house and fainted in his driveway. Now she seemed determined to leave as precipitously as she'd arrived.

Justin felt a twist of wry humor. He must have become more of an ogre than he'd realized over the past five months. Was his manner really that ferocious? One look and beautiful women fainted from fear?

He looked up at Courtney, who seemed poised for flight as soon as Mrs. Moynihan finished her phone call to the cab company. Odd that his subconscious had thrown up the word "beautiful," Justin thought. Superficially she looked plain, but Linda had taught him to look at the bone structure beneath the surface, and he was sure that, in different circumstances, Courtney could be very beautiful. Her face was one that professional photographers and movie directors dreamed of finding. He even had a nagging sensation of familiarity, as if he had seen her before, a long time ago.

Mrs. Moynihan covered the mouthpiece. "The dispatcher says it'll be thirty minutes, Mr. Tanner."

"Tell them not to bother." He was probably more astonished than the housekeeper when he heard himself volunteer to act as chauffeur. "I have to go into town sometime today, so it might as well be now. I'll take Courtney myself."

"No, it's all right," Courtney replied quickly. "Thanks, but I'll wait for the cab."

"They already hung up," Mrs. Moynihan reported. "Do you want me to call again?"

Justin could sense the woman's reluctance to accept his invitation. The refusal started to form on her lips, then her gaze slid toward the zippered pocket of her gym bag. He knew she was silently calculating how much money she would save if she allowed him to drive her into town. Her words of refusal died unspoken.

Courtney drew in a deep breath. "Well, thank you. If it's no trouble, I'd appreciate the ride."

"Don't mention it. That was quite a tumble you took onto the driveway. Would you like to wash your hands before we leave?"

She stared down at her palms, seeming to notice the dirt and scratches for the first time. "Thank you," she said again, still avoiding his gaze. "Some soap and hot water would be great."

"Mrs. Moynihan will show you the guest bathroom."

She picked up her bag, her eyes still somewhat dazed. "There's no need. I know the way."

The housekeeper started to say something, but Justin gestured swiftly for her to keep quiet. They both watched in silence as Courtney turned into the hallway and walked unerringly to the visitor's bathroom, located in an obscure position beneath the stairs.

Mrs. Moynihan's pent-up breath emerged in a huge, accusing sigh. "However did she know where to go? There's nobody can ever find that bathroom the first time they come here."

Justin shrugged, although he felt almost as surprised. "Maybe she just got lucky."

Mrs. Moynihan sniffed. "And maybe she's been casing the house. Why don't you let me call the police, Mr. Tanner?"

"And waste the whole day filling out reports about something that never happened? Whatever she planned to do, she hasn't done it. That faint was genuine for sure. It's easier just to drive her into town and get rid of her."

"If you say so. But I'm turning the alarm system on as soon as you leave here, so don't forget to take your key."

Courtney chose that moment to reappear. A trace of color had returned to her cheeks, and she'd made an effort to brush her hair into some sort of order, but the changes could hardly be considered a dramatic improvement. "Ready?" Justin asked.

She nodded. "Yes, thank you." Her voice was low and carefully controlled, as if she feared unguarded speech might permit some violent emotion to break through.

Justin spoke with calculated casualness. "I thought I'd drive the Bronco. It holds well on these gravel roads."

"Fine."

"It's in the garage. We'd better use the side door."

"Okay."

He gestured to indicate that she should precede him. Courtney turned in the direction of the kitchen, oblivious to Mrs. Moynihan's snort of disgust.

"I'm calling the police," the housekeeper muttered into Justin's ear as Courtney stepped into the garage.

"No, don't. It's not a crime to guess that the side door leads off the kitchen. Most houses are laid out that way."

"How did she know where the kitchen is?"

"You can see it from the hall."

"If she found that garage door by guesswork, then I'm a monkey's uncle."

Justin grinned. "Don't eat all the bananas while I'm gone."

Courtney was waiting by the Bronco when he entered the garage. "What's your name?" he asked, unlocking the doors.

"Courtney."

"Yes, I know. But Courtney what?"

She couldn't quite disguise her almost imperceptible hesitation. "Courtney L-Leonard."

He pushed the opener and the garage door slid upward. "And why did you want to see me, Courtney Leonard?"

This time there was no hesitation. "It was a mistake. A complete mistake. I didn't want to see you."

"How could it be a mistake when you asked for me by name?"

She looked out of the window, apparently fascinated by the landscape. "Somebody gave me your name—at least I thought they did. But they must have meant somebody else. I guess I wasn't paying proper attention."

"Strange sort of misunderstanding, since they gave you my correct address as well as my name."

Her hands grasped the strap of her bag, but she continued to stare at the trees. "Yes, I'm sorry, it was a stupid mistake. I shouldn't have bothered you."

Justin's limited store of patience ran out. "Well, *Ms Leonard*, if you didn't want to see me, and having my address was all a mistake, would you mind telling me how come you're so damn familiar with the floor plan of my house?"

Her head jerked around, her eyes opening wide in what seemed to be amazement. "You found the guest bathroom," he prompted tersely, irritated by his reaction to those huge, fear-haunted eyes. "And the kitchen. And you selected the door to the garage without a moment's pause, although there's a door into the pantry and another door into the basement that you never even considered opening."

All expression disappeared from her face. She dropped her gaze to her lap. "That was just luck," she said, her voice flat. "We've never met, Mr. Tanner, I assure you."

"I know that," he replied softly. "I didn't ask if we'd met. I asked how you managed to find your way around my house. Have you been there before?"

The blankness she imposed on her features was almost eerie in its completeness. "Since I've never met you, Mr. Tanner, how could I have been to your house?"

He was about to suggest that there were dozens of ways, some of them even legal—she might have known his wife, for example—but at the thought of Linda, his throat closed tight with anguish. He stared ahead, the present crowded out by memories. It was a year since he and Linda had last driven into town together. Six months before she died she had already been in too much pain to endure a bumpy ride in the Bronco unless it was absolutely necessary, too weak even to make love. Her tiny reserves of strength had all been saved for her work.

Justin glanced at the silent woman seated beside him, and a wave of white-hot rage flared through him simply because she wasn't Linda. He drew in a deep breath, fighting the irrationality of his anger.

He finished counting to twenty and let out his breath. His anger drained away, and along with it his interest in pursuing the minor mystery of how and why Courtney Leonard knew the location of his guest bathroom. What the hell, he thought. As she said, she'd probably found her way by sheer luck. If there was a more sinister explanation, he didn't care. The electronic alarm system on his house was highly efficient, and if she was a cat burglar, she wasn't a very good one. Moreover, apart from a couple of pieces of antique Indian pottery, his house had nothing in it to attract the attention of a skilled, professional thief.

With the ruthless efficiency that had marked all his personal decisions since Linda's death, he closed his mind to Courtney and her problems. "Where do you want to be dropped off?" he asked curtly.

"The—um—the post office would be fine, if that's not taking you out of your way."

"No, I have to stop off at the supermarket. They're close to each other."

She returned to staring out of the window, and Justin allowed the desultory conversation to lapse. He flipped the switch on the radio, letting the soft rock of a local station fill the too-obvious silence.

They didn't speak again until he was drawing up in the large, community parking lot in the town center. "Are you feeling okay now?" he asked, flipping open the locks on the truck doors.

"Fine, thanks. Just fine."

She still looked awful, but he didn't care. They got out of the truck almost simultaneously, and she walked quickly around to his side. "Thank you for the ride, Mr. Tanner. You've been very kind." She hesitated for a moment, then spoke hurriedly without looking at him. "I'm not a thief or a burglar or anything, so you don't have to worry. I'm not planning to break into your house. Goodbye, Mr. Tanner."

Justin found her attempt at reassurance oddly touching. Even more bizarre, he actually believed her. He held out his hand. "Goodbye, Courtney Leonard."

A heavy hand descended on his shoulders from behind. "Don't you move another step, pardner," a voice bellowed into his left ear.

Justin recognized the familiar, hoarse voice of Sheriff Swanson and resigned himself to a lengthy conversation. The sheriff never used one word where three would do, but beneath his bluff manner he was a sharp and efficient officer.

Justin looked up and saw the sheriff dangling a pair of steel handcuffs a threatening two inches from his nose. "I've got official business to discuss with you, Mr. Tanner, so you'd better stay right where you are or I might decide to run you in."

Courtney's hand turned into a block of ice within Justin's grasp. She gave a convulsive jerk, trying frantically to break loose. Not caring if he inflicted pain, he gripped her wrist tightly. He immediately felt the fear flowing from her body into his, a physical entity, twitching with electric force. He turned to look at her. The naked appeal in her eyes touched some protective instinct he hadn't known he possessed. Despite the fact that she was obviously guilty of something—otherwise why would the mere sight of the sheriff paralyze her with fear?—he discovered that he had no desire to turn her in.

"How you doing, sheriff?" he asked, returning the man's smile. "The out-of-towners keeping you busy?"

The sheriff chuckled dourly. "This is the off-season," he said. "Wait till the ski slopes open. Then my men never get a moment's peace. The chamber of commerce spends a fortune and still can't convince the tourists that this city isn't coke heaven." His gaze ran in frank appraisal over Courtney. "I don't believe I've met your lady friend, Justin."

"She's just arrived in town." Justin spoke slowly, debating exactly what he should tell the sheriff. He could feel Courtney literally shaking. She had long since passed beyond the point of trying to conceal her fear. "She's a colleague from the university," he said finally. "Courtney Leonard from Boston."

"Howdy. Nice to meet you." The sheriff had grown up in Colorado's ranching country, and Courtney had precisely the vague, wild-eyed look that he expected from a research scientist. "You staying out West long?"

"It's n-not decided yet. We have a lot to do."

Justin was surprised Courtney had managed to speak. "What you waving those handcuffs around for?" he asked the sheriff. "I paid that parking ticket one of your guys handed out, even though it was daylight robbery."

The sheriff returned the handcuffs to his belt. "I wanted to thank you," he said gruffly. "We appreciate that donation you made to Barry's memorial fund. It was very generous, and his widow sure is grateful for all the help. Her girl's starting college this year, and they needed the extra cash."

"My pleasure," Justin said lightly. "Barry was a good friend." He nodded toward the far corner of the parking lot. "Looks like you're being called. I can see an arm in a police uniform waving at you."

The sheriff grunted. "That's Tom. He's new. Guess I'd better mosey on over and see what all the fuss is about." The sheriff seemed to delight in talking like a parody of a bad Western, but for once Justin felt not even a quiver of amusement.

The sheriff tipped his hat. "Nice to have met you, Ms Leonard. Enjoy your stay in Aspen. See you around, Justin." He ambled across the parking lot, his easy pace belying his fitness and coordination.

Courtney's fingers still clutched Justin's arm in a viselike grip. He ripped her hand off his sleeve and bundled her back toward the door of the Bronco. He was furious with her for involving him in her problems, furious with himself for having protected her.

"Get in," he said, pushing her into the passenger seat. He slammed the door with a satisfying thud and stormed around to the other side. He slammed the second door and threw the lock, bolting them both inside the truck.

"Okay." He turned around to confront Courtney. "Don't you think it's time you told me what's going on? What the hell are you so scared of?"

Chapter Four

He was furious, Courtney realized, whereas she was mentally exhausted to the point that she didn't really care what happened next. Sheriff Swanson's sudden appearance, complete with handcuffs, had been the last straw. Her body was still trembling.

When Courtney had first arrived in Aspen, way back in the early spring, she had visited the police department and asked for permission to search through the official records concerning her parents' murder. Seeing the sheriff again, she had felt certain her brief flirtation with freedom was over. Instead he hadn't shown even a flicker of recognition. Good old Walnut Park, she thought hysterically. A few months in the tender care of the Nuthouse nurses, and even experienced cops couldn't recognize you anymore.

"I'm waiting for an answer," Justin interjected. "What the hell have you done to be so scared of the sheriff?"

"Nothing."

"Right. Law-abiding citizens always turn catatonic when a police officer stops for a friendly chat."

"You don't have to be a criminal to dislike having handcuffs waved under your nose."

"You were gripping my arm like it was your last hope of salvation. Sheriff Swanson put the fear of God into you."

She attempted a shrug. "Authority figures intimidate me."

Justin grabbed her shoulders, forcing her to meet his eyes. They were a very attractive shade of gray, she thought dispassionately. Smoky. Probably sexy, if she hadn't almost forgotten what sexual desire felt like.

She dropped her gaze. This man wasn't likely to be an impostor; he and the sheriff were obviously old acquaintances. Walnut Park hadn't yet reduced her to a state of paranoia where she suspected the sheriff of being part of a nationwide conspiracy to deceive her.

But if this Justin Tanner was the real McCoy, then the man she had married must be an impostor. But where was he, the original Justin, and why in the world had he singled her out? The chilling thought crept into her mind that perhaps she never had been married, perhaps—as all the doctors kept insisting—she never had known a man called Justin Tanner.

Clenching her fists, Courtney pushed the thought away. Even now, even when she felt drained of every scrap of rebellion and energy, she wouldn't accept that the psychiatrists had been right. She wasn't crazy. Damn it all, *she had been married*! The ceremony *wasn't* a figment of her disordered imagination, and she *had* known somebody calling himself Justin Tanner.

Courtney straightened in her seat. "I'd like to see some identification," she said. "Proof that you really are who you say you are."

For a moment she thought he would refuse, but eventually he reached into his hip pocket and pulled out a bulging wallet. Courtney flipped through the wad of plastic. Driver's license, social-security card, bank card, a dozen credit cards. If this man wasn't Justin Tanner, he sure had done a great job of faking his IDs.

She closed the wallet and returned it to him. "Thank you."

"Quit stalling, Courtney. I didn't turn you in to the sheriff. I think you owe me some answers."

"I guess so." Her situation was so hopeless that Courtney

began to find an element of black humor in her position. She turned to meet Justin's hard, accusing gaze, and laughter escaped from her throat in an inelegant hiccup. "I'm looking for my husband," she said. "Somehow I seem to have mislaid him."

"Very inconvenient for you. Any particular reason why you came to my house looking for him?"

"Because I thought that was where he was." With calculated defiance she added, "Because I thought Justin Tanner was my husband."

She had finally succeeded in startling him. "You think *I'm* your husband!! Are you crazy?"

"Could be," she said. "In fact, it's a distinct possibility." Another hiccup of laughter escaped.

"We're not married," he said tersely. "Take my word for it."

"I know that. But maybe you loaned your name and your house to a friend. Maybe you're part of a conspiracy to deceive me. In case you don't know this, Mr. Tanner, I married somebody calling himself Justin Tanner in Denver on April 22 this year."

He paused for a moment. "It isn't such an unusual name."

"Maybe not, but the Justin Tanner I married owns the house you're living in. Or at least he did in April, when we got married."

If he was acting, then he was brilliant. The anger in his gaze was slowly replaced by understanding and a hint of pity. "Look," he said gently. "You've had a rough day, and that fall you took didn't help. You're still pale, and you look exhausted. Why don't you let me drive you to our local hospital? I'm sure there's somebody there who could help you. I think you could use some professional advice."

"From the psychiatrist maybe?" Courtney asked tightly. His mellow, soothing voice—grimly reminiscent of the staff at the Nuthouse—sparked a flare of anger, but she managed to conceal her feelings. She couldn't hope to run away in the middle of town, and anyway, the car doors were locked. But as soon as he drew up alongside the hospital emergency entrance, she'd make a run for it. They'd allowed her to jog around the grounds in Walnut Park, and she was still faster on her feet than most people, a legacy of her days as a potential Olympic skier.

She slumped down in her seat, pretending apathy. "All right," she said. "Take me to the hospital. I have a terrible headache. Maybe I should get somebody to check it out."

Justin looked at her sharply, as if doubting the sudden meekness of her tone. She pressed her hands to her forehead, and he bent forward, turning the key in the ignition and reversing quickly out of the parking lot.

"Lean back in the seat," he said. "It's just a few minutes' drive."

She complied without protest, and they drove in silence out of town. They were only a couple of miles from the hospital in Aspen Highlands before he spoke again. "Would you tell me something truthfully? How did you know your way around my house? Was it really coincidence or did you go there with...your husband?"

"Justin took me there," she replied flatly. "We lived there when we came back from our honeymoon." She closed her eyes, not bothering to assess the impact of her statement. As Aunt Amelia would have warned her, she was being punished for lying; the headache she had invented was rapidly becoming a pounding reality.

"Can you describe the master bedroom for me?"

"Why?"

"Humor me, Courtney."

She shrugged. "It's a big room, at least fifteen by eighteen. It has a sloping wood-beam ceiling and a big picture window facing south. The walls are white and the bed is a four-poster. No canopy. The quilt is handmade in an Early American ring pattern, but it's new, not an antique. The carpet is beige, medium loop, thickly padded. The bathroom's tiled in sea green and there's a Jacuzzi as well as a huge shower stall. I was too si—'' She cut off her revelation abruptly. No point in handing him the information that she'd been delirious half the time she was married. "I never used the Jacuzzi," she concluded brusquely.

He was silent for several seconds. "I don't know how you managed to get in without damaging the locks," he said finally, "but you've obviously been in my house."

"I've explained how I got in. My husband gave me a key."

"Do you still have it? The key, I mean."

"No," she admitted reluctantly. "I lost my key."

"At the same time you lost your husband?" He didn't bother to conceal his sarcasm.

Her mouth twisted into a humorless smile. "I guess you could say they disappeared together."

The Bronco slowed as they approached the turnoff for Aspen Highlands and the hospital. "When do you claim to have lived in my house?" Justin asked, his voice taut.

"I told you. After we came back from our honeymoon."

"The dates," he said impatiently. "Precisely what dates do you think you lived there?"

"Well, I visited the house before we were married, of course, but I didn't actually live there till we came back from our honeymoon in Mexico. So I guess it was from the end of April until the second week in May."

"Then what happened?"

"I don't kno—'' She corrected herself quickly. "We... um...we...split up."

"You left the house?"

"Yes."

The road forked, and Justin swung the car sharply to the right. "I was in New York from the end of March until the beginning of the third week in May. The house was empty for almost nine weeks.''

His words hung in the air, filling the space between them with almost palpable tension. Courtney sat up very straight, unable to quell the spurt of excitement thrusting its way through her weariness. ''Then it's possible somebody could have used your house while you were gone? Without your permission, I mean.''

He frowned. ''I don't see how. The house was locked and left in the care of Mountain Realty. They're a reputable company; I've dealt with them before. They'd never have permitted anybody to camp in the backyard, let alone live inside the house.''

''But would they have known if somebody broke in and took possession?''

''They certainly should have. They guarantee to check the property a minimum of once a week, inside as well as out.''

''Lots of companies don't do the inspections they're paid for.''

''Mountain gets a lot of work in this area, and their business depends on them being a hundred percent reliable.''

''Are you saying nobody could have been occupying the house without you knowing?''

''I guess I am.''

Courtney closed her eyes and her body slumped into renewed apathy. So much for her hopes of discovering a halfway rational explanation of two Justin Tanners owning the same house. On reflection it was absurd to think that the Justin she'd married had been camping out illegally in somebody else's home. He hadn't looked or behaved like a person dreading imminent discovery. And if her husband hadn't been occupying the house in Copper Creek illegally, then the most logical explanation of the mystery was that *this* Justin Tanner—Justin II as she mentally dubbed him—was in cahoots with the man who'd married her.

But in cahoots to do what, for heaven's sake? And if Justin II was a criminal associate of Justin I, then why hadn't he turned her over to Sheriff Swanson? That would have been a much more effective way to get rid of her than driving her to the local hospital and quizzing her about the dates she'd occupied his house.

She dismissed the questions as unsolvable and therefore irrelevant. People who had spent a lot of time in Walnut Park Mental Health Institute couldn't waste their limited brain power trying to find logical explanations for impenetrable mysteries. If she was smart, she would stop worrying about what had happened last May and concentrate on her plans for escape. She had to make a break for freedom before Justin handed her over to the emergency-room staff at Aspen Hospital. At the moment, there was a chance she wasn't completely crazy. Another few nights with doctors asking her soothing questions, and her hopes of remaining sane would fade rapidly.

She hunched her shoulders away from Justin and stared out of the window. The Bronco drew to a halt at a traffic light, and Justin waited to make a left-hand turn toward the hospital. Courtney was suddenly assailed by a vivid, cameo image of her last drive with her husband. It had been in an ambulance, she realized. They had drawn up at a stoplight and she had stared at the red light, feeling a blinding pain deep in her skull as the signal winked off and changed to green.

She didn't remember getting into the ambulance or where it had finally stopped. She could only remember a short journey in a wheelchair, her body hurting all over and her head feeling strangely light and disconnected. She was pushed along dark corridors to a room with lights so bright they hurt her eyes. A courtroom, she realized with a flash of hindsight.

Courtney swallowed hard, keeping her excitement under control. This was the first time she had been able to visualize the courtroom where she must have been declared mentally incompetent. She pictured the judge, an elderly man who had spoken to her with considerable kindness. Her tongue had felt thick and heavy in her mouth, making it difficult to speak, and she hadn't been able to respond to most of the judge's questions. In the end the judge had turned to Justin, who stood patiently at her side, holding her hand and stroking her knuckles tenderly. For some reason that particular memory caused a thrill of revulsion to course down her spine.

"It's the drugs she's been taking," she heard her husband say. "I tried very hard to counsel her, Your Honor, but she kept breaking her promises, and she wouldn't enter any of the rehabilitation programs I recommended."

"You certainly don't have to blame yourself," the judge said. "I can tell you've done more than could be expected."

"I'm a very old friend of the family," her husband replied, and Courtney could hear the ring of modesty in his voice. Was she recalling his tone so vividly because even then, even through the haze of pain and drugs, she had known the modesty wasn't genuine?

"I felt I owed something to Courtney's aunt," Justin had continued. "Amelia Norris was a wonderful woman. It would have broken her heart to see her niece in this sort of state."

"And I gather her aunt is dead? Miss Long doesn't have any close living relatives?"

"No relatives at all, Your Honor. Courtney is an orphan and her aunt was a spinster. There are no cousins, no aunts or uncles. Nobody except me. That's why I've felt such a burden of responsibility."

"You've done very well, Mr...."

The judge's voice faded into complete and frustrating silence. Courtney tried her best to recapture the image of the courtroom, but without success. The vivid pictures had once again dissolved into an all-enveloping blankness.

She must have made some involuntary sound of protest,

because Justin turned quickly and reached out to touch her on the arm. "Feeling okay?"

She didn't want him to be kind. She wanted to dislike him with a clean, uncomplicated loathing. "I'm just fine," she replied in her best Walnut Park voice, the one she used when she wanted to convince the nurses that she was almost as sane as they were. She could feel his gaze still on her face, so she added quickly, "Except for my headache, of course."

"Of course."

Justin found a parking spot and stopped the car. Long before he had shifted out of gear, Courtney had unbuckled her seat belt and flung herself at the door.

Her foot was already touching asphalt when his right arm whipped out, forming an iron barrier across her waist. His left hand grabbed hold of a hunk of hair. He didn't bother to be gentle. "I knew you were planning to run," he said. "You're not willing to see a doctor, are you?"

She gritted her teeth. "Let me out of this truck, Mr. Tanner. Holding somebody against their will is a criminal offense. It's called kidnapping."

"If the person's a criminal, it's called a citizen's arrest."

"I'm not a criminal, Mr. Tanner."

"Maybe not, but you're one terrified young woman." He jingled the car keys in his hand. "Where are you going to spend the night if you won't see a doctor?"

"In a hotel."

"Aspen hotel prices start at sixty dollars a night for the broom closet and work upward from there."

"There are worse places than a broom closet."

"Hospitals being one of them?" She didn't respond, and after a short silence he spoke again. "How would you like to spend the night with me? In my house, I mean."

Her stomach gave an odd little lurch. "Why would you offer me hospitality?" she asked. "What's in it for you, or are you planning to set up as the town's resident philanthropist?''

"Anything but," he replied, his voice cool. "I'm not in the habit of scooping strays off the streets for the night."

"Then why me?"

"Because you've said some very odd things, and you seem to believe what you're saying. If you're telling the truth, then somebody's been masquerading under my name, and I want to find out who. It makes me mad as hell to think somebody may have been using my name and my house when I was in New York."

Courtney spent about twenty seconds considering the advantages and disadvantages of accepting Justin's invitation. On the one hand, he could well be planning to murder her. On the other hand, she had exactly forty-six dollars and seventy cents in her gym bag. Under the circumstances, she was willing to risk being murdered.

"Thanks," she said finally. "I would very much like a bed for the night."

"Don't think you're getting a free ride. I'll expect full value in exchange for my hospitality."

Courtney shriveled as his words sank in. She looked up and saw his frown.

"I don't mean sex," he said, his voice arctic. "Once I got out of college, I stopped carving notches on my headboard. Besides, you've met my housekeeper. Mrs. Moynihan is a pillar of respectability, and she lives in."

Courtney tried to match his coolness. "Then what did you mean?"

"Simply that I want answers to my questions. If you come back to my house, Courtney, you're going to talk. If somebody's stolen my name, I intend to find out who."

She took her time refastening her seat belt. "All right," she said slowly. "It's a deal."

COURTNEY LET THE hot water cascade through her hair and down her back. The smell of shampoo and an expensive masculine-scented soap tickled her nostrils. The mental fatigue caused by months of bewilderment and frustration began to seep away, gurgling down the drain along with the water. Confidence returned as weariness vanished. By the time she had wrapped herself in a fluffy bath towel and blow-dried her hair, she was convinced that she would have no trouble at all in parrying any difficult questions from Justin.

She padded out of the small bathroom into the sunny yellow spare bedroom. She liked this room. In fact, she liked the whole house. She had often complimented Justin I on his excellent taste in combining sophisticated comfort with just the right touch of mountain rusticity.

Except that the man she called her husband probably hadn't decorated this house at all. Presumably Justin II was responsible for the dark brown carpet in this room, the pale yellow walls and the wild-orchid design splashed across the drapes and matching bedspread. Or maybe Justin II had a wife who'd tended to all the decoration? This room had a subtle feminine undertone.

The possibility that Justin II might be married had not occurred to her before. Just because she'd seen no evidence of a wife didn't mean much these days. It didn't matter either way, Courtney decided. Justin II's marital status was completely irrelevant to her needs and plans.

She patted talcum powder across her stomach, refusing to allow her good humor to dissipate. At the moment she had a lot to be grateful for. She wasn't in Walnut Park. She had a bed for the night. She smelled wonderful, and she was soon going to eat a huge dinner. It seemed like forever since she'd last eaten.

It was not, of course, going to be easy to disguise the fact that she'd spent the past five months in a maximum-security mental hospital. Courtney scowled into the mirror, wishing she had some lipstick and eye shadow to give a bit of color to her too-pale features. *Start inventing your lies now, girl,* she warned herself. A sick relative seemed the best excuse for leaving her husband in a hurry. How about a grandmother dying in Canada? Somewhere abroad, even if just over the border, might validate her excuses for being totally out of touch with her husband.

Courtney straightened her somewhat grubby sweater and cast a final glance into the bedroom mirror. For the first time since entering Walnut Park, she really cared about the way she looked. Justin Tanner II was an attractive man, she reflected. Not suave and sophisticated like her missing husband, but earthy and aggressively masculine. He probably would be absolutely terrific in bed.

Courtney cut off that line of thought in a hurry. It was disloyal and immoral to be married—maybe—to one Justin Tanner, and yet find another Justin Tanner attractive. Aunt Amelia, she thought wryly, would *not* approve.

Enticing smells wafted from the kitchen as she walked downstairs. Justin waited for her in the living room. "Did you find everything you needed?" he asked politely, adding another log to the fire blazing in the grate. Mountain nights were always chilly.

"Everything, thank you. I feel much better for a shower."

"You look like a new woman." He dusted sawdust off his hands as he walked to the small corner bar. "What'll you have to drink? Mrs. Moynihan's baking a chicken casserole for dinner."

"White wine would be great, if you have it."

"I have some Chablis that's cold." He turned on the radio before bringing her some wine, selecting an FM station playing a familiar piano concerto. He handed her the glass and sat down in a comfortable chair beside the fire. "The weather forecasters are predicting snow before the weekend. The skiers will be pleased if the season starts early."

"Yes. Do you ski, Mr. Tanner?"

"In the circumstances, I think you could call me Justin, don't you? And, yes, I ski. With a great deal of determination and absolutely no style. How about you?"

"I've skied quite a bit," she admitted. "A few competitions now and again." An understated way of describing the killing schedule leading up to her inclusion in the women's giant slalom Olympic team.

"Here in Aspen?"

"Occasionally. Colorado is a great place to ski."

He sensed her reluctance to make personal revelations and backed off from his questions. That showed more sensitivity to the state of her emotions than she would have expected. Or, a cynical voice inside her suggested, perhaps he was waiting until the alcohol had loosened her tongue before he set to work.

At this precise moment, he didn't look much like an inquisitor. He looked like an attractive and intelligent man, with a hint of sadness lingering somewhere in the depths of his compelling gray eyes. He leaned back in the chair, his legs stretched out comfortably in front of him as he sipped his wine.

"That's one of the things I like best about my work," he said. "I'm a visiting professor at Princeton University, which means that I can spend a lot of the year working at home. I really enjoy living in Aspen."

"What do you teach at Princeton?"

"The theory of higher mathematics, but I don't teach as many courses as I used to. I'm part of a university research team working on the creation of artificial intelligence."

"You mean computers that think for themselves? It sounds kind of threatening."

"Not really. Although if we succeed, I guess the philosophers and theologians will have to do a bit of professional soul-searching. The ultimate goal is to produce a computer that's genuinely creative, sort of like Hal in *2001*.''

"You know what happened to Hal."

"He developed into a monster. But remember, in the sequel he turned out to be a good guy after all. He saved the world."

"In real life people might not wait around for the sequel. You and your teammates could be lynched first."

He grinned. "That thought has occurred to us. It's one of the things that keeps our work interesting."

"So you don't really have much contact with the regular students?"

"I teach some graduate courses each year, but I can fit those in pretty much as I please. I also act as a consultant to several corporations, since universities don't have the funds to pay a decent salary. Consulting on technical problems takes care of the gray pinstripe part of my personality."

"Then you're not one of those dedicated research scientists who wanders around forgetting to eat and change his socks?"

He smiled, an appealing smile that had the most peculiar effect on the rate of Courtney's heartbeat. He pulled up the leg of his jeans. "See? Perfectly respectable, clean white socks. I turn into a forgetful scientist for about forty-eight hours once a month. The rest of the time I like to eat well and take frequent showers. Proof positive that I'm never going to make it as a genius, I guess."

"I guess. Besides, geniuses are all supposed to have beards and wear glasses."

"I wear glasses when I'm working. That should count for something."

She looked away, perturbed by the unexpected intimacy that had sprung up. "Do you really think machines will be able to make reasoned decisions one day? It doesn't sound possible to me."

"We've already developed computers that are powerful enough to give the *appearance* of making rational choices. Theoretically there's no reason at all why machines couldn't eventually be programmed to think. It's just a question of getting the mathematics right."

Mrs. Moynihan appeared in the doorway. "Dinner's ready. I've put the casserole on the table in the dining alcove. Dessert's in the fridge. Just put your dishes in the sink when you're through, and I'll come down and do them later. There's a program on TV I'd like to watch now, if that's okay with you."

"That's fine," Justin said. "The meal smells wonderful, as always."

Mrs. Moynihan sniffed, refusing to be mollified. When Courtney had returned with Justin, the housekeeper had made no secret of the fact that she disapproved totally.

Strangely enough, Courtney found Mrs. Moynihan's hostility reassuring. The housekeeper was so reproachful, it was impossible to imagine her as part of an ongoing conspiracy.

"Better hurry," Mrs. Moynihan said dourly. "Your food will be cold if you hang about in here."

The dining alcove was a small, open annex directly off the kitchen. Mrs. Moynihan had set two places with brightly colored place mats and the red-handled cutlery Courtney remembered from the brief period of her marriage. In addition to the casserole dish, there was a basket with crusty French bread, a bowl of salad and another bottle of wine. Justin filled both glasses and gestured to Courtney to take a seat.

They exchanged only minimum courtesies as they served themselves the excellent food. The FM station was now playing a selection of Tchaikovsky ballet music, and Courtney gradually relaxed.

"Were you born here in Colorado?" Justin asked, as she started on her second serving of casserole.

Perhaps it was the third glass of wine. Perhaps it was the

fact that he asked the question without any suspicion hardening his voice. In any event, she found herself answering with surprising honesty. "I was born in California, but I was orphaned before I was five and my aunt brought me up. She lived on the East Coast, in New Hampshire, actually. She was almost a caricature of the upright, clean-living New Englander. She could have been transported back into the middle of the nineteenth century, and I'm sure she'd have felt right at home."

"You talk of her in the past tense."

"Yes. She died about ten months ago." Courtney placed her fork neatly alongside a mushroom that had suddenly lost its savor. "I didn't realize until she died how much I loved her. I never told her, you know. That's what haunts me."

"Don't torture yourself, Courtney. People usually know when they're loved, and your aunt sounds like the sort of lady who believed love was expressed in deeds, not words."

Courtney picked up her fork, smiling slightly. "In my rational moments, I know you're right. Aunt Amelia was definitely not in favor of sentimental scenes."

"My wife died in May," Justin said. The words sounded as if they were wrung from him. "She had Hodgkin's disease."

"I'm so sorry. I didn't know—"

"How could you?" He ran his finger absently over the stem of his glass. "She was in so much pain for the last few weeks of her life that I was almost glad to see her die."

"I'm so sorry, Justin." The words seemed hopelessly inadequate. "It must have been terrible for both of you."

"She seemed to handle her pain much better than I did." Justin's face was distorted by the memory of his wife's suffering, and Courtney felt an unexpected impulse to gather him into her arms.

"My aunt died of a heart attack," she commented. "At the time I was angry that she'd gone so quickly she didn't have a chance to say goodbye to her friends. But looking back, I'm glad it happened that way, for my sake as much as for hers.''

Justin pushed his plate away. The pain had gone from his eyes, replaced by a blankness that Courtney understood all too easily. It was the same mask she had learned to put on when the sympathy of the doctors and nurses at Walnut Park became too oppressive.

He sprang up from the table with false energy. ''If you've finished, shall we take this stuff into the kitchen?''

''I'll take the salad and the casserole if you can manage the rest.''

They stacked their dishes in the sink, and Justin withdrew a huge lemon-meringue pie from the fridge. A pot of freshly brewed coffee waited on the counter. ''Wow! I can see Mrs. Moynihan doesn't believe in letting you starve,'' Courtney said.

''I think this creation must be in your honor.''

Courtney allowed her astonishment to show. ''In my honor? I thought she was all ready to barricade me outside the house.''

''Mrs. Moynihan's bark is a lot worse than her bite.''

''Who cares if she bites?'' Courtney asked a few minutes later, as she scraped up the pie crumbs from her plate. ''When you bake this well, you don't need a charming personality.''

''I'm glad you enjoyed dinner.'' Justin reached over to pour her coffee, and their gazes locked. Something in his expression made heat rush up into her cheeks.

His eyes lost their hint of warmth. ''Did your Aunt Amelia ever meet your husband?'' he asked abruptly.

From his tone Courtney knew the real interrogation had begun at last. ''No,'' she replied as calmly as she could. ''Aunt Amelia died before I came to Aspen.''

''And you met your husband here?''

"Yes, I did. Three weeks before I married him." She flung the statement out with deliberate defiance, daring him to comment on her foolishness. He didn't respond to her challenge, at least not directly.

"Why did you marry him?" Justin asked quietly.

She tried to produce some slick, easy answer, but the words wouldn't come. During the long nights at Walnut Park, she had sometimes wondered if the turmoil caused by her aunt's death and the incredible discoveries about her parents had so upset her that she'd mistaken fascination for love. But she wasn't about to confess such doubts to a virtual stranger.

"I was...I was in love with him, of course."

"Of course."

She ignored his irony and sipped determinedly at her coffee. Looking at him now, registering the sharpness of his eyes and the implacable firmness of his mouth, she wondered how she could ever have felt sorry for him. He looked about as sensitive as a stone carving on the cliffs of Easter Island, and about as much in need of her sympathy.

"What does your husband look like, Courtney? Anything like me?"

"No, nothing at all. He's older than you, for a start—"

"How old?"

"Forty-five. He's five feet ten, slender build, with delicate, expressive hands. His hair's dark, and he has the most extraordinary deep blue eyes."

"Do you have any pictures of him?"

She looked away. "No. No pictures. I left here in a hurry. There was no time to pack."

"What about your other belongings? Did you expect to find them here waiting for you?"

"I wasn't sure. Yes, probably."

"Courtney, according to your story, you left here in May. It's now October. Why did you wait five months to come looking for your husband?"

"I was…away." Too late, she remembered her story about the dying relative in Canada. But having just told him all about her aunt, she couldn't suddenly invent another guardian dying in the frozen hinterland of Alberta or Manitoba.

"You were away where?" he asked, making no attempt to soften his questions with a veil of politeness.

"I had to go back to New Hampshire. There was… um…family business to attend to."

"And from May to October, you never once thought of picking up the phone? That was pretty important business you were taking care of, Courtney."

She didn't—couldn't—answer. He repeated his question. "Where have you been for the past six months, Courtney? In jail?"

"No! Of course I haven't been in jail!"

"Then where have you been?"

She waited just a fraction of a second too long, and into the silence came the voice of the radio newscaster.

"Local authorities are checking into security arrangements at Walnut Park Mental Health Institute, a state-licensed private psychiatric facility for the care of seriously disturbed and dangerous patients, located in southwest Denver. Courtney Long, the missing patient, has a history of mental instability and the authorities are afraid she may be a danger to members of the public as well as to herself. The Arapahoe County authorities have issued the following description: Courtney is five feet six inches tall, weighs 123 pounds, has shoulder-length straight blond hair, gray-blue eyes, sometimes described as violet, and identifying scars on her wrists from a recent suicide attempt. Anybody with information about Courtney Long's whereabouts should contact their local law-enforcement agency immediately.

"In sports news tonight…"

Justin got up from the table and switched off the radio, leaving a silence thick enough to cut. He walked over to

Courtney's side, gently taking hold of her hands. Paralyzed with despair, she didn't resist. Justin pushed away the remnants of the lemon-meringue pie and stretched her arms across the table, inner wrists upward. To Courtney's eyes it seemed that the two puckered lines stood out against her skin with all the clarity of neon lights, flashing in a midnight darkness.

Justin said nothing at all. He ran his thumbs over the scars, his taut features softening. He put his arm around her shoulder and raised her to her feet, propelling her carefully in the direction of the hall. Still keeping his arm protectively on her shoulders, he reached into the hall closet and extracted two down-filled jackets. He put one on Courtney, then slung the other carelessly over his shoulder.

He opened the door. "Let's go, Courtney," he said soothingly. "Don't worry about anything. I'll make sure you get all the help you need."

Chapter Five

The rage Courtney had been suppressing for months bubbled up inside her, a seething caldron of uncontrollable emotion. It wasn't fair, she thought wildly. It wasn't fair that a perfectly harmless young woman should have to fight so hard to keep herself out of an insane asylum. Damn it all, she wasn't only sane, she was positively boring. Until Aunt Amelia died, the most eccentric action of her life probably had been to order an anchovy-and-pineapple pizza.

She clasped her hands tightly around her waist, struggling to contain the imminent explosion. If she ranted and raved too much, Justin might decide to deliver her to the hospital trussed up like an oven-ready chicken.

"Watch out for the steps," he advised kindly.

She choked back an irate response. Now that he knew she'd escaped from the Nuthouse, he no longer considered her capable of putting one foot in front of the other.

Clouds covered the moon, and once they moved out of the circle cast by the porch lights the driveway was pitch-black. Justin kept his arm tightly around her and walked her carefully toward the Bronco.

He didn't relax his hold until he could prop her up safely against the passenger side of the truck. "The doors open only from the driver's side," he said, "but don't worry, it won't take but a few seconds to unlock your door.'' His smile was calm, reassuring—and totally *infuriating*.

Her nails dug into her palms. "I'm all right. Don't worry." Her voice, along with the rest of her body, trembled with the violence of her rage. She clenched her teeth together to stop them chattering.

Justin seemed to assume she was shaking because she was frightened. "It won't be so bad, Courtney," he said quietly. "I'll talk to the doctors and see if they can't come up with some new ways to help you."

She didn't trust herself to speak. She closed her eyes and leaned more heavily against the truck. He took the hint and strode around the hood toward the driver's seat.

She heard the key scratch in the lock. It was all the encouragement she needed. Courtney sprang away from the truck and dashed for the concealing thicket of pine trees at the edge of the property. Her feet flew lightly across the autumn-bare flower beds, as she rushed toward the haven provided by the trees.

She was so agile that she just might have made good her escape, but the silence of the mountain night was her undoing. The rustle of leaves, the crack of twigs, even the harsh whisper of her breathing reverberated in the crystal clarity of the night air. Every step she took provided Justin with a fresh sound to follow, and although she was exceptionally fleet, he was no slouch.

She raced through the undergrowth, dodging around trees, sobs of fury tearing out of her throat. Damn it, why couldn't he let her go? What did it matter to him if one insignificant lunatic escaped from her lockup?

It took him a full five minutes to catch her. She made one last, desperate attempt to dodge around a pine tree, but he grabbed her with both hands and forced her up against the trunk of the tree, holding her captive with his body.

They were both panting and sweating despite the cold.

Courtney twisted in a futile attempt to escape his arms. He pressed her even harder against the prickly tree trunk. "What the *hell* do you think you're doing?" he yelled.

"Running for my life!"

"Well, that's great, lady. Don't you realize you could have broken your stupid neck?"

"No! Crazy women don't realize anything, didn't you know that?"

"Why would I know anything about you?" He was still yelling. "I've never been in charge of a mad woman before."

"Is that right? Well, stick around, and you'll have yourself some fun. Us crazies have a real exciting repertoire."

She stared up at him, anger coursing through her body. He held her shoulders pinned to the tree, so she twisted her hips, trying to bring her knee up to kick him in the groin. Just because he'd caught her didn't mean he could load her into his Bronco without a fight.

She had scarcely bent her knee before his body pressed hard against hers, shoulder to thigh, totally preventing her from moving. "Oh, no, you don't, lady. I've no desire to be castrated by a runaway crazy."

"I'm not crazy." Her fingers curled themselves into claws, ready to scratch him. If he leans any closer, she thought, I'll be able to bite him.

The moon came out from behind its covering cloud, lighting his face with a cool, silvery glow. To Courtney's amazement her fingers suddenly uncurled, and she heard herself draw in a tiny, harsh breath. Her stomach contracted with a tension that had nothing to do with anger or fear.

Justin must have felt the change in her. In the erratic beam of moonlight, she saw his eyes darken with an astonishment as great as her own.

"I think we must *both* be crazy," he muttered hoarsely.

His head bent slowly toward hers, but she didn't turn away. His lips touched her mouth with the barest pressure, and her body responded with a leap of pleasure. She opened her mouth on a quiet murmur of astonishment, and his kiss immediately deepened, his tongue flicking against hers. His hands twined in her hair as he held her face captive.

Desire reached out and touched every part of her, transforming her tremors of rage into shudders of longing. She arched her back, molding herself to the hard strength of his body. She realized vaguely that she had never experienced sexual desire this strong, this swift or this exciting. Then she deliberately blanked out all thought and allowed herself simply to feel. And what he was doing felt absolutely terrific.

He had already unzipped her jacket, and his hand was stroking up her rib cage toward her breasts when he abruptly broke off their kiss. Courtney gave a tiny sigh of disappointment. Then reason reasserted itself with the force of a thunderbolt. Good God, what in the world had come over her? What had she been *doing*?

Shaken, she sought instinctively to protect herself. It would be very dangerous to let this man know how vulnerable she felt to his sexuality. In her precarious position, she couldn't afford to trust anybody.

Leaning back against the pine, she stared at him coolly. "Do you make a habit of kissing all the runaway lunatics who cross your path, Mr. Tanner?"

He half turned away. "No," he said, an odd catch in his voice. "I only kiss the ones with blond hair. None of the others turn me on."

Courtney swung on her heel and made another desultory attempt to dash for freedom, but they both knew her heart wasn't in it. Justin caught up with her easily. "Come back to the house, Courtney," he said quietly. "Your face is scratched and your hands are cut. You need to wash up and then apply some antiseptic. I do, too."

"Afraid the doctors might think you've been mistreating me?"

"No. I'm afraid you might get an infection."

"And when I'm all cleaned up, Mr. Tanner? Then what happens?"

He looked at her speculatively. "Then…I guess we talk."

"We did that already."

"But maybe not about the right things. Anyway, you don't have much choice. Wouldn't you rather talk to me than the doctor or the sheriff?"

"Are you offering me a reprieve from banishment, Mr. Tanner?"

He turned away. "For heaven's sake, Courtney, quit with the Mr. Tanner." He walked off in the direction of the driveway.

To her everlasting amazement, she followed him back to the house.

Mrs. Moynihan, fortunately, had not reappeared in the kitchen during their absence. Justin produced a small first-aid kit from one of the cupboards. He handed Courtney a bottle of antiseptic and a tube of all-purpose antibiotic cream. "Why don't you wash up in the guest bathroom? I can use the kitchen sink. I don't have as many cuts as you."

She took the first-aid kit into the bathroom, stripping off her jacket and sweater, then splashing hot, soapy water all over her face and arms. She stared into the mirror as she dabbed on antiseptic cream, wrinkling her nose in disgust at the sight. You look like a corpse with chicken pox, she told her reflection, pulling a twig from her hair with a vicious tug. She had no comb downstairs, so the best she could do was remove the pieces of mountain foliage and smooth her hair back behind her ears. The final effect was not glamorous.

She returned to the kitchen and handed over the antiseptic. "Thanks," Justin said, dabbing lotion onto his cut chin. His abrasions, such as they were, didn't make him look in the least like a corpse with measles. They made him look debonair and dashing.

Courtney scowled. "If I told you that I'm not mad, is there any hope that you'd believe me?" she asked.

"They say it's only the really crazy people who are convinced they're sane."

"I know." Courtney sat down at the kitchen counter, all her combativeness disappearing in a single swoop. "At the hospital I soon learned that the more often I told them I wasn't sick, the less chance I had of making them believe me." She looked up, drawing in a breath that ended somewhere between a laugh and a sob. "What am I supposed to do? Admit that sometimes, in the depths of the night, I've woken up in a cold sweat wondering if—just maybe—they're all right and I'm wrong?"

"Why were you locked up in a maximum-security mental hospital if you're not sick, Courtney? Nowadays, the way the law's written, it's very hard for people to get wrongly confined."

She hadn't realized she knew the answer to Justin's question until she heard herself speak. "It wasn't an accident or a mistake," she said slowly. "I think the man who married me used your name so I'd never be able to track him down. I think he had some reason why he wanted me locked away where nobody on the outside would ever bother about me again." She laughed harshly. "Now I suppose you're even more certain that I'm crazy. Paranoid schizophrenics have the dandiest delusions, isn't that what you're thinking? You ever had the pleasure of meeting a certified schizo before, Mr. Tanner?"

"Not that I know of," he replied evenly. "Here, I warmed up the leftover coffee. Have a cup."

"Thanks." She cradled her hands around the mug, glad of the warmth. Her fingers were freezing.

Justin leaned against the sink, his expression difficult to

read. "Tell me something, Courtney. What reason could anybody have, especially your husband, for wanting you committed to a mental hospital if you're not sick?"

Courtney hesitated. "I have a trust fund," she said finally. "It's worth a little over a million dollars. I did wonder if maybe that was the reason I was gotten out of the way."

"Seems an awful lot of fuss and bother for a paltry million dollars. There must be a dozen easier ways your husband could have gotten his hands on your money. Persuading you to sign a power of attorney, for example."

Courtney shrugged. "That's what I keep telling myself. Besides, he never acted as if he were short of funds."

"That doesn't mean anything. First rule of a successful con artist, my dear. Never let anybody see you're hungry."

"How would you know?"

Unexpectedly he grinned. "From watching television, of course." He moved away from the sink. "All these dirty dishes are making me feel guilty. I have to keep reminding myself I *pay* Mrs. Moynihan to wash them. Let's go back to the living room and you can tell me how you came to be committed to Walnut Park."

"I wish I knew," Courtney said, sitting at one end of the sofa and waiting while Justin plumped up the cushions at the other end. "I must have picked up some sort of bug in Mexico, and when we came back here after our honeymoon, I was so sick I couldn't get out of bed. The last few days, I was vomiting so often, I think I got dehydrated. At any rate I started to get delirious, and Justin said he would take me to a doctor. I remember getting into his car and driving toward Aspen Airport. That's all I remember except being inside an ambulance and arriving at a courthouse."

"You have no memories of the court hearing?"

She couldn't admit that her husband had accused her of being a drug addict. There were limits to how many incriminating facts she could reveal before Justin bundled her back into the Bronco and headed for the sheriff's office. She stared into the burned-out embers of the fire.

"I don't remember anything significant," she said quickly. "I only remember waking up inside Walnut Park."

"But you remember that clearly enough?"

She smiled tightly. "Oh, yes. Waking up in a padded cell is a memorable experience."

"You have scars on your wrists," Justin said quietly. "Do you remember why you tried to kill yourself?"

She twisted around on the sofa. "I never tried to kill myself," she said with passionate conviction. "Maybe my mind is deliberately blocking out incidents that are too painful for me to deal with. But if I'd tried to kill myself, I *know* I'd remember. That's not something my mind could block out."

She could see his skepticism, and she knotted her hands together in her lap, fighting back the familiar waves of frustration. With a supreme effort, she kept her voice low and under control. "You have to believe me, Justin; I'm not the suicidal type. During all the time I was locked up in Walnut Park, I never once considered committing suicide, not even two months ago when they sent me back to the padded cell as punishment for trying to escape." Her mouth twisted. "Murder, I'll admit to considering, but not suicide."

"Didn't the doctors think it strange that your husband never came to visit?"

Courtney examined a scratch on her hand with more attention than it warranted. "My psychiatrist told me I'd never been married. He suggested I was lonely after Aunt Amelia died and my imagination invented a husband to keep me company."

"I see," Justin said. "Well, what about your employers? Didn't they speak up for you?"

"I didn't have any employers." Courtney jumped up from the sofa and paced angrily up and down in front of the fireplace. "Everything changed when Aunt Amelia died," she explained. "I found out that I'd spent the last twenty-two years living a lie, and I wanted to change all that and learn the truth. So I quit my job as a ski instructor in New Hampshire and came to Colorado. I wasn't due to start work out here until the beginning of the ski season, which gave me the entire summer to investigate my past. But I'd only just moved here when I met Justin, and I don't have any friends in Aspen."

Something about the quality of his silence caused her to look up. When she saw his expression her mouth tightened. "Don't give me that damned sympathetic look. I am *not* suffering from psychotic depression over my aunt's death. I am *not* insane with grief or regrets or anything else. I love Aunt Amelia very much, but I didn't go mad when she died."

"You said at dinner how much you regretted the barriers between you and your aunt—"

"But she put them there, not me," Courtney interrupted. She walked over to the window and stared out at the black shadows of trees and distant mountains. "I realize now that she built them deliberately, so I wouldn't question her too closely."

During all the weeks she had spent with Justin I, she had carefully avoided any mention of the incredible discoveries that followed in the wake of her aunt's death, and she had never breathed a word about her past to the Nuthouse doctors. She wasn't quite sure why she wanted to tell all now. She knew only that an oppressive weight seemed to disappear from her shoulders as soon as she decided to speak.

"My aunt lied to me," she said abruptly. "My upright New Englander, my paragon-of-all-the-old-fashioned-virtues lied through her teeth from the day she took me into her home until the day she died."

"What about?"

"My parents, my background. Everything."

Justin walked across the room so silently she didn't know he was standing behind her until she felt the touch of his hand on her shoulder. "You mean you were adopted? She wasn't your real aunt?"

Courtney turned around, wanting to look at him, needing the comfort of eye contact as she told him the incredible, unsettling truth. "Aunt Amelia really was my maternal aunt, but she lied about who my parents were."

He looked puzzled. "Presumably the sister and brother-in-law of your aunt."

"I didn't mean that." Courtney leaned back against the window frame. "Do you have incidents in your childhood you can remember in perfect detail? So that you can smell the smells and taste the tastes, as well as hear the voices and see the people?"

"Sure," Justin said, smiling. "I remember creeping downstairs to snitch a fresh-baked chocolate-chip cookie and seeing my oldest brother kissing his girlfriend on the back porch. He was a senior in high school, six years older than me, and I felt this weird mixture of envy, disgust and intense curiosity. In those days movies weren't as graphic as they are now, and I'd never seen two people in a genuine clinch. Unfortunately, right when things were getting exciting, my dad caught me spying and sent me upstairs with a tanned backside to keep me company. I've had an uncertain relationship with chocolate-chip cookies ever since."

She laughed, surprising herself with the sound. She'd almost forgotten what real laughter felt like.

"What do you remember from your childhood?" Justin asked.

"My nightmare," she said, all trace of laughter vanishing. "It used to come almost every night." She stopped. The mere mention of that dreadful, recurring dream was enough to shorten her breath and turn her skin clammy.

Justin sat in the window seat and drew her down next to him. "Want to tell me about it?"

"No, I don't want to. I hate even to think about it. But I have to tell you if you're going to understand how my aunt lied to me." She grimaced, steeling herself for the ordeal to come.

"I'm in my bedroom," she said finally. "Not the one in Aunt Amelia's house, but nevertheless I know it's my room and that I'm usually happy there. I never get any older in the dream, and from the size of me, I can tell I'm about four. I'm thirsty and I wake up, but I know immediately that something horrible is happening. There's this dreadful noise coming from my parents' bedroom. It's so scary I don't want to listen to it. Then I realize it's my mother, and she's screaming. And then the screaming stops, and the silence is more scary than the noise. I run to the door of my parents' room to find out what's happened, but I don't go inside because I'm too frightened. Instead I sneak downstairs on tiptoe and go out into the garden. It's winter. I know that because I'm freezing cold. I can feel the ice burning against my toes, and the inside of my nose hurts when I breathe. But the worst thing of all is my fear. I run into the bushes and curl up between the branches to wait for my mother to come and find me."

She fell silent, shivering, and Justin put his arm around her. "Tell me the rest," he said quietly. "That doesn't sound like the end of the story."

"It's not. But the last part of the dream's the worst, although I don't know why. I'm still crouched in the bushes and somebody starts calling me. 'Didi, Didi! Where are you, Didi? Time to come inside, Didi.' It's a man's voice, but I know it's not my father's. I have this overpowering sensation of deadly danger, and I keep quiet and still as a mouse, but the Voice never goes away. I don't want to breathe, because if I breathe I know the Voice is going to find me and then something truly terrible will happen.''

She realized that she was rocking back and forth in pain, her eyes shut. She opened them quickly. ''That's the point when I wake up.''

''What a horrible dream.'' Justin kept his arm loosely around her shoulders. His touch was reassuring in its casualness. ''It must have been a terrible ordeal to experience a dream like that every night.''

''When I was little, my nightgown used to be drenched with sweat by the time I woke up. It was such a huge mental effort not to run out of the bushes and tell the man where I was hiding.''

''The man called the child in your dream Didi.''

''I know, and I always recognized that Didi was *my* name, even though in real life nobody ever called me anything but Courtney.''

''Perhaps it was a nickname.''

She managed a smile. Not a very big one, but still a smile. ''Aunt Amelia's ward with a cutesy nickname? Come on, Justin, be real. It wasn't until after my aunt died that I realized Didi must have been the name I'd given myself when I was a baby.''

''How did you find that out after she died? Presumably she didn't materialize in your room, ready to make a full confession.''

''She left me the proverbial deathbed letter that directed me to a safe-deposit box rented under an assumed name.'' She bit her lip. ''Justin, I want you to see this whole story from my perspective. Can we stick with the dream for a moment?''

''Sure. Did your aunt give you any clues as to why you kept dreaming something so specific? Even if your subconscious distorted a lot of the facts, something must have happened to trigger such an intense, recurring nightmare.''

"Yes, she gave me an explanation, and it sounded very believable." Courtney struggled to keep a faint note of bitterness out of her voice. "It was so believable I'm sure she must have spent a lot of time working on the details. She explained that my parents were schoolteachers, Robert and Ferne Long, and they'd been burned in a tragic fire caused by faulty electric wiring in the house they were remodeling. According to her story, the fire started in their bedroom, and they were probably dead of smoke inhalation even before the flames took control. At first firemen assumed I'd died in the blaze. Hours later they found me collapsed behind the shrubbery, barefoot and wearing a short-sleeved nightgown. I was hospitalized with pneumonia, and for weeks it was touch and go whether I'd survive."

"It's not surprising your conscious mind doesn't remember anything about such a traumatic experience."

"Yes. And as soon as I was old enough to understand psychological theories, my aunt explained that I probably felt guilty because I'd survived and my parents hadn't. She suggested my subconscious used the nightmare as a way to reproach me, but she impressed upon me all the time that I had nothing in the world to feel guilty about. There was no way I could have saved my parents, and she encouraged me not to think about the past."

"She never took you for professional counseling?"

"Aunt Amelia? Consorting with *psychiatrists*?"

"Ah! I gather she considered them slightly less reputable than snake-oil salesmen."

"You're right. Not to mention the fact that she claimed most of them were crazier than their patients. She was a great believer in physical exercise as a cure of mental ills, which may be why she encouraged my enthusiasm for skiing."

"Do the nightmares still bother you?"

"Hardly ever. By the time I was a teenager, my subconscious must have decided to ease up on the guilt, and the nightmare came less and less often.''

''I don't understand why you think your aunt lied to you. The dream seems to tie in with everything she told you about yourself. And there's no way she could have controlled your dreams.''

''No, but she could control how I interpreted them.''

''Why would she want to?''

''Because she felt the truth about my parents was too terrible for me to know. For some reason my aunt decided that it would be better if I never found out who my parents really were. Even the letter she left me suggested I might be happier if I didn't pursue the subject.''

Justin's expression was becoming less sympathetic by the moment. ''Okay,'' he said with obvious impatience. ''I've been sufficiently set up for the grand denouement, so I'll ask the obvious. Who were your parents, Courtney?''

She drew in a deep breath. ''My father was Robert Danvers, the Olympic ski champion, and my mother was Ferne Hilton.''

''Ferne Hilton!'' Justin rose slowly to his feet. He stared at Courtney, his body frozen into a posture of disbelief. ''Ferne Hilton was your mother!'' he repeated. ''Ferne Hilton, the movie star?''

''Yup, that's the one. The one who was brutally murdered in Aspen twenty-two years ago. By her husband, no less. My father then obligingly saved the state the expense of a trial by committing suicide alongside my mother's body.''

Justin was ominously silent, and she raised her chin defiantly. ''Now you're convinced I'm crazy, right? Not only do I fantasize a nonexistent husband, but I invent myself a gruesome murder and famous movie stars for parents.''

His gaze became thoughtful as he examined her features with a minuteness that brought heat into her cheeks. ''No,'' he said finally. ''I don't think you're fantasizing. For the firs time since I met you, I'm convinced you're telling the truth. Linda...my wife...was an actress, and she spent a lot of time trying to educate me in the history of the cinema. I've seen all of Ferne Hilton's movies, and once you know what to look for, the resemblance between you and your mother is startling. I've had this niggling feeling all along that I've seen you somewhere before. Of course, I haven't. What I've seen was films of your mother as a young woman."

Courtney tried to speak, but the words wouldn't come. She swallowed hard. "You mean...you *believe* me?"

"I just said I did. What else did you discover in your aunt's safe-deposit box?"

"A file of newspaper clippings from the time of the murder and some family papers. Then there was my mother's jewelry and photos of me with my mother and skiing with my...with my father...."

Courtney got no further. The relief of finding somebody who believed her story sent her emotional system rocketing into overload. She curled up on the hard window seat, covering her face with her hands. She hadn't cried when she woke up in the padded cell. She hadn't cried when the doctors told her she was insane. She hadn't cried when her first attempt at escape was unsuccessful. But now she cried—racking, inelegant sobs that ripped at her throat and convulsed her body.

Justin grabbed a bunch of cocktail napkins from the bar and thrust them into her hands. "Here," he said, sitting down next to her. "Feel free to stop the hysterics whenever you're ready."

After a few more noisy sobs, Courtney sniffed and swallowed hard. Tears continued to course freely down her face. "I'm not in the least hysterical," she said, with a belated attempt at dignity.

Justin brushed her cheeks dry with his thumbs and gave

her a tiny smile. "No, of course not. I can see you're a positive model of self-control."

His eyes rested on her quivering mouth and the tension was suddenly there again, arching between them with undeniable force. The laughter faded from his eyes and his tanned skin stretched taut over his rugged features. She moistened her lips and saw heat scorch along his cheekbones. His hands continued to cup her face as he spoke with studied casualness. "John F. Kennedy reportedly said your mother was the most beautiful woman in America."

Courtney couldn't move. Her body was suffering from a strange new form of paralysis that seemed to intensify the closer he came. She gulped. "I read that, too."

His head continued to move inexorably toward hers. "I guess Kennedy knew what he was talking about. His biographers all claim he was a connoisseur of beautiful women."

Justin was so close that she could feel the heat of his breath against her lips. "My husband..." she whispered distractedly. "I may be married—"

"If he married you under a false name and under false pretenses, it's no marriage."

"Are you sure?"

"I took three weeks of law school before I decided to become a mathematical genius. Sure I'm sure." Almost before he had finished speaking his mouth covered hers, coaxing it open with a passionate, searching kiss.

Waves of desire suffused her body, heating her skin from scalp to toes. Maybe she was crazy after all, Courtney thought. If so, it was mighty tempting to go with the flow. Sanity had never felt half so good.

Justin's arms tightened around her, lifting her so that she rested even more closely against him. She abandoned the struggle to keep her eyes open. Her lashes fluttered closed and her mouth was filled with the taste of him. Erotic, earthy, sensual. She let her fingers wind themselves in the enticing thickness of his hair.

"Mr. Tanner, I have to speak to you! I knocked but you didn't seem to hear.... *Lord love us, Mr. Tanner!*"

The housekeeper's voice faded into shocked silence, and Courtney froze. With no apparent embarrassment, Justin released her from his embrace. She could scarcely credit the evidence of her own eyes, but there actually seemed to be a trace of genuine amusement in his face as he turned and answered the housekeeper.

"Yes, Mrs. Moynihan, what did you want to tell me?"

The housekeeper kept her eyes carefully averted from the window seat. She crossed her hands in front of her solid stomach and planted her feet a little more firmly inside the living room. "I was watching the local newscast on TV," she said. "And there's something I should tell you right away, Mr. Tanner. In private, if you please."

Justin rose, not seeming to care if the housekeeper saw the reassuring squeeze he gave Courtney's hand. "Don't disappear," he commanded softly. "We have a lot more talking to do."

Mrs. Moynihan's snort was audible across the width of the living room. "I'll have that word with you *right now*, Mr. Tanner, if you don't mind."

Courtney watched their departure with a troubled frown. Mrs. Moynihan had obviously seen a news flash about the missing prisoner from Walnut Park Mental Health Institute. Equally obviously she was all set to dispatch Courtney into the hands of the nearest policeman. Even if Justin was prepared to help her, would he be able to prevent his housekeeper from turning her in to the authorities?

Courtney sat on the window ledge and debated the merits of trying to make yet another dash for freedom. It was a safer problem to worry about than the way she had felt when Justin II had kissed her.

Chapter Six

Harvey Nicholson hummed a tune from the Broadway musical *Cats* as he strolled out of his apartment building into the Manhattan sunshine. It felt good to be on vacation. Filming was in hiatus until next week, and he had five days of freedom stretching pleasurably ahead of him. Wednesday. He'd always liked Wednesday. It was an agreeable, well-balanced sort of day, just like he was an agreeable, well-balanced sort of man. He nodded a friendly good-morning to the doorman and turned toward Central Park.

The late October day was unseasonably warm, one of those glorious fall mornings that concealed the city's grime beneath a flattering mantle of golden radiance.

He would take Park Avenue, he decided, breathing deeply. He felt in the mood for an extra walk, and he was in no particular hurry to get to the post office. The day was so fine that even the exhaust fumes from the bumper-to-bumper traffic seemed to have lost some of their power to offend. You could almost convince yourself you were smelling autumn leaves and backyard bonfires instead of carbon monoxide and smoking gasoline. Ah yes, Harvey thought contentedly, this was definitely a day when it felt good to be alive.

He stopped at the intersection of Park and Seventy-second Street, waiting for the lights to change. When the walk signal flashed, he offered his arm to an elderly man whose limbs appeared gnarled with arthritis.

They reached the far side of the road just as the lights changed again. Harvey helped the old man over the curb and onto the safety of the sidewalk. The old codger was profuse in his thanks. Harvey cut him off with a charming smile and an airy wave of his hand. He reflected that such kindly gestures were typical of his thoughtfulness toward the less fortunate creatures of this world. At heart, Harvey congratulated himself, he was an exceptionally benevolent human being.

If the truth were told, he was not only benevolent but brilliant as well. It was typical of his meticulous attention to detail that he had chosen to make time this morning to check out his post-office box, even though there was almost no chance of finding any important mail waiting for him there.

Harvey wove his way in and out of the crowds, still quietly humming. He caught sight of himself in the plate-glass windows of a luxury apartment building and smiled. He really was a fine figure of a man, trim, athletic-looking and so elegantly dressed. The maroon silk cravat was a splendid touch—just the right mix of bohemian nonchalance and New York chic.

He turned into the post office, resisting the impulse to burst into full-fledged song. Damn, but he felt *good* this morning. He located his box in the lobby, number 103, rented under the name of the Reverend Gary Wade. Gary Wade had been one of his mother's legion of lovers, the one whom Harvey most disliked, partly because the poor fool really had been a minister. In those preadolescent days, Harvey had been naive enough to imagine ministers were above temptation, and it had been devastating to see the Reverend Wade succumb to the same artfully cast lures as all the other men who crossed his mother's path. Harvey found it amusing that the wretched man's name was serving a useful purpose at last.

He unlocked his box and swung open the heavy brass door.

As he had suspected, the box was almost empty. He tossed away a pile of circulars, then opened the familiar monthly report from Walnut Park Mental Health Institute. He scanned the formal words. *"Patient's condition stabilized...no longer suicidal, but still totally out of contact with reality... We hope with therapy and medication, etc., etc., etc."*

In other words, Miss Interfering Courtney Long was safely locked away for the foreseeable future. Harvey allowed himself to smile as he tore the letter into a dozen tiny pieces and dropped them into a nearby trash can. He was far too wise to carry the report home. Not for him the errors of lesser mortals. He would never confuse the persona of the Reverend Wade with the real Harvey Nicholson, successful television director.

He was on the point of locking up his box, when a hand thrust another piece of mail into it. A post-office employee, realizing the box was open, bent down and peered through the narrow opening. She smiled tentatively when she saw Harvey.

"One-O-three?" she asked.

He nodded, dangling his key in proof of his identity.

"Well, whaddya know? That's a piece of luck. Here's a mailgram for you." She glanced down at the address label, realized she was talking to a minister, and moderated her voice accordingly. "Just this minute arrived, Reverend. Hot off the plane."

Harvey didn't share the postal clerk's cheery laughter. He took the vivid blue envelope and saw the hospital's return address in the corner. His skin broke out in goose bumps and it was just a few seconds too long before he managed to produce a polite word of thanks for the clerk. A mailgram? Why the hell was somebody in Walnut Park sending the Reverend Wade a mailgram?

With the stern mental discipline he prided himself on, he soon recovered his poise. "Why, thank you, young lady," he said again. He smiled, laying on the charm, although the old bag had to be a minimum of forty pounds overweight. "This was just what I was waiting for. An important message from one of my parishioners, you know."

The postal clerk responded with a blush and a simper. She couldn't have any idea how absurd she looked with only her bulging red cheek and one and a half eyes visible through the hole at the back of the box. "Glad we met," she chirped. "Have a nice day, Reverend."

"Thanks. You, too."

Harvey retreated to a corner of the post-office lobby and slit open the mailgram envelope with fingers that were not quite steady. The letter inside was brief and to the point, and he was scowling heavily by the time he'd finished reading. Damn that scheming little bitch to hell! *She'd escaped from the mental hospital.* Harvey's fists clenched into two tight balls of pent-up fury. How dare she ruin all his careful planning! How dare she leave Walnut Park when he'd gone to such trouble to get her locked up there? Why the hell couldn't women do what they were told?

Harvey crumpled the envelope, then thrust the letter into the pocket of his tweed jacket and strode out of the post office. The sun shone as brightly as ever, but his earlier mood of contentment was totally ruined. Trust some slut of a woman to screw up a glorious day. Now he'd have to skip the sushi he'd promised himself for lunch and dash back to his apartment to find out what the hell was going on. Goddammit! Policemen all carried their brains in their britches, but surely even a bunch of Colorado cowboys ought to have spotted one friendless, penniless lunatic within two minutes of her escape from the hospital.

He reached his apartment building in double-quick time, panting at least as much from mental turmoil as from physical exertion. Of course the bitch thought she was married to

somebody called Justin Tanner, so she was sure to have
headed straight for Copper Creek. Where else would she go?

Harvey pressed the button to summon the elevator and
considered his options. He could call the police in his role
as the Reverend Wade—or perhaps anonymously—and suggest they should concentrate their search for Courtney in the
Aspen area. But that would be risky. They might wonder why
he was so sure Courtney would make for Aspen. And even
if the police didn't ask too many awkward questions, would
Courtney still be there by the time the police organized a
search party? He'd bet his last bottle of hair dye that she'd
make for Justin's house in Copper Creek, but what would
happen once she got there?

Harvey mulled over various possible scenarios as he let
himself back into his apartment. In all probability Justin Tanner would hand the damn girl straight over to the authorities.
In that case Harvey had nothing to worry about. Justin would
confirm in no uncertain terms that he'd never seen Courtney
in his life before, which would only reinforce the doctors'
conviction that Courtney was suffering from extreme delusions.

Harvey removed a bottle of white zinfandel from the pris-
tine shelves of his refrigerator. He poured a glass, sipping
the wine with only a hint of desperation. The letter had been
mailed yesterday. Tuesday. Courtney had escaped sometime
on Monday night. But she might already be back in custody.
No point in missing sushi and wasting his afternoon if Courtney was already locked up again. How could he find out if
she'd been recaptured?

Fortunately the hospital authorities would expect him to
respond to their letter. He would call the hospital right now,
in his role as Reverend Wade, and inquire about Courtney.
If he sounded worried, it wouldn't matter. The Reverend
Wade was an eternal do-gooder. Everybody would expect
him to be worried about his "dear little friend Courtney."

He placed the call. He soon realized that the senior administrator at Walnut Park was far too busy defending his institution to notice whether or not the Reverend Wade sounded overly worried. Harvey could almost hear the man sweating.

"You must understand, Reverend, our security arrangements are excellent, first-rate, top-notch. Courtney Long was a very unusual patient, very unusual indeed. How were we to know she'd be able to get over a twelve-foot brick wall? Not many people have that much athletic ability."

"I quite understand," Harvey murmured, his own confidence returning as the administrator became momentarily more flustered. "Although, of course, I did warn everybody that Courtney had been a member of the U.S. Olympic ski team—"

"We took every possible precaution," the administrator interrupted, his voice rising. "In fact, I suggested to the police that she must have had outside help, otherwise how could she still be free? It's forty-eight hours now, and not a sign of her anywhere. Where's she hiding, and what's she using for money? The hundred dollars she stole from here can't have taken her far."

Harvey's blood froze in his veins. Outside help? Was it possible, in all his brilliant planning, that he'd overlooked somebody who was available to help Courtney? But who? Amelia was dead. Courtney's closest friend from college was working in a hospital in darkest Africa, and her most recent boyfriend had gotten himself dumped about the time Amelia died. Most of Courtney's other friends were professional skiers, and they followed the grueling schedule of the international ski circuit. There was almost zero chance that they knew Courtney was in a mental home, even less chance that they would put their careers at risk by mounting an exotic rescue campaign. Harvey's blood resumed its natural rhythm. Good Lord, he was jumping at shadows!

He mouthed a few soothing platitudes at the sputtering hospital administrator and cut the connection. Harvey stood at the living-room window, sipping his second glass of wine and staring down at the people scurrying below without really seeing them. Ants, that's what most people were. Mindless automatons, waiting for direction from the few men suited to be their leaders.

Well, are you going to call Justin Tanner? The question sprang into his mind, mocking him with its seeming simplicity. Of course, he could disguise his voice. Justin didn't know him all that well, not like Linda. But what could he possibly say? Have you seen a young woman who claims to be married to you? Have you seen a young woman, Courtney Long, who escaped a couple of nights ago from a mental home? Whatever excuse he used, however he identified himself—even if he pretended to be a police officer—the net result of his call would be to establish a link between Courtney Long and Justin Tanner. And that was just what he wanted to avoid.

Harvey carried his glass to the kitchen sink and filled it with cold water. For no reason he could name, his brow was suddenly dewed with sweat, and his fingers felt so clumsy he couldn't turn off the tap.

He finally cut off the flow of water and pulled out his immaculate white linen handkerchief to mop his forehead. There was obviously no help for it. He couldn't control events in Colorado from two thousand miles away in New York, and he needed to be in control. He would have to fly into Denver. He wasn't due at the studio this week, and by the weekend he'd have this little hiccup in his planning all straightened out.

For Ferne's sake he'd given Courtney every chance, but she'd shown no gratitude for his forbearance. She obviously didn't appreciate how generous Harvey had been in his treatment of her. Why couldn't she accept that she was sick and needed help from the Walnut Park doctors?

The world really didn't deal fairly with kindhearted people like him, Harvey reflected. He didn't like killing people, didn't like it at all, but some women didn't deserve to live. He should have realized six months ago that he had a duty to kill Courtney Long. A virtuous man like Harvey had a duty to rid the world of whores like Ferne's daughter.

He picked up the kitchen phone and dialed United. The next flight for Denver left at 2:05 p.m.

Neatly, efficiently, Harvey began to pack.

Chapter Seven

Justin was brewing a pot of coffee when Mrs. Moynihan appeared in the kitchen early on Wednesday morning. "Good morning, Mr. Tanner. You sit down now. I'll get your breakfast."

Her tone of voice left no room for argument. Justin retreated to a corner of the kitchen, burying himself in the pages of the *Denver Post*. If he looked busy enough, he might possibly avoid a lecture.

He should have known better than to indulge in such wishful thinking. Mrs. Moynihan totally ignored his attempt to hide behind the latest stock-market figures. "I didn't sleep much last night," she remarked, beating up pancake batter as if the flour and milk had personally offended her. "I was far too worried."

"I'm sorry to hear that."

"Yes, well, it's not surprising if I felt worried with a madwoman sleeping ten feet away from me."

Regretfully Justin laid aside the *Post*, which obviously was providing no protection at all. "Mrs. Moynihan, I explained last night about Courtney. She's an old college friend of Linda's, a very *good* friend. I met her myself a few years ago, but her physical appearance has changed a bit, which is why I didn't recognize her at first—"

"Of course she's changed. She's loony tunes now. Nutty.

Minus most of her buttons. That's enough to make anybody look different.''

"Mrs. Moynihan, Courtney is perfectly sane." Justin couldn't understand why he was defending Courtney so vigorously. Only yesterday morning he would have agreed wholeheartedly with Mrs. Moynihan. Yet today he was lying through his teeth to protect somebody who might well be a threat to herself as well as the rest of the community. He had an uncomfortable suspicion he was reasoning with his hormones rather than his brain, and hormones were notoriously unreliable. He pushed his fingers impatiently through his hair, then got up to pour himself some orange juice. "Look, Mrs. Moynihan, I explained all this to you last night. Courtney should never have been locked up. She's the heiress to a lot of money, and her relatives wanted her out of the way so that they could use her money. They manipulated her into that hospital.''

The housekeeper pursed her lips. "People don't get locked up when they're not crazy. I looked in on her before I came down, and a babe in arms could tell she's up to no good. Sleeping with no clothes on, she was, and if that isn't asking for trouble—''

"Mrs. Moynihan, she doesn't have a nightgown.''

The housekeeper flipped three perfectly browned pancakes onto a plate and carried them to the counter. "She could've asked me for one. Anyway, Mr. Tanner, I've thought things over and I worked for you and Mrs. Tanner more than four years and you've always been a good employer and she was a real sweet lady. Couldn't have asked for anybody nicer, even though she was an actress. But the law's the law, and I'm going to call the sheriff and tell him that woman's here. It's my duty.''

For a moment Justin was tempted to shrug his shoulders and let her do as she pleased. He had no evidence Courtney was sane, and from the books he'd read last night after she

went to bed, he knew damn well she wasn't telling him anything like the whole story. He had no idea why he chose to
press the issue. "Give us the forty-eight hours you promised
last night, Mrs. Moynihan. Just to track down the evidence
Courtney's looking for, and then I'll turn her in myself, I
promise you."

The housekeeper banged pans into the sink and squirted
hot water over them aggressively. "You're asking me to do
something I don't think's right, Mr. Tanner." She glanced
across at her employer, then drew in a deep breath. "Forty-
eight hours, then, and not a second longer."

"Thank you. I really appreciate your willingness—"

"If something happens to make me change my mind, I'll
report her anyway. Forty-eight hours or no forty-eight
hours."

"I understand that—"

"If you'll excuse me, Mr. Tanner, I have the vacuuming
to do in your office. It's two weeks since I had a chance to
get in there. Usually you tell me you can't be disturbed on
a weekday."

With this final shot, she disappeared into the back of the
house. Justin ran up to his bedroom to retrieve the book he'd
been reading the previous night. He must be a masochist,
going over the same damning information a second time. Did
he want to remind himself how little reason he had to trust
Courtney Long?

Returning to the kitchen, he finished the chilled pancakes.
If he tossed them into the garbage disposal, Mrs. Moynihan
was guaranteed to catch him in the act. He hoped Courtney
would appreciate the sacrifices he was making on her behalf,
Justin thought with an unexpected flash of humor.

He was still leafing through the pages of the book when
Courtney arrived downstairs some fifteen minutes later.

"Hi," she said, hesitating in the doorway. "I hope you
slept well?"

"Like a log. How about you? You're certainly looking terrific. Pink cheeks become you."

She smiled shyly and came a couple of steps farther into the kitchen. "Thanks. I can't believe how well I slept. Good grief, is it already nine o'clock?"

"'Fraid so. Would you like coffee? And there's pancake batter already prepared if you're hungry. Or there's cereal in the pantry. Orange juice is in the fridge."

"Coffee and juice sound wonderful. I'm not a breakfast-type person." She walked over to the fridge and took out the jug of orange juice. When she looked around for a glass, her gaze fell on the book lying open next to Justin's place mat. Her entire body froze. "What are you reading?" she asked, her voice sharp with panic.

He looked at her steadily. "It's called *Snow Flight—Anatomy of a Tragedy*. I expect you've read it. It's a very well-written book."

Her breath squeezed out of her lungs in a harsh whoosh, and she sank down at the table. Her smile was sad, totally resigned, and for some reason it ripped at Justin's heart. "Yes, I've read it."

She set the jug of juice down on the counter with shaking hands. "Well, now you know I didn't tell you the whole truth last night. It's true Ferne Hilton and Robert Danvers had a daughter, but she's supposed to be dead, isn't she?"

"Mmm." Justin flipped over a couple of pages and turned to a color picture of a chubby toddler with a halo of golden curls. He extended the portrait toward Courtney. "Cute kid. Photogenic, too, although I don't think she looks much like her mother, do you?"

Courtney didn't look at the book. "I guess not," she said gruffly. "Not at that age, at any rate."

"Her name was Danielle. Danielle Danvers. That means her initials were D.D. Didi if you say them fast, but the book doesn't mention anything about a nickname."

"Maybe…maybe there's nobody left who knew about the nickname."

"What do *you* think, Courtney? Do you think little Danielle's mother and father called her Didi?"

"I…don't know." Courtney kept her head averted, and Justin resisted the impulse to offer her comfort. He couldn't understand how she kept breaking through the shield of his skepticism. "Want to hear what the book says about little Danielle Danvers?" he asked with a hint of anger. He wasn't sure whether the anger was directed at Courtney or at himself.

Her lips appeared too stiff to move, but somehow she managed to answer him. "I already know what the book says." She stared down at her hands. "Maybe I should just turn myself in to the nearest cop. How many paranoid delusions can a person have and still be considered sane?"

The color in her cheeks had vanished completely. Her face was now almost as white as it had been the day before. Justin deliberately hardened his heart. "The book gives a fairly complete account of the Hilton/Danvers murder," he said. "Apparently the murder was discovered about midnight, when Danielle's nurse arrived back from her Wednesday night off. She found the door to Ferne Hilton's bedroom open and the light on, so she peeked inside to see why. The poor woman was treated to a ringside view of Ferne's body spread-eagled across a bloodstained tangle of sheets—"

"Please, I know what she found." Courtney covered her eyes with her hand, as if shielding them. "Robert Danvers was lying half on top of Ferne's body with his legs dangling onto the floor. At first glance the nanny assumed he'd been trying to protect his wife, but the forensic evidence proved he'd shot himself with the same gun that killed Ferne Hilton."

Justin reached out and touched Courtney very lightly on the arm. "Let's talk about Danielle Danvers," he said after a slight pause. "Jane Grislechy, the nurse, rushed straight out of Ferne's bedroom and into the nursery. Her worst fears were realized when she found the room empty. She called the police, far more worried about the missing child than about the murdered parents. In the end it turned out Danielle hadn't been kidnapped. She was found just before dawn by a young police sergeant. He discovered her wandering barefoot in the backyard, wearing nothing but her nightgown. Although it was only the first week of September, mountain nights are always chilly. Danielle had been exposed to several hours of freezing temperatures. She was rushed to the hospital, but pneumonia had already set in, and the emergency-room doctors weren't optimistic about her chances. A couple of weeks later, the hospital announced with deep regret that Danielle Danvers hadn't responded to treatment and had died peacefully in her sleep."

Courtney looked up with tormented gray eyes. "In her letter Aunt Amelia said she had good reasons for wanting to keep the past secret from me. She deliberately circulated the story that I was dead. She explained that my name was originally Danielle Courtney Danvers, and she had it legally changed to Courtney Long when she adopted me. The records of the adoption were then sealed. Justin, if I wanted to fantasize about being the daughter of famous movie stars, don't you think I'd have enough sense to pick somebody who isn't dead?"

"Yes," he said quietly. "Which makes me wonder why you didn't tell me all this last night."

She laughed tightly. "Oh, sure! I'm busting my gut to convince you I'm not crazy, and you expect me to tell you I'm a dead person? When do you suggest I should have slipped you the news? Right before or right after I claimed there was no reason for me to be confined in a mental hospital?"

He pulled a face, appreciating her point but refusing to concede it. "Either would have been fine."

"Well, it didn't seem that way to me." A very faint flush crept into her cheeks. "Besides, in the end Mrs. Moynihan didn't give us much opportunity for heart-to-heart confidences."

"True, but we have time now. Mrs. Moynihan's girding herself to vacuum the basement." His casual manner suggested he had already forgotten the kiss they had been sharing when interrupted by the housekeeper. He settled more comfortably in his chair. "If you really are Danielle Danvers, why do you think your aunt kept the truth about your parents from you, Courtney?"

She helped herself to coffee before replying. "In part I'm sure it was because she disapproved of my parents' lifestyle. I've already told you what a down-to-earth sort of person Aunt Amelia was. Even if my parents had died from natural causes, she wouldn't have considered them appropriate role models for a growing girl. You can imagine how she felt about flighty careers like acting."

"But she encouraged you to become a champion skier. Isn't that flighty?"

"Not really. World-class skiing is darned hard work. Rigorous training, no boyfriends and not much glamor for women unless you win the Olympics." She smiled slightly. "Everything Aunt Amelia approved of."

"That's all very well, Courtney, but your aunt seems to have constructed an incredibly elaborate cover story. She faked your death, for heaven's sake! It's pushing it to believe she went to all that trouble just because she disapproved of your parents' life-style."

Courtney drew a deep breath. "Actually, in her letter she told me she lied about the past because she was afraid. She never believed my father murdered my mother. The truth is, she thinks somebody got away with committing two murders.''

"I see." Justin narrowed his eyes thoughtfully. "For a person who's spent most of her life with her nose pointed firmly between two ski poles, you've certainly got a colorful past."

"Not to mention a colorful present. It's an offense to break out of a mental hospital once you've been legally sent there, you know."

"Yes, I know." Justin got up and cleared the few cups and dishes into the sink. "Courtney, doesn't it strike you as odd that two totally disconnected mysteries should occur in your life? I mean, your past and your parents' death are surrounded in questions. Then, for reasons you can't even begin to understand, some man whisks you into a phony marriage, consigns you to a mental institution and vanishes into thin air."

"It strikes me as more than odd," Courtney said flatly. "It's just not believable, except that I know I'm telling the truth."

"Has it occurred to you that the two mysteries might be connected?"

Courtney looked up with a mixture of excitement and wariness. "You think that, too?" she breathed.

"I sure think we should consider the possibility of a link. It'll be much easier for us to track down the man who pretended to marry you if we assume he has some connection with your past. I guess our first move should be to check with the real-estate company to see if they can tell us anything...."

Hope flared in Courtney's eyes, then quickly disappeared. "Justin, I really appreciate your offer of help, but you can't involve yourself in my affairs. You gave me a wonderful dinner last night and a comfortable bed, and that's already far more than I could have expected."

"You're surely not planning to investigate all these mysteries by yourself? With every law officer in the state out hunting for you?"

She swallowed hard. "Justin, I have no choice. I'm already breaking the law. I broke it the moment I decided to climb over the wall at Walnut Park. But there's no reason why you should become an accessory."

"I can think of several reasons. Like wanting to find out what's going on and why somebody chose to steal my name."

"Those aren't sufficient reasons," she said after a tiny pause. "But you could do me one favor, Justin, and it's a big one. Please don't tell anybody that you've seen me. And if Mrs. Moynihan insists on telling the police, lie about where I've gone. Tell them I was trying to make for Mexico."

"Stop being noble," Justin advised. He tossed the *Denver Post* toward her. "Your picture's already circulating on the front page of the newspaper, and you've almost no money. How far do you think you'll get without help?"

"I don't know—"

"I'll tell you. Maybe to Aspen bus station if you're *real* lucky."

Courtney thrust her hands into the pockets of her slacks. "I don't understand why you're suddenly so willing to put yourself at risk for me. In the past few minutes, you've changed from virtually accusing me of impersonating a dead child to offering me your unconditional help. Isn't that rather an astonishing transformation?"

He grinned. "Yes, it sure is. But the interesting thing about the human mind is that it can make seemingly illogical leaps of the imagination and come up with an entirely new truth. That's what makes it so tough to create an artificial brain. We have no idea how to program creative illogic into a microchip."

He took her hands and held them for a second. "Courtney,

get smart. Don't look a gift horse in the mouth. If your story's true, somebody who knew my wife was terminally ill took advantage of her final weeks in the hospital to use my home—her home—and to impersonate me. Is it surprising if I'm angry? Is it surprising if I want to find out who exploited Linda's suffering for their own purposes? Frankly, I think I have almost as much at stake here as you."

For a moment her entire body went limp with relief. Then she drew herself up and met his eyes with a grateful smile. "Thanks, Justin, I won't protest any more. Working on this together, I guess we have a real shot at finding out what's going on."

Justin extended his hand. "Partners?" he said.

She took his hand. "Partners."

They stood without moving for a second or two, and then Justin broke away. "Okay, time to get down to business." His voice was all crisp efficiency. "We'd better make some plans in a hurry, because we don't have any time to lose. Mrs. Moynihan only vacuums for this long when she's mad at me, and she's already warned me it's her duty to notify the authorities that you're here. At the moment I've managed to convince her to give us forty-eight hours. I'm not sure how reliable her promise is."

"After five months locked up in Walnut Park, two whole days of freedom sounds long enough to solve anything."

He looked doubtful. "What we really need is to get a look at the records of your commitment hearing. But there's no way we can do that without drawing attention to ourselves."

"No, that would put every cop in Denver on our tail. But maybe we could track down the judge who married me? I could take you to his chambers, I think. They were close to Stapleton Airport."

"The very first thing we have to do is change your appearance. You can't leave the house until you're less easy to identify."

"Hair dye," Courtney suggested promptly. "If I dye my hair auburn, my skin and lashes are so fair it should look almost natural. And a different hair color makes a really dramatic change in a person's appearance."

"Dark glasses would help, too. Thank God, it's always sunny in Colorado so you have an excuse for wearing them. And you'll need some different clothes. The paper described that sweater you're wearing pretty accurately."

"I don't have much money, and Aspen prices—"

"Don't worry about it. I'll drive into town and pick up the hair dye and dark glasses at the drugstore. Fortunately, with all the tourists, I should be able to buy jeans and a whole slew of T-shirts and sweaters without anybody remembering me. I'll buy two sets, in two different stores."

"What shall I do while you're gone?"

Justin rummaged in a drawer and pulled out the keys to the Bronco. He made for the door leading into the garage. "Keep out of Mrs. Moynihan's way and make a list of precisely what we need to investigate."

"Like what's been happening to my trust fund, for example?"

"Right. And whether Mountain Realty has any record of somebody inquiring about this house. Try to make the list comprehensive. We need to move fast with Mrs. Moynihan's deadline looming over us."

Courtney wished that the housekeeper's threat was the worst danger facing them, but she forced herself to smile. "Hurry back," she said. "I've always wanted to be a redhead."

THREE HOURS LATER, feeling strangely shy, Courtney tapped on Justin's bedroom door. He pulled it open, expelling his breath in an appreciative whistle as soon as he saw her.

"Wowee! Would you consider living your life as a permanent redhead? You look spectacular."

She laughed, absurdly pleased by the exaggerated compliment. "Looking spectacular wasn't exactly the object of the exercise. I'm supposed to look inconspicuous."

He feigned dismay. "You failed totally." He propelled her toward the mirror and held up the newspaper photograph alongside her reflected image. "Hmm. The description here says fair hair, and now you're auburn. The paper says gray eyes, but they look more violet than gray. It says pale complexion, which is still true, but I'm not sure it matters. Next time we're in the drugstore we'll buy some tinted foundation. The newspapers say you're wearing a navy-blue shirt and sweater, and actually you're wearing a yellow turtleneck. Which looks terrific, if I may say so."

"You have great taste," she said. "It fits perfectly."

He grinned. "I wish Linda could hear you say that. The first couple of years we were married, she despaired of ever getting me properly trained. She had a twenty-three-inch waist and the first Christmas we spent together I bought her a belt to fit somebody size sixteen. She wasn't flattered."

Justin fell abruptly silent. He can't believe he mentioned his wife so casually, Courtney thought with sudden insight. She covered the little moment of awkwardness by smiling brightly. "Did you manage to find out anything about my trust fund while I was dyeing my hair?"

"Sure did." Justin was more than willing to change the subject. "I called the bank and spoke to one of the clerks in the trust division. Told her I was an IRS inspector. I complained that the bank had failed to file form 2B37C showing movement of funds in and out of your trust fund, and the clerk was humbly apologetic. Which was good of her, since form 2B37C doesn't exist."

Courtney laughed. "Did you agree to overlook the omission just this once?"

"She promised to have the information on my desk by the

first of the month. The whole department's probably going to be in turmoil searching for their supply of 2B37C forms.''

''What did she say about my trust?''

''Courtney Long's trust fund is being used to pay her monthly fees at the Walnut Park Mental Health Institute. There's been no change in the ownership of the trust and no other withdrawals from the fund.''

Courtney sat down on the edge of the bed. ''I guess that blows the theory that I was locked up for my money.''

''Yes, I guess it does.'' Justin hesitated a moment, then added, ''The clerk also informed me it was a strange coincidence I'd called today, because the police had just called from Colorado to inform the bank that Courtney Long had run away from Walnut Park. The bank was instructed to notify the police if anybody attempted to make any withdrawals from the fund.''

Courtney bit her lip. ''I suppose in other circumstances it would be reassuring to find out the police are so efficient. As it is, it's scary to think they've already widened the search as far as New Hampshire.''

''Hey, don't take it to heart,'' Justin said softly. ''We didn't need your money. We have mine.''

''I'll pay you back when this is all over, I promise.''

''Sure you will. I'll even demand ten percent interest if that'll make you feel better. You're richer than I am.'' Justin removed a dark leather jacket from his closet and slung it over his shoulder. ''Come on, let's go and test the effectiveness of your disguise. I think we should check out the realty company before we drive into Denver.''

Courtney found it more nerve-racking than she would have expected to get out of the Bronco and walk casually from the parking lot into the offices of Mountain Realty Company. ''My scalp's itching,'' she whispered anxiously as they pushed on the swinging glass door. ''Is the hair dye streaking?''

Justin's glance held a hint of amusement. "No. Relax, Courtney. Even your hairdresser wouldn't know for sure. If I didn't know better, I'd be willing to swear you were a natural redhead."

The Realtor who had handled the caretaking assignment on Justin's house was out with a client, but fortunately the elderly woman who worked as secretary for the entire care-taker division was at her desk.

She greeted Courtney with polite disinterest and Justin with a warm smile. "Good to see you again, Mr. Tanner. Are you going away again? Nearly time for you to do another stint at Princeton, isn't it?"

"A few weeks yet. Actually, Barbara, I came to check on something that happened while I was away last spring."

"There was nothing wrong, I hope?"

"No, not really. You carried out the inspections according to the usual schedule, I suppose?"

Barbara was clearly offended. "You know the reputation of our company, Mr. Tanner. If anything, we check our cli-ents' homes more frequently than the contract stipulates."

"So there's no possibility anybody could have gotten into my house without you knowing about it? You didn't hand out keys to anybody? A repair guy or a building inspector?"

"Well, of course not, Mr. Tanner. You know how careful we always are." She paused for a moment, then added, "We gave a complete set to your friend, of course, just as you instructed, and we discontinued our inspections once he was in residence. Maybe he gave somebody a spare key?"

Courtney gave a strangled gasp. She glanced swiftly at Justin, whose face was a study in astonishment. Despite ev-erything, Courtney realized, despite all his apparent support, he hadn't *really* believed her story. Until this moment he hadn't really believed somebody had lived in his house.

She watched as he drew in a sharp, tense breath. "My friend?" he queried. "What friend?"

The secretary didn't need very sensitive antennae to sense
something was amiss. She immediately became defensive.
"Well, you wrote to us from New York, Mr. Tanner. I remember the letter because I handled it myself. We gave the
keys to your friend, just as you instructed. Offhand I don't
recall his name."

She swiveled around on her chair and reached into a filing
cabinet, where she rummaged for less than a minute before
finding the folder she was looking for. "Here's the letter you
wrote, Mr. Tanner. Right here in your file."

Justin held the letter so that Courtney could read it along
with him. It was typed on paper embossed with the Waldorf-
Astoria address, and the first paragraph authorized Mountain
Realty to hand over a set of keys to Justin's friend, Gary
Wade, who would be arriving in Aspen on April 10. A second crisp paragraph instructed the realty company to discon-
tinue all routine maintenance and inspection calls until further
notice.

"What did Gary Wade look like?" Courtney asked.

"I don't remember." Barbara sounded defensive again.
"There was nothing special about him, I guess, and we get
dozens of people in and out of this office every day. He
looked like somebody who was a friend of yours, Mr. Tanner. I mean, he was polite and well dressed and everything,
and he showed us a copy of your letter to prove he was who
he said he was."

"That would certainly prove his identity," Justin said. His
irony was totally lost on the secretary. "There's a second
letter here from me," he added. "It's dated May fourteenth,
and it's to let you know Gary Wade has left Aspen."

"I remember that. You instructed us to give the house an
immediate, thorough spring-cleaning, and you enclosed a
money order for two hundred dollars to cover the extra cost."

"What about the keys? It doesn't say anything about them
here."

"There should be another letter." The secretary came around her desk to examine the file. "Yes, here it is. Gary Wade wrote us a note on the fourteenth and returned the keys." Barbara pointed to a long and detailed statement stapled to the inside cover of the folder. "We sent you a full account of how the two hundred dollars were spent," she said.

"Yes, thank you. Your company is always extremely reliable."

"Then there's nothing wrong, Mr. Tanner? We did the right thing handing those keys over to Mr. Wade?"

"You did what you were instructed to do, Barbara. Don't worry about anything. Could you just run me off a couple of photocopies of those letters? I'm having a bit of a hassle with the IRS at the moment. They seem to think I've been renting my house out for profit."

The secretary smiled her relief. In common with the clerk at the bank, she seemed to assume that once the IRS entered the picture, logic and common sense flew out of the window.

"Of course you can have copies," she said, eager to be of assistance now that Mountain Realty was off the hook. "They'll only take a couple of seconds with our new machine."

Courtney grabbed on to Justin's arm as they walked back to the Bronco, dancing a little jig of sheer exhilaration once they were out of sight of the office. "You see? There *was* somebody living in your house. I didn't imagine him! I'm not crazy! I'm not, I'm not, I'm not!"

Justin smiled. "Any chance I could have my arm back? My keys are in that pocket."

"Oh, sorry." She flushed, then flung her arms wide in a new rush of happiness. "I'm not crazy!"

"Seeing you now, nobody would bet money on it," Justin remarked dryly. "Get in the car before somebody sees us."

She pulled herself up into the passenger seat and buckled her seat belt. "You didn't believe me until now, did you?"

"I thought I did," he replied quietly, starting the car. "I owe you an apology. In my heart of hearts, I didn't think it was possible somebody could have been using my house, so I was skeptical about the rest of your story."

Courtney was still riding high. "I accept your apology," she said grandly. "Was that a good forgery of your signature, by the way?"

"Not very. But obviously good enough to fool the Realtors."

"Even for a not-very-good forgery, Gary Wade must have seen your signature someplace."

"True." Justin backed out of the parking lot. "But he could have seen it in a dozen places. When I'm teaching, for example, I sign twenty or thirty notes a day, and half those notes will get pinned up on a bulletin board somewhere. Or what about a clerk at the bank? Or a shop assistant who's seen one of my charge slips?"

"It's weird to think how many near-strangers could forge our signatures if they put their minds to it." Courtney looked at a passing road sign. "Are we driving to Denver?"

"Yes. We need to track down the judge who married you."

She grimaced. "If he exists. I'm beginning to think the whole ceremony was faked. After all, if the judge was genuine, my husband-to-be would have needed to provide proof of identity. Surely he wouldn't risk parading phony ID in front of a judge?"

"Either he arranged an elaborate fake ceremony, or he produced phony ID. Whichever route he chose, he took a hell of a risk."

"If you take a big risk, it usually means you have a lot at stake."

Justin frowned. "Yes, it does. Damn it, Courtney, *why* did

Wade want you out of the way? Why now? What have you done recently that's so threatening to somebody?''

"I've no idea,'' she said, the last of her euphoria dissipating. "I can't imagine how this man's life came into contact with mine.''

"And mine,'' Justin pointed out quietly.

Courtney wrinkled her forehead. "He's somebody who knew a lot about me, even though we'd never met, and he was absolutely sure I wouldn't recognize him.'' She drew in an impatient breath, then burst out, "I still think he must be well acquainted with you. Otherwise, how would he know when your house was empty?''

Justin turned onto the main highway before replying. "A lot of people knew I was taking Linda to New York.'' His voice was carefully even. "Almost everybody who'd ever met us knew she wanted to be with her parents and family when she died.''

Courtney shivered. "That's awful, Justin, truly horrible. It means Gary Wade must have been monitoring the progress of your wife's…your wife's illness.''

"Yes.'' Justin spoke grimly. "Why do you sound surprised? He wasn't squeamish about slashing your wrists and getting you locked up in an insane asylum, so why would he be squeamish about exploiting Linda's death?'' Staring straight ahead of him, he quietly added, "I'm going to find this bastard and nail him to the wall.''

Courtney's smile was only a little tremulous. "Stand in line. It's my turn first.''

Chapter Eight

Harvey's plane was two hours late landing at Stapleton Airport, and it was nearly six o'clock Denver time when he finally made it out of the gate area and into the main concourse.

Harvey fought to control his irritation. He'd learned in the past that he didn't plan well when he was irritated. He moved his heavy garment bag from his left shoulder to his right and wondered why his plane always landed at a gate twenty minutes' brisk walk from ground transportation. Somebody had to land at all those gates close to the exit. Why was it never him?

He drew in a calming breath and focused his thoughts on the task ahead of him. He glanced down at the copy of the *Denver Post* he had bought as soon as he landed. The bitch had managed to get her photograph onto the front page. Seeing her again had given him a nasty jolt, although he should have been prepared. Even in a hospital photo she looked like her mother. Like Ferne. A whore with the eyes of an angel.

Courtney Long, the copy under the picture read. *Escaped from a maximum-security mental facility, and still at large.* There was no mention of Justin Tanner's name. No mention of Courtney's background. In fact, the paper said very little that Harvey considered helpful. No mention of where the police had searched for the runaway. No mention of whether she'd already been spotted anywhere. Three columns on the Bronco football player who'd strained his back, and only a paragraph on Courtney. Just showed the sort of screwed-up priorities journalists had in a cow town like Denver.

He looked at the photo again as he waited in line to use the only functioning pay phone. Was it clear enough for people to make the identification? Probably. Within a few hours, Courtney would surely be safely locked up again, provided the public did its duty. Unfortunately, nowadays you couldn't count on people to do their duty. Not everybody was a civic-minded citizen like Harvey. It was all the fault of the schools, of course. Too many courses in sex education and not enough emphasis on civics and morals.

The truth was he should have killed the damn girl when he had the chance. When he first got her letter and tracked her down in Aspen he could easily have killed her, but he'd feared the consequences of a full-scale murder investigation. Even if he'd managed to hide the body, with a million-dollar trust fund waiting for her signature at monthly intervals, some busybody would have launched a massive manhunt. By arranging to have her locked up in Walnut Park, he'd managed to get her safely out of the way, and best of all, nobody was looking for her. The bank managers, the tax authorities, all the official snoops of modern living knew where she was. So there was no need for anybody to launch investigations into her background. He had obligingly helped the authorities trace her past back as far as Amelia, and there they'd stopped—an ideal situation as far as Harvey was concerned.

But when he'd made his plans, he'd never thought Didi might succeed in escaping. He should have followed his first instincts, Harvey thought, and not allowed those damned violet eyes to get the better of him. Whore's eyes, beguiling him away from his clear duty. Ferne's eyes. He should have killed the bitch the first time he saw her.

The teenager on the phone finally stopped giggling long

enough to hang up. Harvey took her place, dialing the familiar number of Justin Tanner's home in Copper Creek. He was pleased to see that his fingers were perfectly steady. With his usual forethought, he'd provided himself with a stack of small change, so he had no need to use a credit card and leave a record of his call. Harvey's irritation began to recede. He was in Colorado. He was calm. Soon he would be in complete control.

The phone rang once, twice. If Justin Tanner answered, Harvey already had decided to hang up. But he probably wouldn't. Linda had always joked that Justin never picked up the phone if he could avoid it. She used to complain—laughingly—that the house could tumble down around Justin and he wouldn't even notice, provided his computer still churned out its quota of algebraic equations. Harvey hoped the computer and higher math were proving as seductive as ever.

The phone rang for the fifth time. "Mr. Tanner's residence."

Luck was on his side! It was a woman's voice, an older woman's voice. The housekeeper? Must be. His palm was suddenly moist, and he took a firmer grip on the receiver. "This is Rick Padechowski, Linda's brother. Is Justin Tanner there, please?" He flattened his vowels, pushing them out through his nose, pleased with the made-in-Brooklyn effect. A lifetime of working around actors provided some useful skills.

"Who did you say?" the housekeeper asked. "I'm sorry, there's a crackle on the line."

"Rick Padechowski, from New York. Linda's brother." He was taking a risk, but not a very big one. Linda had so damn many brothers, the housekeeper couldn't know all of them. Thank God for Poles, with old-fashioned values and huge families.

The housekeeper obviously recognized Linda's family

name. Her voice warmed several degrees. "I'm sorry, Mr. Padechowski, but Mr. Tanner's not here tonight. Can I take a message? He'll be sorry to have missed you."

Harvey's brain raced. Tanner wasn't there. Could mean anything. Had that bitch made contact with Tanner or not? "That's real bad news," he said. "I'm in Denver for just a few hours, and I was hoping we could get together."

"In Denver? You're in Denver? That's where Mr. Tanner's gone. He's taking that wo—" The housekeeper fell abruptly silent.

Harvey's hands were suddenly wet. He took out his handkerchief and wrapped it around the phone to stop it slipping. The housekeeper had been about to mention a woman. Was it Courtney? Oh, God! How the hell was he going to find out whether the bitch had gotten her hooks into Justin Tanner?

"Justin's in Denver!" he exclaimed, managing to sound thrilled. "Well, there's a piece of luck. Can you tell me where he's staying? It would be great if the two of us could get together for a drink."

"He didn't give me a number where he could be reached." Disapproval darkened the housekeeper's voice. "But I did hear him say...that is, I believe Mr. Tanner's business was in the neighborhood of the airport."

The sweat chilled on Harvey's forehead. No, he told himself. There were a hundred reasons why Tanner might have business near the airport, and none of them would have anything to do with Courtney. He cleared his throat. "That's a big area," he said jovially. "Any idea which hotel he might use?"

Even over the long-distance wires, he sensed an odd little hesitation in the housekeeper's response. "He sometimes stays at the Stouffer Inn or the Hilton, but I don't know if he'll be there tonight." She added, almost to herself, "He didn't want me to tell people where he'd gone, but I'm sure he'd want to see you, Mr. Padechowski, you being related to his wife and all.''

Excitement twisted through Harvey, mixed with just enough fear to give a pleasurable edge to the sensation. Could he risk a face-to-face meeting with Tanner? Could he bump into Tanner in a hotel restaurant and pretend it was coincidence? Maybe, if Tanner was alone. But if the Courtney bitch was with him, he couldn't possibly afford a face-to-face encounter.

He dripped charm into the phone. "Well, thanks a lot for all your help, Mrs....er..."

"Mrs. Moynihan," she supplied helpfully.

"Ah, that's a good Irish name to be sure. If you aren't lucky enough to be Polish, thank the Lord for being Irish, I always say." He heard Mrs. Moynihan's chuckle, and his mouth tightened contemptuously. God, older women were so easy to manipulate! "Goodbye, Mrs. Moynihan, and thanks again. I'm really looking forward to seeing Justin."

He hung up, wiped his hands one last time on his handkerchief, then dropped the crumpled square into the nearest trash bin. He really couldn't bear carrying soiled linen around with him.

Harvey followed the signs out of the airport to a waiting cab. "Are Stouffer's and the Hilton both close to the airport?" he asked the driver.

"'Bout five, mebbe ten minutes away. Stouffer's is a bit closer."

"Take me to the Stouffer Inn, then."

The cabbie flicked down his meter and cut into the stream of traffic without a backward glance.

Harvey ignored the squeal of brakes sounding at the rear and leaned back against the cracked leather seat, for once indifferent to the dusty floor and dirty windows. He was going to find Tanner, he was sure of it. He could feel it in his bones.

The cabbie filtered right. "Hotel's over there," he offered. "Couple more minutes."

Harvey peered through the murky cab window. He was actually looking forward to seeing Tanner again. At Linda's funeral there had been something deeply gratifying about shaking hands and talking with the man whose identity he'd stolen. Tanner was one of those husky, aggressively male sort of men whom Harvey most despised. Harvey thought of how brilliantly he'd manipulated Tanner, and his body was suffused by a warm glow of satisfaction, the little glow that always came when he proved his superiority to ordinary men. Some people might think that masculinity was proved in the bedroom, but Harvey knew better. It was power that counted, being in control. And he was in control again, of his own life and of Courtney's.

By this time tomorrow night he would have found Courtney. By this time tomorrow night, she would be dead, dispatched by Harvey to join her mother and the other whores he'd been compelled to take care of.

He would be able to fly back to New York in time for the weekend. Harvey smiled at the agreeable prospect. He would be able to eat at that delightful new oyster bar on Third Avenue. He would order saffron rice and tender, silvery oysters stuffed with dark green spinach. Harvey never ate meat. The sight of all that red blood was far too distressing.

He hoped there wouldn't be too much blood when he did his duty and rid the world of Courtney. But whatever happened, Harvey wasn't a shirker. Ferne's daughter was a menace to honest men. Despite the blood he would do what he had to.

IT WAS AFTER five by the time Courtney finally managed to direct Justin to the building that she thought might house Judge Simmons's offices. They had used the phone directory to draw up a list of all the Simmonses in the vicinity of the airport, but it had taken two hours of circling the warehouse-lined back streets before they finally arrived at an office park with a few stretches of grass and trees to break up the bleakness of the surrounding landscape.

Courtney perked up. "Justin, I think this is it. I'm sorry it took me so long. I didn't think it would be this hard to locate."

"The streets around here all look alike," Justin said, but she could tell he thought she was pretty dumb to have gotten herself married without even knowing the address or the full name of the judge. In retrospect Courtney considered that pretty dumb herself.

Gary Wade, or whatever his name actually was, had swept her off the commuter plane that had brought them from Aspen and whirled her out to the main concourse of Stapleton Airport. He'd bought her two dozen pink rosebuds from the flower stand. Then he'd rushed her into a cab and they'd driven to Judge Simmons's offices. They'd been married within an hour of landing at the airport. They'd been on their way to Mexico an hour later.

At the time she'd thought the breakneck speed of the ceremony was wonderfully romantic, even though she was already beginning to feel a little bit sick. With the miraculously clear vision of hindsight, she wondered cynically just how early in their acquaintance her "husband" had started drugging her. There seemed almost no other explanation for her total suspension of even the most basic common sense.

"You know we're probably not going to find any trace of this judge," Justin remarked abruptly. "If your wedding ceremony was phony, the judge was probably phony as well."

"I know." For the first time since he had agreed to help her, fear tugged at her heart. "Justin, what are we going to do if we can't find any proof to back up my story? Where do we go from here?"

"We've already found something," he said. "We know

somebody was masquerading under my name in my house, presumably for the express purpose of deceiving you. We have the name he used for the realty company, and you can give a full description of what he looked like.''

''Do you think that's going to be enough to get me released from Walnut Park?''

''No.'' He squeezed her arm reassuringly. ''Look, Courtney, we're going to find out more, lots more. This deception Gary Wade perpetrated held up as long as nobody questioned it. Now that we're starting to investigate, the whole scheme's bound to unravel sooner or later.''

''But I don't have a later. Mrs. Moynihan's going to blow the whistle on me in a few hours.''

''She can only do that if she knows where you are. If she won't agree to give us more time, we'll hide somewhere.''

''Thank you,'' she said softly, knowing she would never be able to accept his offer.

He looked at her sideways, then smiled. For some reason her stomach gave a little jig of happiness. ''Come on,'' he said. ''Let's go and beard the lion in his den. Or Judge Simmons in his office, if he should happen to be there.''

They walked through the revolving glass door into the lobby. ''Building still look familiar?'' Justin asked.

''Yes,'' Courtney murmured, excitement beginning to bubble up inside her. ''Yes, this is the place. I remember the dark brown carpet and the sea-grass paper on the walls.''

''And here's the judge,'' Justin said, reading from the directory. ''B.R. Simmons, District Judge.''

Courtney stared at the board, eyes wide with astonishment. ''He exists!'' she said, stupefied. ''There really is a Judge Simmons.''

''Seems like it. Suite 305. Shall we go up?''

Her fingers were rubbing up and down the side seams of her slacks in mindless rhythm, and she quickly shoved her hands into her pockets. "He probably won't be there," she said. "It's after office hours."

"Let's find out." Justin crossed the lobby and pushed the elevator button. The doors slid open immediately and they stepped inside. He crooked his finger under her chin and gently twisted her around to face him. "Look, be grateful we found him. That means we have a lead to follow."

She felt tears well up in her eyes. "If Judge Simmons is a real judge, then I'm really married. To a man who wants me locked away in a lunatic asylum."

"Even if that's true, you can get an annulment just by signing a couple of forms."

She managed a smile. "Did you learn that your first or second week of law school?"

"Second. It's advanced stuff."

The elevator doors slid open on the third floor, and Courtney automatically turned left into the corridor. "Wrong way," Justin said, grabbing her hand. "Suite 305 is in the other direction."

Courtney frowned, but the signs painted on the walls indicated Justin was correct, so she followed.

The door to Judge Simmons's office was closed, but a young woman responded promptly to Justin's buzz. She smiled, although she didn't invite them into the suite. "The office closes to the public at four-thirty," she said, her voice pleasant but firm.

"We're sorry to bother you so late in the day, but we only just arrived in Denver and we need some information from Judge Simmons. It's really urgent," Courtney said.

Some of her inner desperation must have shown in her voice, for the young woman's manner softened noticeably. "The judge and his clerk left over an hour ago, and I'm just the receptionist. What did you need to see him about?"

"My cousin's wedding," Justin said quickly. "She moved to New Jersey with her husband and lost her marriage certificate. She's nine months' pregnant, but when she applied to the county court for a copy of the certificate, they couldn't find any records. Naturally she wants to get the mix-up straightened out before the baby's born.''

"Well, I can understand why she might be a bit anxious! Honestly, those clerks at the county building couldn't keep their paperwork in order if the recording angel was standing next to them. My name's Nancy, by the way. Come back at ten tomorrow, and I'll see the judge makes time for you. You know what date the wedding took place and everything?''

"Yes, we have all that information.''

"You shouldn't have a problem then, because our records are a lot better than the county's. Judge Simmons may even recall your cousin's wedding. He has an amazing memory for names and faces.''

Courtney was silent until they left the building. "What's bothering you?'' Justin asked her.

"I don't think we were married in that office. I recognized the building but not Judge Simmons's office.''

"We didn't see much of the office,'' Justin pointed out.

"I could see the reception area behind Nancy's desk. It had a beige carpet. The office where I was married had orange carpeting. That's not a color you forget too easily.''

"The judge probably redecorated,'' Justin said, brushing dust off the Bronco door as he unlocked it. "Maybe all his staff threatened to quit unless he got rid of the orange.''

"Maybe. But there's another thing. If you'd asked me to find the office where I was married, I'd have turned left, not right.''

"Courtney, I suggest we don't worry about it until tomorrow. We'll see the judge in person then.''

She didn't argue, although she was positive that her wedding hadn't taken place in suite 305.

Justin leaned across and took her hand. "Courtney, I'm not doubting you. I'm not sitting here saying to myself that

I think you're crazy. Maybe you weren't married in that particular office, but there could be lots of explanations for that. Maybe Judge Simmons moved from offices at the other end of the hallway. Maybe he had the entire suite redesigned from floor to ceiling. Whatever the truth, we can't uncover it tonight, so let's leave it until tomorrow. We have plenty of other problems we can work on. Okay?''

"Okay." She turned to look at him, then admitted the truth. "After six months of being treated like a mindless fool, I get uptight when I feel I'm being patronized."

"I can understand why." Justin glanced out of the window. "It's getting dark, and my stomach is sending out peevish reminders that it didn't have any lunch. Could I interest you in some dinner before we tackle the next item on the agenda?"

"You sure could. Now that you mention it, I'm starving."

Justin headed the Bronco back toward the main road. "I don't know many places to eat around here. One of the hotels near the airport might be our best bet. Linda and I have stayed at a couple of them, and their restaurants aren't bad. In fact, we might as well check into a hotel, since we're obviously not going to leave Denver tonight."

"Sounds good to me. And after dinner, maybe we could call the hotel in Mexico where I spent my honeymoon. I don't know what they could tell us, but they might remember something useful."

Justin glanced at his watch. "The Stouffer Inn is the closest place from where we are now. Want to go there?"

Courtney's stomach emitted an audible growl. She grinned. "I guess my stomach just voted in favor."

The hotel lobby was crowded, but the receptionist found them a room without difficulty. She glanced down at the registration card Justin had filled out. "Mr. and Mrs. Tanner from New Jersey? Would you and your wife like a king-sized bed, Mr. Tanner?"

Justin glanced at Courtney, an unmistakable gleam of amusement in his eyes. "I think we'd prefer separate beds tonight, wouldn't we, dear? You know how restless I am when we change time zones."

Courtney was annoyed to feel her cheeks flame. "Whatever you prefer, *dearest*. You're the one who has trouble sleeping, not me."

When they were alone in their room, Justin turned to her with a hint of apology. "It seemed easier and safer to book us both into one room."

"Of course. I understand perfectly." Her voice was brisk in the extreme. No way would she let him see how conscious she was of his presence in the confines of the hotel bedroom. "Besides, why waste money paying for two rooms when one will do?"

He smiled. "I hear thrifty Aunt Amelia talking."

"Good grief, you certainly don't! Aunt Amelia wouldn't have sacrificed her reputation for anything as mundane as saving money." She drew herself up ramrod straight and pretended to frown. "You should know, young man, that a woman's virtue is valuable beyond price."

He unzipped his overnight bag, laughing. "I'd have enjoyed meeting your aunt."

"She was fun to be with, even though she would never let you get close. Since finding out about my parents, I've often wondered how she felt about having a sister who was a walking sex symbol. Ferne Hilton made her first film when she was sixteen, you know, and men were already going wild about her."

If Justin noticed the impersonal way she named her mother, he made no comment on it. "From what you've said about your aunt, I imagine the fuss over your mother's looks simply confirmed her low opinion of mankind's common sense. I can almost hear her saying 'Beauty is only skin-deep.'"

"I guess so." Courtney tossed her gym bag onto the nearest bed and searched for the plastic pouch of toilet articles she'd bought two nights previously. Dear God, she thought, was it only two nights since she'd been lying in bed at the mental hospital, praying Nurse Buxton wouldn't notice anything amiss? It seemed half a lifetime ago.

She held up the toiletries. "Can I take five minutes in the bathroom? Then I'll be ready to go down with you for dinner."

"Take your time. I need to give Mrs. Moynihan a call."

Courtney swung around. "Your housekeeper? Why do you need to call her? You won't tell her where we're staying, will you?"

"I'm calling to check for messages, and I'll tell her we're in Denver, but not the name of our hotel." He touched her lightly on the arm. "Courtney, try to trust me. Please?"

She flushed. "It's harder for me to trust people these days than it used to be."

His hand moved up and just skimmed over the surface of her hair. "Men like Gary Wade are the exception, Courtney, not the rule."

"But I trusted my aunt, too. I…loved her."

"And I'm sure she loved you. She may not have told you the truth, Courtney, but that doesn't mean she was untrustworthy. She dealt with a difficult situation in the way she thought best."

"Best for who?"

"You, Courtney." His eyes met hers, and then he stepped back, breaking the moment of intimacy and shooting her an impish smile. "Hey, please hurry up, because my stomach has given up on polite messages. Right now we're talking stabs of downright aggression."

She found herself returning his smile. "In deference to your stomach, I'll be superquick."

YOUR PARTICIPATION IS REQUESTED!

Dear Reader,

Since you are a lover of fiction – we would like to get to know you!

Inside you will find a short Reader's Survey. Sharing your answers with us will help our editorial staff understand who you are and what activities you enjoy.

To thank you for your participation, we would like to send you 2 books and a gift – **ABSOLUTELY FREE!**

Enjoy your gifts with our appreciation,

Pam Powers

SEE INSIDE FOR READER'S SURVEY

What's Your Reading Pleasure...
ROMANCE? <u>OR</u> SUSPENSE?

Do you prefer spine-tingling page turners OR heart-stirring stories about love and relationships? Tell us which books you enjoy – and you'll get 2 FREE "ROMANCE" BOOKS or 2 FREE "SUSPENSE" BOOKS with no obligation to purchase anything.

Choose **"ROMANCE"** and get **2 FREE BOOKS** that will fuel your imagination with intensely moving stories about life, love and relationships.

FREE!

Choose **"SUSPENSE"** and you'll get **2 FREE BOOKS** that will thrill you with a spine-tingling blend of suspense and mystery.

FREE!

Whichever category you select, your 2 free books have a combined cover price of $11.98 or more in the U.S. and $13.98 or more in Canada.

And remember... just for accepting the Editor's Free Gift Offer, we'll send you 2 books and a gift, ABSOLUTELY FREE!

YOURS FREE! *We'll send you a fabulous surprise gift absolutely FREE, just for trying "Romance" or "Suspense"!*

® and ™ are trademarks owned and used by the trademark owner and/or its licensee.

Order online at
www.FreeBooksandGift.com

Offer limited to one per household and not valid to current subscribers of MIRA, Romance, Suspense or "The Best of the Best." All orders subject to approval. Books received may vary. Credit or debit balances in a customer's account(s) may be offset by any other outstanding balance owed by or to the customer. Please allow 4 to 6 weeks for delivery.

YOUR READER'S SURVEY
"THANK YOU" FREE GIFTS INCLUDE:

▶ 2 Romance OR 2 Suspense books

▶ A lovely surprise gift

The Reader Service — Here's How It Works:

Accepting your 2 free books and gift places you under no obligation to buy anything. You may keep the books and gift and return the shipping statement marked "cancel." If you do not cancel, about a month later we'll send you 3 additional books and bill you just $5.24 each in the U.S., or $5.74 each in Canada, plus 25¢ shipping & handling per book and applicable taxes if any.* That's the complete price and — compared to cover prices starting from $5.99 each in the U.S. and $6.99 each in Canada — it's quite a bargain! You may cancel at any time, but if you choose to continue, every month we'll send you 3 more books, which you may either purchase at the discount price or return to us and cancel your subscription.

*Terms and prices subject to change without notice. Sales tax applicable in N.Y. Canadian residents will be charged applicable provincial taxes and GST.

If offer card is missing write to: The Reader Service, 3010 Walden Ave., P.O. Box 1867, Buffalo, NY 14240-1867

BUSINESS REPLY MAIL

FIRST-CLASS MAIL   PERMIT NO. 717-003   BUFFALO, NY

POSTAGE WILL BE PAID BY ADDRESSEE

THE READER SERVICE
3010 WALDEN AVE
PO BOX 1341
BUFFALO NY 14240-8571

NO POSTAGE
NECESSARY
IF MAILED
IN THE
UNITED STATES

"HOW WAS MRS. MOYNIHAN?" Courtney asked, when the waitress had brought them each an oversize platter of New York strip steak and baked potato.

"She was fine. No important messages except that one of Linda's brothers called to say he was in Denver for the evening and wanted to get together with me for a drink."

"I'm sorry you missed him."

Justin buttered a slice of crusty bread with careful attention before speaking. "Look, I wasn't going to tell you this, Courtney, because I don't want you to get into a panic over nothing. The thing is, I must be more a creature of habit than I realized. Mrs. Moynihan told him I was probably staying near the airport, at the Hilton or at Stouffer's. I don't know which brother it is, because Mrs. Moynihan must have misheard his name. But it's possible he'll try to make contact with me here."

Courtney's pleasure in her sour-cream-slathered potato vanished instantly. She put down her fork. "How many other people know where we are, do you think?"

"Nobody, as far as I know. Mrs. Moynihan certainly hasn't been in touch with Sheriff Swanson, if that's what you're worried about. Courtney, it's no big deal. To be perfectly honest, I don't know Linda's brothers all that well— if you count in-laws she has seven of them—and I'm darn sure he's not going to waste his evening tracking me down. It would be different if Linda were still alive." He stopped abruptly, then picked up her glass and pushed it into her hand. Courtney had the impression he changed the subject as much for his own sake as for hers. "Hey, kid, don't look so tragic. Eat your steak, drown your sorrows in wine, and then we'll go call Mexico. Everything's going to be fine, I promise."

She drank the wine at a speed that would have horrified Aunt Amelia, aware of an odd, irrational twinge of envy. Justin's voice became gentler and his eyes darkened whenever he mentioned his wife's name. Courtney reflected sadly that she couldn't even imagine what it would feel like to be the recipient of so much tenderness.

She shrugged off her unusual mood of self-pity. "I guess I overreacted," she said, picking up her fork. "Even if your brother-in-law finds you, he'll have other things on his mind besides turning me in to the local police."

"Atta girl. Here, have some more sour cream. I can see a naked piece of potato."

As soon as she was eating normally again, he took charge of the conversation, asking her questions about her skiing career, drawing her out until she actually found herself reminiscing about her less-than-thrilling romance with a famous skier on the men's Olympic team. She realized what Justin was doing, of course, but when he regaled her with stories about his own misspent youth, she found herself laughing and relaxing exactly as he'd planned. By the time the waitress returned to present a bill, Courtney was no longer quite sure why the news about Mrs. Moynihan had seemed so threatening.

"Ready to make that call to Mexico?" Justin asked, when he'd signed the charges to their room.

"Ready."

They strolled toward the elevators. Courtney, afloat on wine and good food, felt almost as if she were coming home after a pleasant date. She deliberately fostered the mood. "How's your Spanish?" she asked, smiling sleepily. "If it's no better than mine, we'll probably take until midnight to get the hotel number out of the directory service in Acapulco."

"Hah, I'm not just a pretty face, you know. I speak quite good Spanish."

She stared at him with exaggerated surprise, and he grinned down at her. "Speaking of faces...I packed an empty can of shaving cream. I need to pick up a new one from the gift shop over there."

Justin went to the section housing men's toiletries, and Courtney wandered over to the paperback books. She was skimming through the blurb on a bestselling biography when she had the strangest sensation that she was being watched. She put the book down, afraid she might drop it, and pivoted slowly on her heels.

A man stood outside the gift shop, half hidden by a group of people admiring a display of posters. Justin! Her mind screamed the name, even though her vocal chords seemed paralyzed. No, not Justin. Not the real Justin, but the man who had married her.

She clutched her stomach, feeling the sickness start to swell within her. For a split second neither of them moved. His brilliant blue eyes burned with hatred so fierce that it struck her body with physical force. She gave a little cry, doubling over as if protecting herself from a blow. When she straightened up again, he was already running across the lobby.

Too late, her legs regained the power of movement. She dashed after him. She pushed her way around a group of businessmen, then ran as fast as she could through the central seating area. He seemed to be zigzagging haphazardly, and that made him difficult to follow. She kept losing sight of him in the ebb and flow of guests crossing the lobby.

Then it was all over. At one moment she had him in plain view. The next moment a row of pillars hid him from sight. The moment after that, he had disappeared completely.

She pushed open the heavy service doors, which seemed to be the only place he might have gone. The short corridor was empty. Her head jerked around wildly. Service elevators, but no light indicating movement. Concrete stairs, but no sound of footsteps. Two doors. She banged on the door marked Janitor, pummeling until her fists were sore. No response.

She banged on the other door, the one marked Housekeeper. Silence. Only silence. Justin…Gary…whoever the hell he was…had once again vanished from her life.

Courtney slumped against the wall, shaking so hard she could scarcely breathe. She spread out her fingers and placed her palms flat against the coolness of the wall's painted surface. You saw him, she told herself. You will find him again. It was not an illusion. You are not crazy. He was here. You— are—not—crazy.

Courtney had no idea how much time passed before Justin found her there, still spread-eagled against the wall, her breathing finally regular, her heart still pounding.

"What happened? What the hell's going on around here? Have you any idea how much attention you attracted with that hundred-yard dash across the center of the lobby?"

She stared at Justin, not really hearing what he said. "I saw him. Outside the gift shop. He was here and then he disappeared."

"Who did you see? A policeman? What do you mean, he disappeared?"

Courtney blinked, then shook her head. "Not a policeman. My husband." She corrected herself carefully. "The man who pretended to marry me."

Justin's look was straight and hard. "Are you sure? I kept your wineglass pretty well filled at dinner, you know. And this has been a tough few days for you."

"I'm sure." She pushed herself away from the wall. "I am absolutely, one hundred percent, positively sure. The man who impersonated you is—was—right here in this hotel. I lost sight of him behind those pillars in the lobby, and I thought he might have come in here. But he wasn't anywhere. He just disappeared."

"He was probably on the next floor already by the time you got in here." Justin took her hand and led her over to the concrete steps. "Take a seat, Courtney. You look about ready to keel over."

She sat down, not saying anything, her mind still numb with shock.

Justin sat beside her on the step, his knee touching hers in casual intimacy. "There are about 240 million people in the United States," he said. "Speaking as a mathematician, do you realize what the odds must be against meeting that man by coincidence?"

"A few trillion to one, I guess."

"Close enough, give or take a couple of billion." Justin frowned. "On the other hand, can you suggest any possible way he could have known you would be here? We didn't know ourselves until ten minutes before we checked in."

Courtney's hands tightened around her knees. "He must be following me."

"Then where did he pick up your trail? Was he standing outside the grounds of Walnut Park on the off chance you might jump over the wall?" Justin crashed one fist into the other and sprang to his feet. "Damn it all to hell! None of this makes even a lick of sense."

Courtney got up and brushed off her slacks. "I guess we have to do what we planned to do all along. Go back to our room and call Mexico. You said yourself, if we keep investigating, something's going to start unraveling eventually."

Justin grimaced ruefully. "Did I really say that? Aunt Amelia should have taught you never to remind a gentleman of his more foolish sayings."

Courtney laughed. "She probably did. I was a hopeless pupil."

"Well, come on. Let's go and place that call to Mexico. Maybe we'll get lucky. Maybe Gary Wade left without paying the bill, and they remember him clearly."

HARVEY WAITED UNTIL there had been silence for a full five minutes before he carefully unbolted the door of the janitor's office. The shock he had felt on first seeing Courtney had changed into a cold, furious anger, and he still shook with the force of it.

There was no need for him to speak to Tanner now. It was all too obvious what had happened. Courtney had gone from Walnut Park to Copper Creek and had somehow managed to persuade Tanner to help her. What magic spell had the bitch cast on Tanner that they were already working as *partners*, for God's sake?

They both knew far too much, and neither of them had any sensitivity to Harvey's point of view. They didn't seem to understand that a genius was subject to different rules from ordinary mortals.

He would have to kill her very soon, he thought. He simply couldn't afford to have the pair of them connecting too many links in the chain. They already knew about Gary Wade. There was no way of guessing what they might find out tomorrow.

Harvey realized he was sweating. He reached for his handkerchief, then remembered he'd thrown it away in Stapleton Airport. He'd have to buy a new one tomorrow. No, he didn't have time for shopping. He was going to be busy.

Harvey took the service elevator to his room. He had a lot of thinking to do. Tonight he would make his plans.

Tomorrow he would kill her.

Chapter Nine

Courtney and Justin arrived promptly at ten for their appointment with Judge Simmons. The judge was an elderly man with a dramatic crop of white hair and bushy gray eyebrows. His face was striking in the extreme, and Courtney was positive she had never seen him before in her life. Drugs or no drugs, she thought, surely she would recognize such distinctive features?

The judge listened courteously to Justin's story of confused records at the county building, and a nine-month-pregnant cousin in New Jersey.

"I don't recall any couple called Tanner," he said when Justin had finished. "But I'm afraid my memory is no longer as accurate as it once was."

The crispness of his tone belied his words, and Courtney had a horrible suspicion that the judge's wits were still sharp enough to detect several flaws in the story she and Justin had invented.

"You've no idea how scatterbrained my cousin is," she said. "Honestly, how could any woman lose her wedding certificate when she's about to give birth?"

The aloofness of the judge's expression softened slightly. "Naturally, with a baby on the way, I'll do everything in my power to help your cousin. My secretary is the guardian of all our records." He depressed a button on his intercom.

"Brenda, would you check our wedding list for April 22 of this year? Mr. and Mrs...."

"Padechowski," Justin supplied quickly.

"Mr. and Mrs. Padechowski are anxious to help their cousin straighten out a little problem."

"Certainly, sir."

The judge rose to his feet. "Now, if you will excuse me, Mr. and Mrs. Padechowski, I have an appointment in court."

Thanking him profusely, Courtney and Justin made their way into Brenda's office. The secretary was also more than willing to be helpful. Like the judge, she had no memory of any couple called Tanner, but she pulled out an appointment calendar and quickly searched through an efficient, cross-referenced index. Nobody called Justin Tanner or Courtney Long had been married by Judge Simmons during the entire year.

"It's very strange," she said, looking up with sudden curiosity. "I don't remember the couple at all, and yet the name Courtney Long rings a definite bell. I know I've heard that name somewhere recently."

Courtney's lungs gave up on breathing until the secretary frowned and shook her head, abandoning her search for the elusive memory. "Your cousin is certainly very confused. How could she possibly make a mistake about something as important as her own wedding?"

How indeed? Justin and Courtney exchanged frantic glances. Good grief, Courtney thought, we've got to get better at inventing lies. Justin was looking at her in a half-laughing appeal, and she plunged into the lengthening silence.

"Oh, dear," she murmured. "I can see we'll have to tell you the truth. It's what my grandmother was afraid of all along. She never did believe that horrid Justin Tanner actually married my poor cousin. Granny said poor little Courtney invented that story because she's pregnant and ashamed to tell her family the truth.''

"And it looks like Granny was right, as she always is," Justin interjected piously. "Our cousin should have known she'd get found out sooner or later."

"Yes, and Granny will have a heart attack if the pair of them carry on living in sin. She doesn't realize times have changed since she was a girl. Oh, dear, I can see there's going to be a major family fight, and I wish we weren't involved."

Brenda was looking at them both rather oddly, and Courtney decided it was high time to beat a retreat. Neither she nor Justin would ever manage to earn their livings as actors, she thought.

"Time to go, dearest," she murmured, grabbing Justin's arm. "We'll have to decide how we're going to break the news to poor old Granny."

"Yes, you're right, honey. We mustn't let her work herself into a rage. It's so bad for her heart." Justin bestowed a final, dazzling smile on Brenda and made for the door. "Thanks again for all your help," he said, and whisked Courtney out of the office.

Courtney ought to have been worried by the secretary's near recognition of her name, but somehow the entire episode struck her as irresistibly funny. She managed to restrain her giggles until they were safely out of sight. "I don't think Brenda believed a word of my brilliant story," Courtney said, when she finally controlled her laughter.

"Oh, I don't know. I thought dear old Granny was rather a convincing touch. The poor old lady was beginning to seem quite real, even to me."

Courtney laughed again, then sobered. "I guess that little session proves I was never legally married. Oh, God, Justin, I can't tell you how wonderful that news feels."

The elevator arrived and they stepped inside. "You didn't recognize the judge, I gather?"

"No, I never saw him until today."

"In one way that's great news. On the other hand, what do we do now? The hotel in Mexico told us a couple were registered in their honeymoon suite under the name of Mr. and Mrs. Tanner, but that's all they could tell us."

"We agreed last night that information was useless."

"And this morning we discovered Judge Simmons has no record of any marriage. We're really galloping ahead."

The elevator reached the ground floor, and Courtney walked out, wrinkling her nose. "Can you imagine Sheriff Swanson's reaction if I told him I was the victim of some master plot to keep me locked away from civilization and then produced those bits of information as eviden—"

"Wait!" Justin interrupted. "We're forgetting something. You *did* recognize this building, and you remembered Judge Simmons's name, even though you don't recognize him in person."

Courtney's eyes sparkled. "Of course! That means I went through some sort of a wedding ceremony in this building, even if the real Judge Simmons didn't perform it!"

"Right. Watch out for the can of paint. They're redecorating the office suite over there."

Courtney stood stock-still in the middle of the lobby. "That's it!" She gasped. "The smell of paint. It was overwhelming in the office where I was married. Gary Wade must have discovered an office suite that was changing tenants, and he used that for our wedding."

"It's a possibility," Justin remarked, then added thoughtfully, "Have you noticed something? This Gary Wade never invents people out of thin air. He always impersonates somebody. Why does he do that? Why use Judge Simmons's name when he could have made one up with much less trouble?"

"Maybe he was afraid I'd look at the directory when we came into the lobby of the building?" Courtney suggested.

"That's possible, although he could have invented a dozen

quick explanations as to why the judge's name wasn't listed. But that doesn't explain why he used my name for six whole weeks. That had to create extra risks for him.''

"You think there's some deep significance to his decision to impersonate people rather than simply invent names?''

Justin considered her question, then grinned. "Hell, I don't know. At least I had three weeks of law school. I never took a single day of psychology classes.''

They had reached the Bronco by this time, and Courtney's euphoric mood dissipated in a rush. "Gary Wade saw me last night in the hotel and you know what that means, don't you? He's going to find some way to turn me in to the authorities. The Denver police are probably out in force looking for me.''

"I'd already thought of that,'' Justin agreed quietly. "An anonymous phone call is all too easy. That's why I suggest we should go back to Copper Creek as fast as we can, pick up some supplies from my house and then hightail it out of state. It's going to be a lot easier to blend in with the woodwork once we're away from Colorado. And we'd better pick up another bottle of hair dye, since Wade has seen you. By now the authorities are presumably looking for a redhead. How do you feel about tackling life as a brunette?''

"Sounds great to me, especially the bit about hightailing out of Colorado. Except, where are we hightailing to?''

"Hop in the truck,'' he said, unlocking the door. "We've got several hours to discuss that while we drive to Aspen.''

They headed out of the parking lot, following the signs for Interstate 70. "I think we've been approaching this problem from the wrong angle,'' Justin said, as soon as they were on the road. "We've focused our energies on trying to discover Gary Wade's real identity, and we've tried to trace back what he did during the time you two were together. But when you think about it, that's just what he's gone to a lot of trouble to conceal. We've got to stop concentrating on what he did and start asking ourselves a different set of questions. Why did he want you confined in a mental hospital? Why couldn't he risk revealing his real name? Does he have a criminal record, maybe? Once we know the answers to those questions, maybe we'll also know who Gary Wade really is."

Courtney stirred in frustration. "I came to live with my aunt before I was five, and I'm nearly twenty-seven now. Justin, it's depressing to sound so boring, but I haven't done *anything* in those twenty-two years to make me a danger to anybody."

"Come on, you're underestimating yourself. You don't win yourself a slot on a U.S. Olympic team without creating a few bitter rivals—"

"Sure, I had rivals. But I broke my leg in three places when I was nineteen. Nobody needs me locked away in Walnut Park to keep me off the Olympic ski team. I couldn't even make the state finals these days."

His gaze was sympathetic. "Does it still hurt?"

She knew he wasn't referring to physical pain, and she felt her stomach clench tight with remembered anguish. "Less and less as time goes on," she said, striving to sound matter-of-fact. "I used to get physically sick with frustration whenever I stood at the top of a run, but Walnut Park seems to have put those frustrations in better perspective." She smiled ruefully. "Maybe I should write Gary Wade a note of thanks when we eventually find him."

"I'd save the ink if I were you. Okay, so if he isn't connected to your ski career, what connection can he possibly have to your life?"

"Justin, I think this is where we came in."

"You were never the mistress of an important senator or a company president or an international arms smuggler—"

The idea was so absurd, she smiled. "The only person I was ever mistress to was Ed, the downhill skier I told you about. And that guy had exactly two thoughts in his head:

how fast could he come down a mountain, and how fast could he bed his woman of the day. Usually his score was about equal: one minute, forty-two seconds for each.''

''Slow and sensitive lover, huh?'' Justin glanced into his rearview mirror, frowned slightly, then switched lanes. ''I guess that means we're both thinking the same thing. If Gary Wade isn't connected to your career or your love life, he has to be connected to your distant past. Which means everything happening to you now is somehow tied up with your parents' murder.''

It was exactly what she herself had been thinking, for days if not for weeks, but hearing the idea put into words made her shudder.

''Courtney?''

She expelled her breath in a long sigh. ''Yes,'' she said. ''I agree with you. My incarceration in Walnut Park is somehow connected to my parents' murder. It's the only explanation that makes any kind of sense.''

''But why now?'' Justin demanded. ''Why after twenty-two years of indifference is Gary Wade suddenly frantic to get you locked away?''

''I may know the answer to that. For twenty-two years nobody except Aunt Amelia knew Danielle Danvers was still alive. Even I didn't remember that Courtney Long had once been Danielle Danvers. Then my aunt died and I found out who I really was.''

''Did you tell anybody else?'' Justin asked quickly.

''No, not directly.''

''But indirectly?''

''Perhaps. When Aunt Amelia died, I became obsessed with finding out the truth about my parents' death. You see, the official police version of events didn't tie in with my nightmare—''

''Dreams aren't factual reality, Courtney. They're interpretations of our subconscious hopes and fears.''

"But fear is precisely what my dream is all about. It's an endless replay of my deepest fear."

"Losing your parents, you mean?"

"No, not exactly. Don't you see, Justin, once I knew who I was and what had happened to my parents, my nightmare took on a whole new significance. The most terrifying part of the dream, worse even than my mother's screams, has always been the soft, compelling voice of the man calling to me. I know the voice isn't my father's, but I recognize it. I know the man calling Didi is supposed to be a friend, but I've seen him do something so dreadful that even with my child's mind, I know I can't trust him anymore. His voice paralyzes me with fear because I recognize that he's evil."

Justin drove in silence for a few seconds. "What you're suggesting," he said finally, "is that somewhere in your subconscious you carry the knowledge of who killed your parents."

Courtney felt the fear clamp tight and hard at her throat. "Yes, that's what I'm saying. And you know what, Justin? I'm scared as hell of finding out precisely how much I know. I have this irrational fear that if I put a name to that man's voice, he'll be able to find me. That's why I always wake up from the dream with him still calling me. I know if I step out from behind the bushes, I'll see his face...." Her voice died away to a whisper. "I'm too scared to see his face. I don't want to see it."

"You shouldn't be scared," Justin said, reaching out to touch her very lightly on the arm. "When you think about it, putting a name to that man's voice is probably the one thing in the world that will keep you safe from him."

"How?"

"Once you remember what really happened that night, we can confront the authorities with our knowledge. The murderer will be found, and the law will take care of him. And you'll be safe."

"That's a great scenario, Justin, but the fact is the police would be reluctant to accept the word of *anybody* recalling events from almost twenty-three years ago. Now that I've been certified insane, there isn't a chance in a million that the police will believe anything I say."

Justin looked at her, skidding the Bronco onto the verge of the road. "*That's* why he wanted you locked away!" Justin exclaimed, swiftly correcting the skid. "Damn it, Courtney, you've just hit on the explanation for this whole stupid mess! You're officially crazy, so everything you say is suspect. In fact, dredging up stories about a twenty-two-year-old murder is likely to confirm the doctors' opinions about your mental health. You'll have to produce independent, factual evidence for every claim you make. Otherwise the police will simply dismiss your story as another one of your paranoid delusions."

"Great! Well, having worked that out, we have no problems at all!"

"We certainly have fewer than we had before. At least we have a motive that begins to make sense."

"But Justin, we still have to find out who this guy really is! Nobody found evidence of an outside killer twenty-two years ago. How the blazes are we going to find it when the trail is stone cold, and we have half the police in Colorado earning overtime by chasing me?"

"The trail isn't cold," Justin said calmly, accelerating to overtake a huge truck. "And we have some things to work on that the police don't. We know your father didn't kill your mother, because the murderer has come back to find you. We know he sometimes calls himself Gary Wade. We know he's somewhere close. Most of all, we know he's running scared."

Courtney began to feel queasy. "Gary Wade," she murmured. "You're saying he murdered my parents and then arranged for me to be sent to Walnut Park to protect himself.''

"It seems likely, don't you think? Especially if he's afraid you witnessed the killing."

Courtney found it amazingly easy to accept the idea of her pseudohusband as the killer of her parents. So easy, in fact, that she knew the realization must have been hovering on the edge of her consciousness for weeks. A sudden horrible thought struck her, and she choked on an involuntary gasp of bitter laughter. "To think I was worried because we'd never slept together! I wonder what weird scruple held him back?"

She stuffed her fist against her mouth as nausea began to swell uncontrollably in her stomach. "Oh, God, if I'd slept with him and then found out he killed my parents...."

She gagged and turned for the window, pushing it down with frantic speed. Fortunately she'd not eaten breakfast, and the dry retching stopped as the blasts of fresh mountain air blew cold and cleansing against her cheeks.

When she finally pulled her head back inside the Bronco, she realized Justin was driving off the highway onto a nearby exit. "We're in West Vail," he said quietly. "Time for a break. Tea and toast sound good to you?"

"At least the tea part," she said ruefully. Embarrassed, she gestured toward the window. "Sorry about that."

"Don't apologize," he said, parking the truck outside a small café. "I'll order while you find the rest rooms if you want to freshen up."

Alone in the small washroom, Courtney looked at herself in the mirror above the single sink. She still hadn't gotten used to the sight of herself with auburn hair. Her cheeks seemed as pale as ever, but her eyes had lost their defeated look and her chin had once again acquired its stubborn upward tilt. A vast improvement over four days earlier, she decided.

She washed in the hottest water the tap would provide, then rinsed her mouth at the drinking fountain. "You'll do," she informed her reflection. "Just remember you're not going to let that murdering bastard send you back to Walnut Park."

She ate the whole wheat toast Justin had ordered with surprising appetite, and by the time she'd consumed her second cup of tea, she felt almost human again. She glanced up from draining her cup to find Justin's eyes fixed intently on her face.

"You're an amazingly brave woman, Courtney," he said softly. "We're going to make this thing come right for you, you'll see."

His words flooded her with a warm glow of pleasure. "I don't feel in the least brave on the inside," she admitted.

"I think the cliché goes, *Most of us don't.* But you're sure putting up a hell of a good facade." He stood up. "Ready to face the road again?"

"Ready," she confirmed. "That tea just hit the spot."

He put his arm around her as they walked to the car, and she was a little disconcerted by her intense reaction to the ripple of his hard muscle against her side. It seemed almost indecent to be experiencing even a hint of sexual desire in her present situation. Anyway, Justin had made it clear he was still in mourning for his wife.

They stopped at the passenger side of the car, and he put his finger under her chin, tilting her face gently upward. He dropped the briefest of kisses on the end of her nose, pushing a stray lock of hair out of her eyes. "Remind me we have to buy brown hair dye when we pass a drugstore," he said.

Courtney swallowed. "All right." Justin gave her another feather-light kiss, then walked around to unlock the car door.

Neither of them spoke until the Bronco was safely back on I-70. "You haven't explained how Gary Wade discovered little Didi was still alive," Justin said.

"I think I probably told him myself."

At Justin's startled glance, she explained. "I told you. Once I read Aunt Amelia's letter, I was obsessed with learning the truth about my parents' death. They were both famous, so there was lots of material for me to work on. Eventually I compiled a list of all the people who'd been with my parents during the final weeks of their lives. As you know, they were acting in a movie called *Snow Flight* up at Aspen, so they were in daily contact with literally dozens of people. When I finalized my list of names—thirty or so—I hired a private detective and asked him to find out their current addresses."

Justin stared at her with dawning amazement. "And then you contacted them saying you were *Danielle Danvers*?"

"No, of course not. I didn't want them to think I was crazy. I wrote them all letters signed Courtney Long, although that was pretty dumb because my original name had been Danielle *Courtney* Danvers and my dad's name was Robert *Long* Danvers—"

"Quite apart from that, didn't it occur to you that some of these people might not want to have the circumstances of your parents' murder investigated?"

"No," she said simply. "In those days I guess I was pretty naive."

Justin muttered a few choice expletives under his breath. "Okay, so what did you write these people?"

"Some of the people on my list were dead, of course, and there were a couple the detective couldn't trace. But he turned up about twenty-five survivors, scattered around the country. When I wrote them, I pretended to be a sports reporter commissioned to produce a biography of Robert Danvers. Then I asked them for interviews."

Justin's silence was eloquent. "How many people replied?" he asked finally.

"Almost all of them, although some said they were too busy to give interviews."

Justin turned to look at her, his eyes grave. "You realize you've just reduced our pool of suspects from about one hundred million American males to one of the men who answered your letter? How many people is that?"

"Maybe thirteen or fourteen."

"Sounds like a manageable number for us to investigate."

"If I can remember their names. A copy of the list is with my luggage, wherever that's disappeared to."

"Hmm. Who can you remember?"

"Well, as far as the men are concerned, there's Emil Zoran, who was the director of *Snow Flight*. He lives in Beverly Hills, and so does the producer, Kit Krane. I remember their names because they're both so well-known."

"Zoran won an Oscar last year, didn't he?"

"Yes, and I've seen pictures of him and Kit Krane. Neither one of them could possibly be Gary Wade. Kit Krane is bald and not a fraction over five foot three. Emil Zoran is about six foot four and must weigh three hundred pounds minimum."

"How about the cameramen, gofers, assistant producers and makeup men?"

Courtney sighed. "I don't even remember their names, much less their addresses. I remember some of the women, though, and maybe they could give us some leads."

"There was your nurse, Jane Grislechy. Her name was in that book I was reading."

"Yes, I remember her address because it was a nursing home. Twin Oaks, somewhere out on Long Island."

"Since she discovered the murders, she'd be a good person to track down. How about Pauline Powers? She's another one who ought to be easy to trace. Isn't she something to do with women's fashions?"

"Yes, she has her own design house in New York, and I think her private address was somewhere in Manhattan's East Sixties."

"No telling if she'd agree to see us, of course. Did you manage to interview any of the people on your list already?" Justin glanced into his rearview mirror as he spoke. "Hold on," he said abruptly, accelerating to an illegal seventy-five miles an hour. After driving for several miles at breakneck speed, he rounded a bend in the highway, then braked sharply and skidded off the road onto a ramp provided for runaway trucks.

"What's the problem?" Courtney gasped.

"A tan-colored Buick Skylark has been behind us ever since we left Denver. I didn't pay that much attention to it until we turned off at Vail, but it was still there when we came back on the road."

"Is it…does it look like a police car?"

"It doesn't have markings or flashing lights, if that's what you mean. Anyway, we seem to have lost it. Damn!"

"Maybe it was…him."

"If it was, he's not following us anymore."

"He doesn't have to," she said in a small voice. "Where would we be going on this road except back to Aspen?"

"He's not going to be fool enough to follow us to Copper Creek," Justin said grimly. "He must realize that would be putting his head straight in the noose."

Courtney gave a hollow laugh. "Funny, but from my perspective it doesn't seem that he's the one whose neck is at risk."

"Then your perspective's wrong. If by any fortunate chance he should turn up at Copper Creek, it would save us a hell of a lot of trouble. We'd simply grab him and make him talk. Damn it, Courtney, the whole object of this is to do just that!"

"I guess so."

"I know so." Justin sounded annoyingly confident. Self-confidence, Courtney reflected, was one of the many advantages of not having spent several months in a mental institution.

"Okay." He rejoined the flow of traffic. "Back to business. Who have you interviewed on that original list, and what did they say?"

Courtney decided wallowing in fear and doubt would get her nowhere. "Two of the people who replied to my letter lived in Aspen," she said, doing her best to sound as crisp as Justin. "The detective in charge of the original investigation lives in an apartment on the edge of town, and Ferne Hilton's ex-dresser runs a boutique in Snowmass." Her briskness crumbled a bit. "I interviewed them both before I...before I met Gary Wade."

"Did they say anything useful?"

She shook her head. "A little, not much. The dresser was willing to gossip, but she didn't really have much to say. She'd worked for Ferne Hilton no more than a couple of months before the murders, and their relationship seems to have been strictly professional. She did say one thing that was interesting, but it wasn't anything new. She claimed my mother stormed off the set the afternoon of the murders, threatening to kill her husband if he so much as looked at Pauline Powers again."

"It was Pauline Powers's first movie, right?"

"Right. She was playing the young-but-not-so-innocent maiden. Typecasting, according to my mother's dresser."

"Still, that's a reason for your mother to shoot your father, not the other way around."

"Well, I questioned the detective on that point, but he swears everything fits. The dresser's statement is considered important because it gives a reason for my parents to be fighting in the first place. The detective insisted everything at the scene of the crime bore out the original police story. Ferne Hilton and Robert Danvers had a blazing row, things got out of hand, and my father went for his gun. Or maybe my mother went for it, and he snatched it away, then decided to use it. The detective pointed out to me that the fingerprints, the position of the bullet wounds, the sweater fluff under my father's fingernails, all the forensic evidence, in fact, bore out that Robert Danvers killed his wife at the culmination of a violent argument, then committed suicide from remorse.''

''Something about the detective's story bothers you. I can tell from the tone of your voice.''

''He struck me as terribly defensive, that's all. As if something about the police version bothered him, but he wouldn't allow himself to think about it.''

''You mean he was bought off?''

''Not that,'' she denied quickly. ''It was more as if he didn't want to rock the boat on a highly publicized case, and he had plenty of excuses for keeping his mouth shut about his doubts, whatever they were. The circumstantial evidence all fitted—at least superficially. In that book I read, everybody connected with *Snow Flight* agreed tension between Ferne Hilton and Robert Danvers had been getting visibly higher. So the police had a nice, neat case. Motive, means and opportunity all presented to them on a shiny silver platter.''

''Maybe that's why your police detective was uncomfortable. The whole scene was just too neat. Murders usually aren't.''

''You know that from watching TV, of course.''

He grinned. ''How else? Linda was forever telling me about all the careful research that goes into those police shows. Some of the writers spend a whole ten minutes reading police manuals before they turn in their scripts.''

The inevitable moment of silence followed his unthinking mention of Linda's name, and Courtney interjected quickly, ''I tried to check out the house where the murders took place, but no luck.''

The pain in his eyes was veiled. ''The house didn't jog any memories?''

''It didn't exist anymore. The mountain chalet I remember has been converted into a bunch of condominiums built around a swimming pool. So much for my hope that I'd go back to the house and the meaning of everything in my dream would suddenly become crystal clear.''

They had finally entered the town of Glenwood Springs and crossed the bridge leading to Aspen. Justin glanced into his rearview mirror as he prepared to enter local traffic. He swore softly.

''What's wrong?'' Courtney asked.

''We're being followed again.''

''By the tan Buick?''

''No,'' he said tersely. ''By the police.''

Chapter Ten

"How do you know it's following us?" Courtney asked, dry-mouthed. She leaned over and looked in the mirror. "It's still quite a long way back."

Ignoring irate hoots and angry gestures, Justin wove the Bronco in and out of traffic until they were driving directly in front of a supermarket delivery truck.

"I don't know for sure. But its lights are flashing, and I'm not waiting around to find out." He reached into his pocket, fumbling for his wallet. "Quick," he said, handing it to Courtney. "Take a twenty. We're out of sight from the rear. I'm going to swing right into the motel parking lot up ahead. You jump out and go back to the drugstore we passed down the street. Buy hair dye and dark makeup. Looks like we're going to need it real soon."

"What are you going to do?" She scrabbled for the twenty with shaking fingers.

"Drive on a quarter of a mile, then pull over to the side of the road like any other law-abiding citizen. If the police are chasing speeders, so much the better. If they're looking for you, then I'll tell them you skipped out on me in Denver."

"Justin, you can't get yourself involved in my—"

He swung the car hard right. "Get out and don't argue. For God's sake, hide yourself inside a store before the squad car catches up.'' He pushed her unceremoniously out of the door. ''I'll pick you up here as soon as I can shake the cops.''

''I can't just stand in the parking lot—''

''Order a cup of coffee in the motel restaurant, but come out as soon as you see me. *Now move*, damn it!'' He pulled the door of the Bronco shut and immediately nosed out again into the flow of traffic.

She could hear the police siren getting ominously closer. The sound jolted her into action. She dashed into an alley alongside the motel and made her way to the back of the building. As she had hoped, another alley stretched parallel to the road, almost filled by giant garbage Dumpsters. She raced along, flanked by trash on one side and scraggy bushes on the other, until she saw a Dumpster marked Discount Drugs. A metal-barred door, similarly signed, carried a warning notice painted in large black letters: Fire Exit—No Entry.

Unwilling to risk setting off an alarm, Courtney didn't attempt to enter. Heart pounding, she searched for the alley that would lead her back to the front of the store. She was still squinting into the sun when the fire door suddenly opened. Courtney and a young girl in a pink nylon uniform stared at each other in mutual astonishment.

Courtney spoke quickly. ''I'm lost.'' She forced an innocent smile. ''I took the wrong door out of the motel, and now I can't find how to get in the front of the store.''

The suspicion in the assistant's eyes cleared. She tossed the plastic container she was holding into the trash and returned Courtney's smile. ''You can come in this way, if you like. It'll be quicker. Otherwise you have to go clear to the end of the alley before there's any way to get back to the front of the store.''

With country-town trust she held open the heavy door, squeezing herself flat so Courtney could avoid the Dumpster.

Courtney produced another of her sincere smiles. ''Thanks very much,'' she said, following the assistant down a short corridor that seemed to contain nothing except two rest rooms. "Er...lovely day, isn't it?"

"Yes, I guess it is. You from out of state?"

"From Illinois," Courtney improvised, then wondered why in the world her subconscious had picked a state about which she knew absolutely nothing. It would serve her right if the shop assistant had been born and raised there.

Luck, however, remained on her side. "Oh, Illinois," the girl said, pushing open a swinging door. "I wouldn't like to live there. What do you want to buy?"

"Shampoo," Courtney answered. There was no point in letting the shop assistant know she planned to buy hair dye.

"It's in aisle three. You have a nice day now."

Courtney bought medium ash-brown hair coloring and a bottle of makeup labeled as suitable for dark complexions. She also bought mascara to blacken her lashes and a palette of various gray and mauve eye shadows. She was no makeup expert, but with these supplies she thought she would be able to effect some fairly distinctive changes in her appearance.

The woman at the cash register expressed not a smidgen of interest either in Courtney or the items she had purchased. Courtney made her way back to the motel, attaching herself to small groups of pedestrians and striving to appear inconspicuous. She walked slowly, wanting to minimize the amount of time she would have to hang around in the motel parking lot. Even so, it was three-fifteen, and she had stretched out a cup of coffee and a cranberry muffin for thirty agonizing minutes before she saw Justin's blue-and-silver Bronco appear in the parking lot.

She tucked three dollar bills under her plate and hurried outside. Justin already had the door of the truck open. He was moving back into the road before she had a chance to close it.

"Climb over the seat into the back," he ordered. "You'll have to lie down for the rest of the trip."

The fear Courtney had been feeling for the past hour coalesced into an ice-cold lump in the pit of her stomach. "The police were looking for me?" she asked, obeying his instructions.

"Not only for you, for me, too. They had the license number of the Bronco, and they knew you'd changed the color of your hair."

"Gary Wade tipped them off."

"I guess so. Either that, or Mrs. Moynihan decided it was time to do her civic duty. The state trooper was singularly uninformative as to how he'd come by his information."

"So how did you shake them in the end?"

"I swore I'd learned the error of my ways. I told them you ran out on me in Denver last night as soon as I'd bought you dinner. I'm not sure they believed me."

"But they let you go. Obviously, since you're here."

"Get your head down. Yes, they let me go, but they followed me for a good ten miles, and I had to drive another ten before I could find a side road where I could double back to get you."

She sat up. "Justin, you know how grateful I am for everything you've done—"

"For God's sake will you get your damn head down!"

Courtney wedged herself more or less lengthwise on the back seat. "Do you really think they'll concentrate their search in Denver?"

"That's where I said you'd left me. I tried hard to sound annoyed. The troopers couldn't make up their minds whether I was a fool who'd been taken in by a pretty face, or a master criminal who was scheming to keep a certified lunatic out on the streets."

"There's nothing to stop them coming after you again, and there's no road we can take to Aspen except this one. Independence Pass is closed at this time of year."

"Exactly. Which is why I'd rather not have you visible for the rest of the drive."

Courtney subsided into an uneasy silence, and Justin flipped the car radio to a local all-news channel. The knowledge that the police were out in force looking for her did nothing to soothe Courtney's lacerated nerves, but eventually the drone of the newscaster's voice recounting the latest stock prices took the edge off her fear, lulling her into drowsiness.

Justin's voice murmuring her name brought her back to her surroundings. "We're almost home," he said softly, as she pulled herself into a half-sitting position. "And I've been thinking about who may have turned you in to the police. If it was Mrs. Moynihan, it wouldn't be smart for us to walk back into my house arm-in-arm."

"You're right," Courtney said, rubbing her eyes. "What if she thought I'd given you the slip somewhere in Denver? At least that way you're telling her and the state troopers the same story. But what excuse are you going to use for leaving the house as soon as you arrive home?"

"I'll tell her I've decided to make a flying visit to Stanford University. She knows they've been asking me to go out there, because she's taken a couple of telephone messages from the head of the math department."

"Won't she think it's strange if you leave tonight? I mean, why all the rush? Presumably Stanford's been waiting for weeks. They could wait a couple more days."

Justin acknowledged the problem with a grunt. "There's one solution that might work," he said finally. "I could storm around the house and pretend to be angry at the way you'd tricked me. Maybe I could complain that you'd never have deceived me if I hadn't been spending too much time alone recently."

"Would Mrs. Moynihan fall for that?"

"She might. She's the one who keeps saying that shutting myself away from the world won't bring Linda back." Almost to himself, Justin added, ''Maybe it's time I faced up to the fact that *nothing* will bring Linda back.''

Courtney tried to think of something appropriate to say, but her mind remained obstinately blank. Her body, perversely, was not feeling blank at all. Still not entirely awake, her mental barriers were down, and her body tingled with awareness. Looking at Justin's taut, controlled features, tenderness grew inside her, and she felt an overwhelming desire to offer him comfort. No, that wasn't true. If she was to be honest with herself, what she felt wasn't a desire to comfort. It was a desire to share with Justin passion that was so intense he would forget all about Linda.

The crunch of gravel under the wheels of the Bronco alerted her to the fact that they were almost at Justin's house. She dragged her errant thoughts back to the matter at hand. ''Where do you want me to stay while you're talking to Mrs. Moynihan?'' she asked.

''In the Bronco. Would you mind? I'll be as quick as I can.''

''Of course I don't mind. Justin, without your help I'd have been locked up inside Walnut Park hours ago. There's no way I can ever thank you for all you've done.''

''I'm in your debt, too,'' he said quietly. ''I was rapidly turning myself into a self-pitying hermit before you came along. I needed a reminder that there's more to the world than the algorithms in my computer....'' He braked sharply, his voice dying away into silence. ''Sheriff Swanson's car is parked in my driveway,'' he said. ''I can see it through the trees.''

''We could turn around....''

''No, we need to get the police off my tail if we're ever going to make it out of the state. It's better if I go into the house and convince them I'm all right.''

''I can't stay in the Bronco. He might check it.''

''Could you hide in the trees at the edge of my property?''

"The sheriff will find me in five minutes if he comes looking. It's not even dark."

"Then we'd better make damn sure he doesn't look." He swiveled around in the driver's seat. "Grab the navy-blue sweater from my overnight bag. If you put that on, it'll keep you warm and make you harder to see. The sun's already gone down. In another half hour, it'll be night."

She leaned over the back of the seat, reaching into the carpeted cargo area to unzip Justin's bag. "There's a knit hat on the floor back here, too. A gray one."

"I wondered where that had gotten to. Tuck your hair up, and you should be almost invisible among all those tree shadows."

She pulled on the sweater and shoved her hair haphazardly under the knit cap. "How do I look?" she asked.

"You look...young," he said in a husky voice. "And very innocent."

Courtney's body was flooded with unexpected heat. It was the extra sweater and the woolen hat, she told herself firmly. She had to swallow hard before speaking. "Appearances can be deceptive."

He didn't answer for a long moment. Then his eyes darkened, lingering on her mouth as he spoke. "You'd better get out of here before somebody sees you. If I drive you any closer to the house, we're sure to be spotted."

He leaned across the front of the Bronco, tilting the passenger seat forward and opening the door. Courtney clambered out somewhat awkwardly. The leg she had broken skiing tended to cramp if she didn't stretch it out frequently, and her muscles felt knotted.

"Keep warm," he called softly, as she sprinted along the side of the road toward the safety of the coppice.

"I'll be fine." She heard Justin turn on the ignition. The Bronco soon overtook her, and by the time she had reached a reasonably safe hiding place behind a giant spruce, Justin had already arrived at his destination. The noise of the engine ceased abruptly, and she almost persuaded herself that she could hear the crunch of Justin's footsteps on the gravel driveway. Then, for endless minute after minute, there was nothing except the tiny sounds of animals and insects preparing themselves for the night ahead.

Despite the cap and extra sweater, it was cold now that the sun had gone down, but Courtney didn't want to walk around. Sounds carried clearly in the silence of the night. She wasn't sure if she had really heard Justin's footsteps or only imagined them, but either way, she didn't dare to risk making some movement that might attract the sheriff's attention toward the woods. She shifted her weight from one foot to the other, twisting herself between the low-lying branches of the spruce in the hope of finding a sturdy branch to rest against. Standing still was amazingly tiring.

She heard the muted sound of a door opening and peered through the branches toward Justin's house. It was difficult to see the driveway through the intervening trees, but eventually she heard the sound of a revving car engine. Wheels crunched over loose driveway gravel, and a few seconds later she saw the sheriff's car pass along the road. As far as she could tell, the car had only one occupant.

Courtney's body went limp. Until she'd seen the sheriff driving away, she hadn't realized how tense she actually was. She gave a little crow of mingled exultation and relief and was about to burst out of her hiding place when she remembered Mrs. Moynihan. On second thought it would be much safer to stay where she was.

Time crawled by. At first she decided she must have imagined the whisper of sound. "Didi, I know you're there.... I've been waiting for you to arrive. Where are you, Didi?"

She shook her head, convinced that she had fallen into some weird, waking form of her nightmare.

"Didi...I know you're out there somewhere. I followed

you from Denver. Tell me where you are, Didi, so I can come and get you.''

She huddled deeper into the embrace of the tree, barely feeling the scratch of needles and pointed twigs. Her entire body was suddenly drenched with ice-cold sweat.

''Didi! I'm going to find you this time, Didi.'' The voice was nearer. Soft, penetrating, gently persuasive, it pounded against her ears, tempting her to run out and surrender herself. Only some primal instinct of self-preservation kept her cowering between the concealing spruce branches.

''Didi! You should have stayed where I put you and then you'd have been safe. Now I have to take care of you another way. Come here, Didi.''

''No,'' she whimpered, pressing her hands over her ears in a childish effort to block out the terrible voice. ''No. Go away. I don't like you. You hurt my mommy and my daddy.''

A crackle of dry leaves and a swoosh of branches sounded somewhere to her left. She whirled around, but she could see nothing except trees and dancing shadows. ''Wh-where are you?'' she whispered. ''Where have you gone?''

A chattering squirrel ran up a distant pine. The shadows thickened, closing in on her, until they seemed to join hands and smother her in their darkness. She tore at them, but they formed again as fast as she destroyed them. Gasping for air, she began to push her way through the branches of the spruce tree. She had to breathe!

The voice spoke softly behind her. ''Hello, Didi. I knew I'd find you eventually. Why didn't you come when I called?''

She didn't run, she didn't cry out, she didn't even turn to look at him. She knew she would die if she saw his face. She felt something slip around her throat. Something smooth. Silky. Inevitable.

"I really wish you'd stayed in Walnut Park, Didi." The voice was sad, almost wistful.

"I'll go back there. I will."

"No, of course you won't, Didi. We both know that." The silk around her throat was drawn tighter. Now, when it was far too late, she began to struggle, clawing at his face and trying desperately to twist out of his grasp. She could have kicked him in the groin, but her injured leg collapsed under her. She screamed—a loud, ringing scream that echoed uselessly in the empty night.

Her attacker hit her viciously across the side of her head. "That was naughty," he said. "You shouldn't make a noise."

The silk tightened inexorably around her neck. The shadows returned, veiling her eyes. The voice whispered its final apology into her ear. "If you'd been a good girl, I wouldn't have needed to do this. But you're bad, like all the others. Bad, bad, bad."

In the distance she heard a funeral drumroll, and a heavenly cymbal crashed as the skies went black. Courtney felt angry. How could they hold her funeral when she wasn't dead? She *wasn't* dead. Not yet. Not quite.

Or maybe the sound hadn't been a funeral drumroll. Maybe it had been the approach of a car. *Justin!* she screamed. *Justin, help me!*

One tiny rational part of her mind knew she hadn't spoken the words out loud. Knew that she had neither breath nor strength left for screaming. She was dying. Her mind shouted a last, final plea. Then there was only darkness. Space. Nothing.

Chapter Eleven

Justin stowed his hastily packed suitcase in the rear of the Bronco, anxious to be on his way. The sheriff had been relatively easy to get rid of, but Mrs. Moynihan had proven much harder to placate. Rigid with disapproval, she had watched him throw clothes and toilet articles into his case. She had made no offer to help.

"You're going to meet up with that crazy woman, aren't you? No good trying to lie to me, Mr. Tanner. I don't think she skipped out on you in Denver. Her type knows how to stick to a good thing when they see it."

Justin tried hard not to look guilty. He really was lousy at lying. "I told you, Mrs. Moynihan, Professor Karleck has asked me to deliver a couple of lectures at Stanford. I decided to take him up on his offer. It's more than a year since I gave any guest lectures."

The housekeeper's expression remained severe. "I wanted you to get out and about more, Mr. Tanner, but not like this." She watched as he added a pile of sports shirts to his packing, and her mouth quivered with unexpected emotion. "Mr. Tanner, there's nobody else around to tell you the truth. Your wife was sick for so many months, and then after she died… Well, anyways, what with one thing and another, it's been so long since you had a conversation with a normal woman, you can't recognize a crazy when you see one. That Courtney woman is trouble, Mr. Tanner, nothing but trouble.''

He was touched by the housekeeper's concern, although at this precise moment it was damned inconvenient. "You're right about one thing," he said, snapping shut the locks of his suitcase. "I've been closeted in my office far too long, feeling sorry for myself. Linda wanted me to look back with joy on our life together. She wanted me to remember what a great marriage we had. She didn't expect me to become a living monument to her memory."

Mrs. Moynihan snorted as she followed him down the stairs. "Sounds like you finally realized it wasn't your fault she got sick and you didn't. There wasn't nothing more you could have done to make her better, Mr. Tanner, so you can stop blaming yourself for what happened. Mrs. Tanner shared a lot of love during her life. There's plenty of folks live to be a hundred and don't achieve so much."

"Anybody ever tell you you're an interfering old Irish-woman?" Justin asked, the warmth in his eyes belying the bluntness of his question.

"They may have, now and again, but that doesn't alter facts. Courtney Long is a crazy woman, you mark my words."

Justin paused in the front doorway. "If anybody should happen to inquire, tell them I've gone to Stanford."

"And how'll I reach you if there's any important messages?"

"I'll call you."

"And not from California, I'm willing to bet." The house-keeper's glare would have intimidated many a lesser man.

Justin gathered her stiff, unyielding body into a brief hug. "Thanks, Mrs. Moynihan. I really appreciate what you're doing for me."

He stepped outside before she could say anything more,

but he heard her disapproving sniff right through the solid-oak panels of the front door.

Total darkness had descended during the forty-five minutes he'd spent inside the house. He squinted, maximizing the light from the porch as he unlocked the truck and pulled himself up into the driver's seat.

Justin scowled when the Bronco didn't start on the first try. His sense of urgency was out of proportion to the situation, but he still couldn't shake it. Courtney was probably cold and certainly bored, but Sheriff Swanson had returned to town, and she wasn't in any imminent danger of arrest.

The truck finally started. Justin rolled down the window a crack and let the night air refresh him as he drove fast along the familiar gravel road. He reached the stand of trees that marked the corner of his property. The thicket loomed dark by the side of the road, and he scanned the bushes, looking for some sign of movement. No Courtney. He opened the window a bit further, wondering whether he should beep the horn to attract her attention.

When he heard the scream, for a split second he told himself it was an animal, but his body reacted more swiftly than his mind.

"Courtney?" Justin was out of the truck and running toward the trees even as he shouted her name. Out in the open, the sound of somebody fleeing became unmistakable. On the far side of the coppice, a human body was crashing through the undergrowth. Justin switched course, racing toward the sound, but it was almost impossible to run fast and listen at the same time for the direction of the noise.

The running footsteps stopped. Then the momentary quiet was broken by the sudden roar of an igniting engine. Headlights flared in Justin's face with blinding brilliance. A car shot out of a dirt track, gathering speed as it vanished around a bend in the road and headed toward town.

Justin didn't waste even a second chasing the car or straining to read the dust-covered license plates. He swung around and plunged deep into the stand of trees. The thicket, which earlier had seemed so inadequate a hiding place, now seemed as dense as a forest. He channeled his rage and panic into an ice-cold, disciplined logic and began a methodical crisscrossing of the thicket.

He found Courtney on his second diagonal run, crumpled in a patch of open ground between three large evergreens. Her hat—his hat—had fallen off, and her hair spilled over her face, obscuring it from view. Pale moonlight filtered through the branches and highlighted the rich, lustrous gleam of artificial auburn color. He knelt down and pressed his fingers against her wrist, searching desperately for a pulse. He couldn't find one.

He rolled her over, noticing with an odd detachment that his hands were numb but perfectly steady. Her neck was wrapped in a long, paisley silk scarf, knotted at intervals to make a more efficient noose. He unwound it carefully, clenching his jaw when he saw the hideous bruises already forming in a ragged chain around her neck. Frantic with haste, he bent down, covering her mouth with his and blowing air into her lungs. Rage fueled his desperate efforts. Linda had died; he damn well wasn't going to let Courtney die, too.

He delivered a solid blow to her chest. "Breathe, damn you, breathe!" he cursed. With the heels of his hands, he maintained a rhythmic pumping motion against her rib cage while his mind shouted might-have-beens. Why hadn't he found her two minutes earlier? The would-be murderer obviously had been interrupted in his task. She could have stopped breathing only seconds earlier.

The stir of warm breath against his face was so feeble that for a moment he didn't register its significance. Then he felt the shudder of her chest moving and heard her draw in a shallow, rattling breath. Dear God, she was alive!

Heart pounding like a trip-hammer, Justin cradled her head in his arm. He felt his mouth stretch into an asinine grin. He had never heard anything more beautiful than the rhythmic rasp of air in her lungs!

After a couple of minutes, she opened her eyes. "Hi," he said softly, then had to stop and clear his throat. "You sure do get yourself into a heap of trouble every time I leave you alone."

Courtney attempted a smile but couldn't quite make it. Justin's heart gave an odd lurch as he looked down at her. "Don't say anything," he murmured. "Rest your throat."

Her hand flew to her neck. "He...was...here," she croaked. Justin had to put his ear almost to her mouth in order to hear what she was saying.

He saw the terror in her eyes, although she tried to conceal it, and a wave of murderous rage welled up inside him. He held her close against his chest, rocking her to and fro as he would a frightened child. "You mean Gary Wade?" he asked. "The man who impersonated me did this?"

"He called me...Didi." It was torment to listen to her, and she winced with the effort of speaking.

Justin got to his feet, then swung Courtney into his arms and placed his forefinger lightly against her dry, cracked lips. "Don't talk anymore. I'll take you back to the house, and we'll find something to ease your throat."

She didn't protest. She seemed only half-conscious as he placed her carefully inside the Bronco. When she leaned back against the headrest, her bruised neck was fully exposed. Justin's body shook with rage. Goddammit, but he was going to find the bastard who'd done this!

He drove the short distance home at breakneck speed, then lifted Courtney out of the truck and carried her to the house almost at a run. He turned off the alarm system and let himself in through the front door, expecting Mrs. Moynihan to appear in the hallway at any moment. Instead, as he climbed the stairs, he heard the sound of canned laughter and bursts of applause coming from her room. Game-show time, he realized. So much the better. He'd have more time to decide exactly what he was going to tell her.

He settled Courtney on his bed, propping her against a pile of pillows before going into his bathroom to dampen a towel with hot water. He wiped her face, then held the steaming cloth against her throat, talking soothing nonsense until the color gradually returned to her cheeks. He fixed a second hot towel and handed it to her with an encouraging smile. "I'm going to make up a mixture of lemon juice and honey for you to drink. My mother swears that'll ease a sore throat better than anything you can buy in the store. I'll bring you some water, too, if you think you can swallow it."

She nodded. "Thank you, you saved my li—"

"Rest your throat, Courtney. We'll talk when you've had something to drink."

She had scarcely moved when he returned to the bedroom ten minutes later, but her eyes seemed alert once again, and her face already looked less swollen. He supported her against his arm while she sipped the mixture of sweetened lemon juice. She didn't complain, but he could feel the shudder of pain that coursed through her body each time she swallowed. Finally she drank a little of the water, refusing with a quick shake of her head his offer to hold the glass.

"Better?" he queried, when she leaned over to put the glass down on the nightstand.

"Good as new." The rasp of her voice proved otherwise, but he thought she looked sufficiently recovered to answer a few questions. He didn't want her to feel threatened, so he eased away, leaning back against the headboard. He missed the slender weight of her nestled in his arms, and he was shocked to realize that his desire to hold her comprised more than a noble wish to offer sympathy.

"I shouldn't be here," she whispered. Whispering was apparently easier for her than talking out loud. "Mrs. Moynihan won't approve."

"Her approval doesn't matter a damn at the moment. Courtney, do you remember anything about your attacker? Anything at all that might help us to identify him?"

"I wish I did. He…came up behind me, whispering the same sort of things he says in my dream. I felt as if I were a little girl again, cowering in my parents' backyard, hiding from his voice like I do in my dream. But the adult part of me knew it was Gary Wade."

"*How* did you know that if you didn't see him?"

She frowned. "His touch, his smell, even his voice. And he said I should have stayed in Walnut Park. He acted almost as if I was *forcing* him to kill me."

Justin forgot his intention to keep a safe distance and rolled over onto his side, propping himself up on one elbow. He gently propelled her head around until she was forced to meet his eyes. "You realize this attack has changed everything, don't you, Courtney?"

Her gaze slid away from him. "How do you mean? N-nothing's changed. I'll be fine in just a few minutes."

"Of course the situation's changed. We have to go to the police, Courtney."

"No!" She winced. "Justin, *please* don't go to the police!"

"We have to tell them about the murder attempt—"

"What murder attempt?" she croaked. "They'll probably say I tried to commit suicide again."

"How can they? *I* found you with a silk scarf twisted around your neck. *I* saw a man running away from the woods. *I* know you didn't try to commit suicide. Courtney, with everything else we've discovered, the police will have to listen to us."

"I'm certified legally insane, Justin. Why should the police believe anything I say?"

"Because I'm backing you up."

"We can prove somebody calling himself Gary Wade used your house illegally. That's all we have proof of, nothing else."

"We have proof he's come back and is trying to kill you."

"What proof?" She smiled wearily. "*I* told *you* I saw Gary Wade in the airport hotel. You never saw anything, except me behaving strangely. True, you saw a man running out of the woods, but *I* told *you* he attacked me. *I* told *you* he called to me just like the man in my dream. All you know is that somebody was trespassing. Can you imagine Sheriff Swanson's response to a piece of 'evidence' like that?"

"We don't have to report anything to the sheriff except the fact you were attacked."

"Maybe. But even if the authorities agree to conduct an investigation, I'll be locked up in Walnut Park while they conduct it. And in the meantime, Gary Wade will have covered his tracks and polished his alibi. He'll bury himself so deep in his protective cover, nobody will ever flush him out."

"At least you wouldn't be in physical danger."

Courtney's mouth trembled into a travesty of a smile. "Physically I might be safe. Mentally I'd be in the worst danger possible. Have you any idea how difficult it is to keep hold of your sanity when everybody around you is terminally crazy—and the medical staff keeps insisting you're crazy, too?"

Tears welled up and quivered on the ends of her lashes. She dashed them away with an impatient flick of her hand, then knotted her fingers tightly in her lap. "I'm not going back to Walnut Park," she said in a low voice. "I won't do anything that would put me back there, Justin. If you try to turn me in, I warn you, I'll run away."

She looked stubborn, tired, vulnerable and heartrendingly courageous. Justin wanted to end the argument by pulling her into his arms and kissing her into submission. Instead he got up and walked over to the window. There was nothing to see except snow-peaked mountains, darker shadows against the darkness of the night. He knew that if he had a grain of common sense he'd ignore Courtney's pleas and call the sheriff. None of her protests had any real validity. She was simply terrified of being sent back to the hospital.

With a shrug he admitted to himself that his common sense seemed to have taken a holiday. His knowledge of mental institutions was strictly secondhand and highly colored by horrific images from movies like *One Flew Over the Cuckoo's Nest*. But the truth was, he couldn't tolerate the thought of Courtney locked up in Walnut Park's maximum-security wing. He wanted to help her solve the mystery of her parents' death so that she would be liberated from her past and set free to enjoy her future. And, for his own sake almost as much as for Courtney's, he needed to find out who Gary Wade really was. He had a strong urge to deliver a series of well-placed punches before Wade got handed over to the authorities. His caveman reflex was obviously closer to the surface than he'd ever realized.

He turned around and looked at Courtney. "If we're not going to the police," he said, "do you have any brilliant suggestions about what we should do next?"

Courtney was about to reply when a furtive squeak of the bedroom door startled them both. Mrs. Moynihan stood on the threshold, wielding an old-fashioned hunting rifle.

"I hope to God that isn't loaded," Justin said. "Please put it down carefully, Mrs. Moynihan."

The housekeeper's mouth dropped open with almost comic astonishment. Gathering her wits, she lowered the rifle, propping it up against the wall before walking into the bedroom. She flicked a brief, hostile glance toward Courtney as she passed the bed.

"Lucky for you I couldn't find the bullets," she said to

Justin with unconcealed belligerence. "I thought you were on your way to California."

"My plans have changed."

"That's all too easy to see. And it's even easier to see who's persuaded you to change them."

"Is it?" Justin walked back to the bed, deliberately holding the housekeeper's gaze as he picked up Courtney's hand and squeezed it reassuringly. He didn't care if Mrs. Moynihan got the wrong impression about their relationship.

"Would you look a little more closely at Courtney?" he said. "At her neck, to be specific."

Grudgingly the housekeeper swiveled. Her eyes narrowed, then her hand flew to her mouth, and she choked back a gasp of horror. "Oh, my Lord, the poor young lady! Whatever in the world has happened to her?"

"Somebody tried to kill her," Justin said. "If I'd left the house five minutes later, I probably wouldn't have been able to revive her."

"Saints and angels preserve us! What in the world is going on around here? Was it a burglar, do you think?"

"The man who attacked Courtney followed her here from Denver. He's the same person who managed to get her certified insane six months ago."

Some of the sympathy faded from Mrs. Moynihan's expression. "And how would you be knowing a thing like that, Mr. Tanner?"

"Because I recognized her attacker," Justin said, stretching the truth. "Unfortunately he was too far away for me to catch."

Mrs. Moynihan pursed her lips, giving no indication of whether or not she accepted her employer's version of the events. "Have you called a doctor for the young lady, then? And how about the police?"

"Er...not yet."

"Well, you'd better call the police right away or they'll

have no hope of catching the man you saw. You should be able to give them a good description at least."

Courtney flashed him a look of desperate appeal, and Justin tightened his grasp on her hand. "We're not going to the police," he said quietly. "We can't tell you the whole story, Mrs. Moynihan, but we have some leads we need to follow up on our own."

"Huh! With a murderer *and* the police on your heels? You'll end up in jail if you don't get yourselves killed first."

Courtney spoke for the first time. "We'll be safe when we leave Colorado," she said hoarsely. "The murderer will never be able to track us out of state."

"That's as may be." Mrs. Moynihan looked down at Courtney, her nurturing instincts clearly at war with her suspicion. "I have a couple of prescription-strength painkillers if you'd like them, Ms Long."

"Thanks very much, but I can't risk taking anything that might make me drowsy. We have to leave here soon." Courtney swung her legs over the side of the bed and struggled to her feet. "Mrs. Moynihan, I'm really grateful..."

She got no farther with her thanks. Her knees buckled beneath her, and she would have fallen if Justin hadn't taken a rapid stride forward to catch her. He felt her tense for a moment. Then she relaxed, allowing him to support her.

"Mrs. Moynihan's right about one thing," he said, his voice soft. "You need a doctor."

"Justin, I'm fine now, truly I am. I'll take a shower and I'll be as good as new."

He looked down at her, torn between admiration and annoyance. "Yeah, I can see how fine you are. A tap with a feather might not knock you over. Two feathers would put you flat on the floor."

"We have to get out of here!" She clenched her teeth, struggling to control her panic. "There's no *time* for me to lie around in bed feeling sorry for myself!"

"I promise we'll fly out of Aspen Airport tomorrow morning. In return you have to promise to stay here and get a decent night's sleep."

"You don't want to fly out of Aspen," Mrs. Moynihan interjected. "You know how small the airport is, and the sheriff's warned everybody working there to be on the lookout for Courtney. Probably for you, too, Mr. Tanner. Go to Aspen Airport, and you'll walk straight into the arms of the police."

Mrs. Moynihan flushed with irritation when she realized what she'd admitted. She had never intended to reveal herself as being so firmly on their side.

Justin grinned but tactfully made no direct comment on her change of heart. "Thanks for the warning," he said.

"Well, I don't want to work for a man who gets himself arrested," the housekeeper mumbled crossly. "I've got my reputation to think of. You're a couple of fools, the pair of you, but I reckon I'm gonna have to let you do whatever crazy thing you've set your hearts on. You'll do it anyways."

She thumped over to the door. "I'll heat up some chicken soup," she added belligerently. "You can eat up here where you'll be more comfortable. I don't suppose either of you had any dinner."

She left the room, and Justin realized that Courtney remained locked in his arms. He made no attempt to release her.

"I guess I can stand by myself now," she murmured.

"I guess you can."

Still, neither of them moved. Justin wondered why this particular woman aroused his latent sexual instincts, when he'd spent most of the past year totally indifferent to the female half of the population. He was becoming obsessed with the need to make love to her. Even now, his response to her closeness was frankly erotic. Holding her like this, he could tell that her breasts were small but firm, her hips taut and sexy, her legs long and sleek and slender. He imagined her lying naked beneath him, her breasts soft and full in his hands, her nipples swollen beneath the teasing touch of his tongue. His imagination created a vivid picture, and his body responded with embarrassing promptness.

"How does your throat feel now?" he asked, easing himself away from the betraying contact of thigh to thigh. He wished he hadn't given up smoking. At least a cigarette would have provided something to do with his hands—other than hold Courtney.

"Better. It gets better all the time."

"You still sound husky." He looked down at her, tempting himself. "You sound very sexy."

Color ran up into her cheeks and she turned away. "I have to take a shower. Bits of leaf are sticking to me in some very strange places."

Lucky leaves, Justin thought. "Keep the bathroom door open in case you faint," he said, making his voice as casual as he could. "Here, let me find you a clean towel."

He left her in the bathroom and sat down at the bedroom desk to draw up a list of what they needed to do next. He had gotten as far as writing "Priority—check with Didi's nanny," when Courtney turned on the shower. Through the open door he could hear the sound of splashing water. An all-too-clear picture of her soap-slicked, naked body came into his mind, leaving him hard and hot. He imagined her bending over to soap her legs. He imagined her legs wrapped around him. He imagined thrusting deep inside her. He imagined her writhing with pleasure as he brought her to climax. It took all the self-discipline he possessed not to groan aloud.

Justin walked as far away from the bathroom as he could, offended by the reaction of his own body. Barely an hour had gone by since Courtney had survived a brutal attempt on her life. Speaking and swallowing were still painful for her, but he was fantasizing about what a terrific sexual partner she would make.

Gritting his teeth, Justin turned his attention back to the list. "Contact the starlet, what's her name, who caused so much trouble on the Snow Flight set." Not a very coherent note, he admitted, but mental discipline had its limits.

Those limits were stretched to the utmost when Courtney emerged from the bathroom clad in his toweling robe and nothing else. The shoulders of the robe were way too big, and despite frequent adjustments, the front gaped open to reveal tantalizing glimpses of Courtney's satin skin and provocative breasts.

"I hope you don't mind." Courtney gestured to the robe. "My clothes were so dirty I couldn't bear to put them on again."

"No, of course I don't mind." His voice was somewhere between a growl and a bark. He couldn't remember having so much difficulty breathing since the day a classmate in junior high sneaked him his first-ever copy of *Playboy*. He'd forgotten what hell unfulfilled sexual fantasies could be.

He greeted Mrs. Moynihan's arrival with gushing, heartfelt relief. The housekeeper rewarded his enthusiasm with a suspicious look. "Eat your food while it's hot," she admonished. "You sit here on the bed, Courtney, and I'll hand you the tray. It's best if you rest your legs. You may as well stay where you are, Mr. Tanner. Then you'll have the desk to put your bowl on."

Feeling long-suffering and noble, Justin directed his gaze away from Courtney and toward his bowl. Homemade cream-of-chicken soup had rarely looked less appealing.

"I'll be back with your dessert in fifteen minutes or so," Mrs. Moynihan commented. "Make sure you eat a good meal." She marched out of the room, leaving the door wide open.

Courtney gave a throaty chuckle. "Your housekeeper

knows she disapproves of me, she just can't make up her mind why. She feels she has so many good reasons."

"Don't take it personally. Mrs. Moynihan views ninety-nine percent of the population as thoroughly undesirable. And that's on her good days."

"You included?"

"Probably me especially. Her father was a union leader back in the old country, and Mrs. Moynihan disapproves of all employers on principle."

"Her cooking makes up for everything." Courtney leaned back against the pillows, savoring the creamy soup. "I was thinking while I was in the shower," she said finally. "We need to check out each of the people I wrote to in connection with my parents' death. But we can't do that systematically because the original list of names and addresses is in Aunt Amelia's safe-deposit box, and I don't have the key."

Justin crumbled a crust of bread. "How about asking the private investigator you hired for a copy?"

"Do you think we could? Supposing the Colorado police have notified him to be on the lookout for me?"

"That's stretching their efficiency a bit, don't you think?"

"Maybe, maybe not. They notified the bank that administers my trust fund."

"You're right. We'll have to reconstruct that list some other way."

"It's infuriating to think we already know the murderer is one of fourteen or fifteen men on my list, and I can't remember a single name." Courtney arched her back in pure frustration. The bathrobe opened almost to her waist. Justin allowed himself one long look before burying his nose in his glass of ice water. The cold water didn't do much for his overactive libido, but it effected a marvelous revival of his powers of reasoning.

"Hey, wait a minute!" he muttered, getting up and retrieving the book about the movie *Snow Flight* from the drawer of his nightstand. "We ought to go through this to check the names in the index and under the photos. You may recognize some of them."

"Of course! Why didn't I think of that?" Courtney reached for the book. "If we're lucky, maybe we can reconstruct the entire list that way."

"I've just thought of something else." Justin sat beside her on the bed, helping her flip through the pages. "There's a good chance I may recognize the name of the man who impersonated me. After all, we already decided he must know me."

Courtney frowned. "I'm not sure I understand."

"Well, if you recognize some name from your list, and it turns out I know that person too, I'd guess there's a fair chance he's the man who impersonated me. Otherwise, it's too much of a coincidence, don't you think?"

Excitement made Courtney's eyes sparkle. "You're right! Oh, Justin, we're really getting somewhere with this mess at last!"

They pored over the pictures together, excitement gradually draining away into depression. The names Courtney had already remembered occurred repeatedly, but the rest of the support crew rarely merited a mention by name. Those few cameramen or assistant set designers who were named rang no bells in Justin's memory, and none in Courtney's.

"Although," he said, snapping the book shut, "it's not surprising we're coming up empty. Given this man's penchant for aliases, he may have changed his name several times since *Snow Flight* was made."

Courtney sighed. "And I used dozens of sources to draw up that original list, not only this book. In fact, most of the people I mentioned to the private investigator had been quoted in newspaper reports."

Justin stared gloomily at the book's cover picture, a glamorous shot of Ferne Hilton and Robert Danvers. "If only

Linda were here! She knew everybody in the film world. I'd bet big money that if any of these people are still working, Linda would have known where."

They looked at each other in startled silence, recognition slowly dawning. "That's it!" Courtney whispered. "*Linda's* the link between my parents and the man who impersonated you. My parents were movie stars. Your wife was a TV star. The man who murdered my parents is—was—somehow connected to Linda's career."

"That's how he knew exactly when this house would be empty," Justin muttered, distaste making his stomach roil. "He wasn't keeping tabs on me or on my movements. He was monitoring the progress of Linda's illness through professional contacts."

Courtney's eyes clouded with sympathy. "Justin, I'm sorry. I didn't mean to bring up painful subjects."

"You're not. The man who attacked you did that."

She cleared her throat tentatively. "Then we just need to compile a list of everybody who worked on the soap with Linda—"

"Unfortunately it's not quite that easy. Her career was really taking off when she got sick. In the six months before…she was bedridden, she'd done commercials, guest appearances on network shows, even a cameo appearance in a movie."

"Still, it's a whole new angle for us to work on. Linda's career."

They were staring at each other so intently neither of them heard the sound of Mrs. Moynihan's footsteps on the stairs. She came into the bedroom carrying a large serving tray. On the tray were two dishes of vanilla ice cream, a carafe of coffee and a selection of chocolate mints.

She scowled as she served her supply of goodies. "You'll ruin the mattress, Mr. Tanner, sitting on it like that." She clattered empty soup bowls back onto the tray.

Justin wisely made no comment. Courtney smiled with genuine warmth. "The soup was delicious, Mrs. Moynihan. Thank you for choosing things that are easy for me to eat."

"Humph. Can't have you getting any sicker than you are already. Have you decided where you're going tomorrow?"

"The East Coast?" Courtney said, looking questioningly toward Justin.

"Yes," he agreed. "New York, I think. We can take the first flight out of Denver."

"You'll need to be up at the crack of dawn," Mrs. Moynihan observed.

"Before five. That way we'll catch the nine-thirty flight out of Stapleton and be in Manhattan around midafternoon, East Coast time."

"Going to stay at the Hilton like you usually do?"

"No." Justin didn't elaborate. He glanced at the housekeeper and saw the hurt in her expression.

"We'll stay at the Grand Hyatt," he said slowly, confident that Mrs. Moynihan would never betray their whereabouts once she'd tacitly agreed to support their cause. "I've heard it's a decent hotel, although I've never stayed there myself."

"Humph," Mrs. Moynihan said as she picked up the tray of dirty dishes. It was the closest she could ever come to giving her approval. "The bed's made up in the guest room whenever you're ready, Courtney. You'll be needing an early night if you're to be up and about so early."

Amused by Mrs. Moynihan's heavy-handed determination to preserve the proprieties, Justin smiled at her with guileless charm. "Thank you, Mrs. Moynihan, but we won't be needing the guest room. Courtney's sleeping in my room tonight. She'll feel much safer with me to keep her company."

Courtney thought the point was debatable.

Chapter Twelve

Courtney watched As Justin made his way back down the aisle of the plane. Her heart began to thud with the same anticipation that had bedeviled her all night long.

"Another twenty minutes and we'll be landing." Justin slipped into the seat beside her. He sounded energetic, cheerful and damnably in control. He smiled kindly. "Are you exhausted?"

Only from lying next to you all night and pretending to sleep, Courtney thought ruefully.

This morning he was wearing gray tailored slacks, a turtleneck knit shirt in pale blue and a lightweight tweed jacket. He looked the epitome of the successful professional man, spiced with just enough rugged masculinity to be irresistible.

Courtney could barely keep her hands to herself. She had read somewhere that the threat of physical danger often heightened a woman's sexual awareness. So far her body seemed to be subscribing to that theory. She reminded herself for about the twentieth time that her attraction to Justin was simply a product of her desperate situation. But her body had no interest in sensible reminders. It manufactured hormones with increased determination and trembled with desire every time Justin came within touching distance.

Last night could hardly be termed romantic. Mrs. Moynihan had been hell-bent on preserving her employer's chastity, and Courtney had been escorted to bed swathed neck to ankle in a pink flannel nightgown.

Justin had eyed her armor plating somewhat wryly, although he, too, had made an effort. Pajamas obviously didn't form any part of his wardrobe, so he'd slept in a pair of faded cutoff jeans. He hadn't bothered with anything at all on top, which left Courtney's hormones free to do their worst. His current outfit did nothing to dispel her memory of broad, muscular shoulders and a tanned chest liberally matted with crinkly brown hair.

Sadly, Justin had not turned out to be a restless sleeper. Neither his broad shoulders nor his masculine chest had come within reach of Courtney's tense body.

The consequence of all this unfulfilled sexual tension was that Courtney felt less alert than the average zombie. Justin had insisted that she would succumb to nightmares if left to sleep alone. He had not considered the possibility that if forced to lie two feet away from him, she might not sleep at all.

"Exhausted?" she said brightly, realizing he was still waiting for her reply. "Not at all. I slept *wonderfully* last night. How about you?"

Justin looked at her oddly. "Oh, I had a wonderful night, too," he agreed, his voice hearty. "Since we're both so well rested, we should be able to hit the ground running."

Courtney mustered a smile and pulled herself bolt upright in her seat. "We sure should."

Her jaws were aching, but she'd be damned if she was going to stop smiling first. She injected another scoop of artificial brightness into her voice. "There are so many people for us to see in the New York area. There's Jane Grislechy—"

"I already have the phone number of the nursing home where she's living."

"Good. And we must try to contact Pauline Powers right

away. She's a very successful person, and we might have to wait a long time before she agrees to see me. Did I tell you that she gave several interviews at the time of the murder, insisting that Robert Danvers would never have killed my mother?''

"She could have been looking for a little extra publicity, of course.''

Courtney was crestfallen. "I hadn't thought of that.''

"Don't worry, it's definitely a lead worth following. She may have had genuine doubts about the police verdict. After all, she was rumored to be having an affair with Danvers, so she ought to have known his state of mind. Why don't you concentrate on her? That cover story you invented about being a sports journalist should hold up. Your skiing credentials are impeccable.''

"What will you do while I'm pursuing Pauline?''

"I ought to work on Linda's career and her contacts, don't you think? Last night I remembered a good friend of Linda's who has a photographic memory and an extensive library on the movie industry. I'll call him as soon as we get to the hotel and try to arrange a meeting for tonight. He might come up with some useful information. He might even be able to identify the people Linda worked with who also worked on *Snow Flight*.''

"Wonderful.'' Courtney was unable to think of anything more to contribute. She wondered if their room in the Grand Hyatt would have two beds. Nowadays, unfortunately, most hotels did.

The fasten-seat-belt sign flashed on overhead and the stewardess began to intone her prelanding announcements.

Justin buckled his belt, leaned back in his seat and closed his eyes. "I slept like hell last night,'' he said conversationally. "My only consolation is that I think you did, too.''

HARVEY NICHOLSON PAID off his cab outside the Grand Hyatt hotel. He'd called that stupid Irish housekeeper again in his role as Linda's brother. She had sounded much more cautious this time, and it had taken all of his cajoling skills to extract the name of Justin's hotel from her.

Tanner ought to be checked in by now. Would Didi be with him? Harvey was sure that she would. He had watched all the early news shows before catching the 10:45 flight out of Denver. There had been no mention of Didi's death on any of the channels.

He was angry that his hard work had been wasted. He was not, however, all that surprised. Women were creations of the Devil and sometimes had to be killed more than once. Harvey realized at last why everything had gone wrong recently. His only regret was that it had taken him so long to recognize the truth, which was simple enough: *Ferne's spirit had come back and was hiding inside Didi's body.* It was a perfectly logical conclusion. Ferne was Didi's mother. What more suitable instrument could Ferne find to exact her vengeance on Harvey?

Harvey knew now what he should have recognized from the very beginning. He would have to kill Ferne/Didi again and again until they both finally stayed dead. If he'd known from the start that Ferne and Didi were one person, of course he'd never have allowed Didi to live. Kind gestures, Harvey reflected sadly, invariably led good men like him into trouble.

It was raining, a state of affairs that always depressed Harvey. He turned up the collar of his imported British raincoat and glanced sourly at the functional, modern facade of the hotel. Harvey was not a lover of modern architecture, and he would never have chosen to stay in a glass-and-steel box when the Plaza offered all the comfort and elegance of an earlier, more refined age. Still, you couldn't expect Tanner to have any taste. He was a computer jock, for God's sake. Harvey thought the world would be a much better place if all computer experts were gathered into a single giant warehouse in the Nevada desert and condemned to communicate only with each other.

He entered the hotel and smiled pleasantly at the doorman. It was, of course, a mark of his sterling character that he managed to hide every sign of his justifiable irritation. Despite all the trouble Didi was causing, Harvey's good nature remained unimpaired. Help across the road for a cripple, smiles for a doorman—it was all in the day's work for Harvey.

His troubles had always been caused by women, he reflected. Women like his mother and Ferne Hilton. Those psychiatrists who tried to convince Harvey that all women were not like his mother didn't know what they were talking about. And that last one—the crazy doctor who actually suggested that Harvey might benefit from intensive therapy in a mental hospital! Well, Harvey would have laughed if the suggestion hadn't been so insulting.

It was his brother who needed therapy—his brother who was the alcoholic. Harvey never drank to excess. Harvey had a successful career. So what if he liked to change his name occasionally and pretend he was somebody else? It was a free country, wasn't it? He was a successful director, even if they'd said he was a terrible actor. His whole life was organized to perfection. Except for that bitch Didi Danvers. She was like a missile out of control, hurtling toward him and threatening destruction.

Harvey crossed the crowded lobby and made his way to the reception desk. The two women and one man on duty all looked as harassed as Harvey could wish. He waited patiently for an opportunity to speak, then inquired if Mr. Justin Tanner had checked in.

"Mr. Tanner?" The clerk typed the name into her computer. She was speaking into the phone at the same time and never even glanced at Harvey. "Yes, Mr. and Mrs. Tanner have checked in."

"Could you tell me their room number, please? I'd like to go up and see them."

"We're not allowed to give out room numbers, sir. Perhaps you'd like to call on one of our house phones. The operator will connect you if you ask for them by name."

He hadn't expected any other reply. With all the dangerous people in the world, hotels these days had a duty to be cautious. It was only right and proper.

Harvey smiled again at the desk clerk, who'd obviously already forgotten him. "Thank you very much. I'll call my friend," he said.

He merged quickly with a crowd of businessmen crossing the lobby and found a seat behind a giant plant. He could see everybody from here without being seen himself. He didn't like to admit it, but his legs were trembling. In a minute he would work out some brilliant plan for discovering Didi's room number. Right now he just wanted to sit and let the feeling of anticipation consume him. In the final analysis, what did it matter if that crazy psychiatrist had accused him of being impotent? Harvey knew the truth. Soon he would kill Ferne/Didi again. Soon his power would swell until he felt strong, invincible, potent, *masculine*.

It was a very good feeling.

THE HOTEL ROOM boasted two queen-size beds, a miniscule closet and a modest bathroom. Courtney decided destiny was not on her side, or the room would have boasted a miniscule bed and a queen-size closet. She and Justin had stopped at a discount clothing warehouse on the way in from Long Island, and she now owned a suitcase filled with a modest wardrobe. In comparison with the recent past, she felt positively encumbered by her possessions.

"Why don't you take a shower and dye your hair brown," Justin suggested, when they had completed the taxing task of bestowing their clothes on the four available coat hangers.

"I can't imagine anybody in Manhattan who'd be looking for you, but it can't hurt."

"Okay." Courtney found the package of hair dye she'd bought—surely a lifetime ago—in Glenwood Springs. Neither she nor Justin mentioned the fact that the person most likely to be on the lookout for her was the would-be murderer. "What are you going to do while I'm turning myself into a brunette?"

"I'll call the nursing home and arrange for you to see your ex-nurse, hopefully tomorrow morning. Then I'll try to set up that appointment for you with Pauline Powers. I'll say I'm your literary agent and the interview is very important. It sounds more impressive if you're not doing the calling yourself."

Courtney grimaced. "Good luck. Whoever calls, I suspect she'll keep us hanging around for a week just so we realize how important she is."

"I'm more optimistic. She's so successful she may feel no need to play silly games. Her fashion empire must be one of the largest in the world."

"Will you come with me if she agrees to the interview?"

"Probably not. People tend to reveal more when it's one-on-one."

"How do you know that?" she asked, then sighed. "All right, let me guess. You saw it on TV, right?"

His eyes gleamed. "Hey, it's a great educational medium, don't knock it. Some of the scriptwriters can even read."

She hid a smile. "So what'll you do while I'm talking one-on-one with Pauline Powers?"

"With luck I'll be talking to Geoff Buck, Linda's friend. If he's free tonight, I know he'll see me."

An hour later Courtney emerged brown-haired from the bathroom. She stared sideways in the full-length mirror. It was a very odd sensation to keep seeing herself reflected back in different colors. She'd not even had time to get used to being a redhead.

Justin hung up the phone. "Does it look natural?" she asked, lifting a strand and searching for traces of blond or auburn. "What do you think?"

Justin grinned. "Ever hear the joke about the sailor who was asked if he preferred blondes, redheads or brunettes and he replied yes? I'm beginning to feel like the sailor. You look terrific in all three shades."

"I'm expecting my hair to fall out in hanks any minute now. Aunt Amelia always claimed that hair dye rotted the roots."

"What Aunt Amelia probably meant is that women who dye their hair *deserve* to have it fall out at the roots."

Courtney's smile held a touch of wistfulness. "I wish you could have met her, Justin."

"I do, too." He walked across the small room and stood beside her, admiring her reflection in the mirror. "That skirt and blouse look great. Until today I never shopped with a woman who could pick out three outfits, complete with underwear, stockings and shoes, in twenty minutes."

"You probably never shopped with an escaped lunatic before. Having the police on your tail makes speedy decisions easier."

He laughed. "True. Well, Ms Escaped Lunatic, how do you feel about having cocktails tonight with Pauline Powers?"

Courtney's eyebrows lifted. "She agreed to see me so soon?"

Justin looked pleased with himself. "Your literary agent— in other words, me—impressed upon her the urgency of sharing her insights for this important biography of Robert Danvers. Naturally she agreed that her input was vital. She's leaving for a dinner appointment at eight. She volunteered to meet with you in her apartment at six-thirty. You have ninety minutes, kid. Make them count.''

Courtney, who had been thrilled with her wool skirt and peacock-green silk blouse after months of wearing institution polyester, instantly turned to the mirror. Pauline Powers made the *Women's Wear Daily* list of America's ten best-dressed women every year without fail.

Courtney began twitching pleats and tugging at her waist-band. What had possessed her to buy something as out of style as a blouse with a cossack collar? What, that is, other than the chain of purple bruises decorating her neck?

Justin rested his hands on her shoulders. His gaze locked with hers in the mirror. ''You look perfect.'' He ran his fingers gently down the silk sleeves of her blouse, then clasped his hands lightly around her rib cage. ''You have the sort of figure that makes even discount-house specials look spectacular.''

Hypnotized, Courtney watched his tanned fingers tease lightly up her arms. She twisted around, seeking contact more real than reflections in a mirror. Justin bent slowly, making a harsh sound deep in his throat before covering her mouth with his own.

His kiss was determined but gentle, seducing her with its sweetness, gradually summoning such intense excitement that she shivered with the force of it. His hands reached beneath the silk of her blouse, caressing her bare skin and the fragile lace cups of her bra. Afloat on a sea of pleasure, she pulled up his shirt, exploring his body as he explored hers. His skin burned beneath her fingertips, taut flesh over hard muscle. Suddenly the heat was no longer confined to her fingers. It was within her, a slow, strange fire that spread throughout her entire body. She surrendered to the blaze.

She had no idea how long it was before he finally broke off their kiss. She knew only that she grew chilled as soon he lifted his mouth away from hers.

He moved away quickly, glancing at his watch. "Guess you'd better hurry. You have less than thirty minutes to make your appointment with Pauline Powers."

"Yes. How about you? Did Geoff Buck agree to see you?"

"We arranged to have dinner in his apartment."

"That's good. We're doing well for our first night in town."

"He's looking over all his material on Ferne Hilton and Robert Danvers. He has quite a bit of stuff on their murder."

Justin's voice sounded husky and breathless. Courtney didn't need to ask why. He had moved, but she could still feel his breath against her face, still feel the heat flowing from his body into hers. Her blouse hung open, and he reached out to touch her. Fire blazed against steel, consuming her.

She wanted to be closer. She must have made some tiny, involuntary movement toward him because he swung around, breaking away. "Time for you to go," he repeated. His eyes were suddenly bleak, and she guessed he was remembering Linda.

"Yes." Courtney tucked her blouse back into the waistband of her skirt and reached into the closet for the coordinating blazer. She smoothed her hair and renewed her lipstick. "All set," she said. She couldn't have sounded more cheerful or less genuine if she'd been a tour guide at Disney World.

"Take a cab both ways." Justin handed her two twenties. His friendly smile was back in place, but his eyes remained shadowed. "Logically I know there's no way we could have been followed from Colorado to this hotel. We both walked up and down the aisle of the plane half a dozen times, and there wasn't a soul on board we recognized. But we didn't think we were followed to Aspen, either, so take care, Courtney."

"Don't worry," she assured him. "I'm not going to give that creep a chance to get near me."

A MANSERVANT WELCOMED Courtney into Pauline Powers's penthouse apartment in the fashionable East Sixties. "Allow me to take your coat, madam."

Courtney handed over her jacket, and they walked together through an entrance hall tiled in black and white marble and illuminated by a massive crystal chandelier. The overall effect, Courtney decided, was something between a royal palace and a Mafia morgue.

The living room was similarly austere, a symphony in gray and silver, without any touch of color to give the room a decorative focal point. Even the small fire burning in the marble fireplace seemed overwhelmed by the vast expanses of cool gray and silver.

Courtney understood the lack of color as soon as Pauline Powers made her entrance. The ex-movie starlet had certainly not forgotten how to command the attention of her audience. A set of double doors was flung open at the far end of the room, and Powers paused in the doorway to milk every ounce of dramatic effect from her arrival. She wore a stunning, full-length gown of sapphire-blue satin. The entire room had been created to form the perfect backdrop for her brilliant, glittering presence.

"I'm so sorry to be late," she murmured. She advanced regally into the room, a living crown jewel approaching its setting, then held out her hand, almost as if she expected it to be kissed.

Much amused, Courtney bestowed a suitably humble handshake. She admired the performance although she refused to participate in the show. "I appreciate the gift of your time, Miss Powers," she said briskly. "I know how very busy you are, but I suspect you're also anxious to see the truth told about Robert Danvers." She flipped open a spiral notebook, thoughtfully provided by Justin. "Shall we get right to work?" she asked.

Pauline Powers was too old a hand to allow herself to be outmaneuvered. She recognized, however, that Courtney meant business and decided to go along for the time being. With a slight smile, she arranged herself on the room's only white chair, a wingback placed strategically at one side of the fireplace. Her dark hair gleamed against the heavy brocade, and the firelight cast a warm glow across her impeccably painted features. "Your agent tells me you plan to write the definitive biography of Robert Danvers."

Courtney ignored the hint of sarcasm. "Yes, I do, Miss Powers. You may remember I wrote to you myself some nine months ago. I'm a sportswriter with a special knowledge of championship skiing, and I want my book to emphasize Robert Danvers's achievements as an athlete. But if this is going to be a well-rounded biography, I know I have to deal with the tragedy that ended his life. That's what I'd like to talk to you about."

Pauline Powers looked at her shrewdly. "You really care about this story, don't you? Why is that? You're too young to have known Robert personally."

Courtney was about to trot out some glib response when she made a startling discovery. She genuinely wanted to write the book she'd just outlined for Pauline's benefit. "Robert Danvers was a relative of mine," she said, sticking as close as she could to the truth. "It's very important to me to tell his story." She drew in a deep breath, wondering how far she dared go. "The fact is, I don't think Robert Danvers killed his wife, and I'd like to clear his name."

"A woman with a mission?" Pauline Powers fitted a Turkish cigarette into a long ivory holder. She flicked a diamond-studded lighter, lighted her cigarette and carefully blew a series of perfect smoke rings. "He's been dead twenty years, honey. Right now he's too busy playing the harp to care one way or the other what people say about him.''

''That's true. But if Robert Danvers didn't kill his wife, somebody else did. I'd like to find out who committed a double murder and got away with it.''

Pauline blew several more smoke rings. ''That's an ambitious project.''

''But not impossible. I've read all the newspaper accounts published at the time of the murder, and a lot of people weren't satisfied with the official version of what happened. People seem to think that Ferne Hilton and Robert Danvers were quite happy together in their own perverse sort of way. You yourself were one of the people who said that Danvers had no reason to kill his wife.''

''The police didn't pay much attention to my statement.'' Pauline's voice remained neutral. ''They made no secret of the fact that they thought I was protecting my guilty conscience.''

''Because you were having an affair with Danvers?''

''That was their reasoning, yes. Ferne Hilton had all the money, you see. The police theory was that she threatened to divorce Robert when she realized he was being unfaithful. According to the detective in charge, things got out of hand and their argument escalated all the way up to murder.''

''You don't accept that theory?''

''Honey, Robert Danvers was probably unfaithful to Ferne Hilton within a week of their marriage. If she wanted to divorce him for adultery, she'd have done it years earlier.''

''Perhaps this was one affair too many. The proverbial straw that broke the camel's back.''

Pauline rose from her chair, frowning as she stubbed out her cigarette. She stared moodily into the fire, then suddenly swung around in a swirl of rustling taffeta. ''What the hell!'' She shrugged ruefully. ''Three husbands and a hundred million dollars later, I guess my pride doesn't matter so much.

I'm more interested in seeing somebody write the truth than in protecting my reputation.''

She walked over to a corner bar, where two or three decanters and some cut-crystal glasses were already set on a silver tray. "Would you like a drink?" she asked, pouring herself a hefty serving of what looked like neat Scotch.

"No, thank you." Courtney tried not to move. She didn't want to do anything that might distract Pauline from her apparent urge toward confession.

The ex-actress set her empty glass back on the tray with a grimace. "Damn stuff's loaded with calories and ruins the complexion, but sometimes I think if I see another piece of lime floating in Perrier, I'll puke."

She lighted a second Turkish cigarette. "I was madly in love with Robert Danvers. He was the best-looking bastard I'd ever seen, and he knew it, too, damn him. When we were filming *Snow Flight*, if he didn't have a gaggle of women swooning as he came down the slope, he considered it a lousy day. Mind you, watching him ski was like watching an eagle in flight. He was perfect." She puffed nervously at her cigarette, drawing in deep lungfuls of smoke, then lapsed into a brooding reverie.

Courtney broke the silence. "Was Robert Danvers in love with you?"

"I always claimed he was, even to the police." Pauline's smile was mocking. "The truth is, I doubt if he'd have noticed I was alive unless I'd practically dragged him into my bed. Robert was always willing to oblige a hungry female, but I'm not sure he went out actively looking for partners."

"But he did sleep with you?"

"Oh, yes. Robert slept with different women as casually as other men try out a change of tie. In fact, knowing how attached most men get to their favorite clothes, I'd say he changed women more easily than most men change ties."

Courtney could not keep the intense disapproval out of her voice. "He sounds like a despicable man."

Pauline laughed. "Despicable? Honey, he was the charmer to end all charmers. He was even quite honorable in his own way. He never pretended to be in love with any of the women he bedded, me included. He'd whisper plenty of sweet nothings while he was seducing you, but even then he never said anything about *love*. Anybody who spent more than ten minutes with Robert Danvers knew he was a one-woman man."

"You think he really loved his wife?"

"Honey, he *worshiped* Ferne Hilton. Said she was the only woman who could make him laugh and cry within the space of five minutes. Sometimes, when they were together, you would swear you actually saw the passion vibrating between them."

"Does that mean Ferne Hilton loved her husband as much as he loved her?"

"At least as much. And she was even faithful most of the time, I think. They had a child, you know. Didi. I guess you heard about her. Personally I think children should be kept behind bars till they're twenty-five and safe to have around civilized adults, but this girl was a cute little thing as kids go, not as spoiled as you'd have thought. She followed her father around on skis whenever she got the chance, and he took her on some pretty difficult runs."

A faraway look came into Pauline's eyes. "She really was a cute kid. Mop of curls, chubby red cheeks, huge violet eyes. I can see her now, skiing down Aspen mountain, with Robert calling out encouragement. He and Ferne both thought that child was God's gift to the universe. They spent a lot of time with her, unlike some Hollywood parents."

An enormous lump seemed to have lodged itself right in the middle of Courtney's throat. She swallowed hard, then swallowed again. "She...the child...she died, didn't she?"

"Yes, soon after her parents were killed." Pauline stubbed out her cigarette and wrapped her arms tightly around her waist. "Hell, this session isn't turning out to be much fun. I thought confession and catharsis were supposed to feel good. I haven't thought about that damn kid in years."

Courtney was more than willing to switch topics. "If there were so many questions being asked, why do you think the police insisted Robert Danvers committed the murder?"

"They had no other suspects, and there were so many reporters crowded into the town you couldn't turn around without falling over a camera or a guy with a notebook. TV news wasn't as big then as it is now, but every night there was an update on the story, and the Aspen police weren't exactly coming out smelling of roses. The chief didn't want any bigger scandal than he already had, and he was ecstatic when the forensic evidence came in."

"It supported his view, didn't it?"

"I wouldn't say that, but at least it didn't rule it out. After that he made damn sure nobody asked any more difficult questions. Robert became the official villain of the piece. Very convenient for everybody."

"What about my…" Courtney corrected herself quickly. "What about Ferne Hilton?"

Nobody had ever accused Pauline Powers of being a fool. She looked at Courtney intently, then drew in a sudden sharp breath. "My God! How was Robert related to you?" she asked sharply.

"He was my…my cousin."

Disbelief and puzzlement warred in Pauline's expression. "What about Ferne? Was she your cousin, too?"

Courtney flushed uncomfortably. "No."

"You know you look a lot like Ferne, don't you? I can't think why I didn't notice it right off the bat. Other people you interviewed for this biography must have told you the same thing."

"No, not really."

Pauline's voice was hard. "Who are you, Courtney?"

She flushed. "I'm a journalist writing a book about Ro—"

"Don't try to feed me that garbage," Pauline interrupted. "I didn't make a fortune in the rag trade by believing horseshit." She strode over to the bar. "Hell, I'm going to have another Scotch. Screw the calories. Sure you won't change your mind?"

"No, thanks."

From the bar Pauline spoke over her shoulder. "I don't know what's going on here, but I'll tell you something I've never told anyone before. Everybody knew Robert and I were having an affair. Nobody seemed to realize Ferne was involved with somebody as well. Robert let something slip one night when we were together."

Courtney's hands tightened around the notebook. "Did he mention any names?"

"No, none. But from the way he spoke, I knew it was some man working on *Snow Flight*. To be honest, I've often wondered myself who it might have been. Maybe one of the extras? There were a bunch of young guys hanging around who'd been hired chiefly because they looked terrific in tight ski pants."

Courtney opened her notebook to a fresh page and handed it to Pauline, together with a pencil. "Can you remember any of the names of those men, Ms Powers? Could you write them down for me?"

"Honey, they were just extras. People referred to them as a group. 'Extras to the middle of the slope.' 'Extras take a break.' 'Extras, ski in formation.'"

"How about names of cameramen? The assistant producers? Bit players?"

Pauline picked up the pen and scratched about half a dozen names. She was interrupted by a discreet cough from the butler. "Your companion for this evening has arrived, Miss Powers. He's waiting for you in the den."

Courtney swore silently at all dinner companions. Pauline, strangely relieved, abandoned any attempt to complete the list. She drifted over to the white-brocade chair, once more securely immersed in her role as Famous Fashion Designer.

She picked up her cigarette holder and gestured regally toward the manservant. "Thank you, Soames. Tell my friend I'll be right there. I'll wear my sable cape tonight, if you'd ask Maggie to fetch it."

"Very good, madam." The manservant disappeared on silent feet.

Pauline held out her hand in dismissal. "Goodbye, Ms Long. If you have any more questions for me, send them to my secretary. I warn you I probably won't answer them."

"I appreciate your seeing me on such short notice, Ms Powers, and your honesty—"

"Honey, I don't know what the word means. Quote me on most of this stuff, and I'll deny ever seeing you." She picked up a silver kid purse from its resting place on the bar and swept from the room. "Good night, Ms Long, or whoever you are. Soames will see you out."

Chapter Thirteen

Contrary to Justin's instructions, Courtney didn't bother with a cab. Instead she walked back to the hotel from Pauline's apartment. She took Fifth Avenue and strolled downtown, absorbing the sights and sounds of the city at night.

In Denver she had felt permanently oppressed by pursuers. Here, on the crowded streets of central Manhattan, she felt safe. It was ridiculous to worry about being identified as an escaped lunatic in this frenetic environment. One more run-of-the-mill crazy wouldn't merit so much as a raised eyebrow. Native New Yorkers hadn't even turned to look at a woman in full evening dress, promenading twin piglets on jeweled leashes. If *that* sight didn't warrant a second glance, Courtney decided she must be the next best thing to invisible.

The rain had stopped late in the afternoon, and the sidewalks were already dry. She felt illogically euphoric as she crossed over Park Avenue and made her way toward the Forty-second Street entrance of the Grand Hyatt. Maybe she was leaping to reckless conclusions, but everything Pauline Powers had said tended to confirm Courtney's belief that Robert Danvers had been unjustly accused of killing his wife. It would be wonderful—more than wonderful—if she could prove her father innocent.

The hotel lobby was as crowded as the streets, and she joined a group of at least a dozen people waiting for an elevator. Pauline's scrawled list practically burned a hole in her pocket. The former actress had written down eight names, and at least four of the males seemed to strike vague chords of recognition. Which meant that any one of those four might have impersonated Justin Tanner.

James Stuart, for example, the lighting director. The spelling was different, but how could she have forgotten him when he had such a famous namesake? And Freddie Whistler, sound engineer. She remembered writing him a letter, remembered thinking Whistler was an appropriate name for a sound technician. She frowned, racking her brain. Did Whistler live in L.A. or New York? For the life of her, she couldn't remember the details. *Damn* those months in Walnut Park, when it had taken all her mental energy just to remain convinced of her own sanity. She had forgotten so much during those endless weeks of incarceration.

Her stomach rumbled just as she was about to step into the elevator. The other waiting passengers surged forward, but she hesitated, glancing down at her watch. It was still only nine o'clock. Too early for Justin to be back.

"Are you taking this elevator, lady, or are you planning to stand there all night and admire the scenery?"

She smiled apologetically at the man holding the door open. "Sorry, I changed my mind. You go ahead."

The elevator doors swooshed closed on the man's exasperated mutterings, and Courtney returned to the main lobby. There was no point in pacing up and down their room, generating ulcers while she waited for Justin's return. She'd call their room number, and if he didn't answer, she'd go to the coffee shop and order some dinner. A giant bowl of soup sounded very appealing. Her throat remained too sore for solid food.

She let the phone ring ten or eleven times before she finally hung up. She asked a bellboy for directions to the coffee shop and followed a bespectacled, white-haired priest who happened to be walking in the appropriate direction.

The lobby was still so crowded that she felt comfortably anonymous, but she glanced over her shoulder a couple of times to see if anybody was watching her. Her existence seemed to be a matter of monumental indifference to everybody, and she settled down in the coffee shop to enjoy her meal.

At ten o'clock, replete with clam chowder and Irish coffee, she decided it was time to go up to her room. She made her way back to the elevators, found one waiting and stepped inside.

Food seemed to have sharpened her wits, for another name on Pauline's list was beginning to mean something. "Nick Harris," the former actress had scribbled. "Lousy actor but beautiful face."

Nick Harris, actor. Yes, the name was definitely familiar. Courtney could almost visualize herself in the living room of Aunt Amelia's house, typing Mr. Harris a letter. Hadn't his address been somewhere in Manhattan's East Eighties? And the detective had noted something interesting about the actor. Something about his present career, perhaps? No, that wasn't it.

Courtney sighed in frustration. If Nick Harris really did live in Manhattan, maybe she and Justin could pay him a visit. Maybe, if luck was on her side, she would find his name and address listed in the telephone directory.

The elevator came to a halt on the fourteenth floor. Courtney hurried toward her room, compelled by a pleasant sense of urgency. She would check the phone book before Justin returned. How terrific if she could actually present him with an address and phone number for Nick Harris!

She pulled her room key out of her purse and inserted it into the lock, jiggling impatiently until the key turned. She'd always been a klutz with locks.

At the very moment she pushed open the door, the sound of footsteps alerted her to the fact that somebody was already inside the room. "Justin?" she said, annoyed with herself for lingering over a second cup of coffee when he must have been upstairs waiting for her. She never had been able to resist Irish coffee.

She stepped into the room, and the door immediately banged shut behind her. She whirled around, her heart slamming in sudden terror against her ribs.

"Oh, my God, *Justin*!" This time, her voice was thick with horror.

She made a frantic dash for the door. The man smiled, stepping smoothly to bar her exit. "I don't know why you're surprised to see me, Didi. You must have known I'd come back."

Her teeth were chattering. She clenched her jaw until it hurt and the chattering stopped. "Justin will be here in a minute. He's coming right up—"

"Then I must hurry, mustn't I?"

The spray of mace hit her full in the face just as she started to scream.

JUSTIN PAID OFF the cab and edged his way around a bellboy pulling a trolly full of suitcases. "Excuse me," he murmured automatically as he almost bumped into a group of people leaving the hotel. One of the men gave him a startled look, before acknowledging his apology and hurrying outside.

Justin was almost to the elevators before he remembered why the man had looked so familiar. Of course? It had been the producer from Linda's soap. Harvey Nicholson. Darn! He'd only met the man three or four times, but if he'd been quicker at putting name and face together, he could have asked Harvey some useful questions. In real-life investigations, as opposed to TV movies, Justin suspected more useful information was uncovered by coincidence than by all the detective skills combined.

An exotic, heavily made-up woman joined him in his wait at the reception desk. She was at least six feet tall, and her outfit of thigh-high leather boots and black miniskirt emphasized the length of her legs. Wafts of Opium perfume drifted under Justin's nose when she leaned across the counter to accept her key from the desk clerk. "Thank you, darling. Any messages for me?"

Her voice was low, too low for a woman. Startled, Justin looked more closely. He saw the faint shadow of beard beneath the makeup and realized she was a man. Feeling like a hick fresh up from the boonies, he resisted the urge to stare. Good grief, he thought, I must have been out of circulation way too long if I can't separate the men from the girls without looking twice.

"May I help you, sir?" The bored desk clerk turned to Justin, not even glancing toward the "woman" as he/she glided off toward the elevators.

"Justin Tanner. My room key, please. 1439."

The clerk checked behind him. "I'm sorry, sir. Both those keys are out already."

Justin frowned. "I handed my key in to the desk when I went out. Could you check again?"

"There's nothing here, sir, but we can give you a spare key if you'll show me some identification."

Justin was swept by a sudden and intense foreboding. He pulled out his wallet and pointed to his driver's license and a string of credit cards, barely able to conceal his impatience as the clerk keyed his name into the computer. "Mr. and Mrs. Tanner, Room 1439."

"Yes. As I told you."

The clerk produced a mechanical smile as he opened a drawer and handed over the spare key. "Here you are, sir. Enjoy your night."

Justin ran across the lobby to a waiting elevator and hurriedly touched the button for the fourteenth floor. He might be imagining dangers where none existed, but why wasn't his room key at the desk? Had the murderer conned his way into possession of the key? All it took was a couple of phony credit cards and the knowledge of which room your quarry was registered in.

Justin was cold with dread by the time the elevator reached the fourteenth floor. He sprinted along the carpeted hallway. Room 1439. Silence. The soundproofing couldn't be that good.

The smell of gas hit him full in the face as he thrust open the door. He rushed into the room, already gagging when he stumbled over Courtney's body.

She was lying half in and half out of the bathroom. Holding his breath, Justin scooped her into his arms and carried her into the hallway, propping her up against the wall. Thank God, she was still breathing.

He took her hand and carried it to his cheek, whispering endearments and soft words of encouragement as he waited for the relatively fresh air in the corridor to revive her.

Her fingers tightened around his, but she spoke without opening her eyes. "I think I'm going to be sick."

Justin shot to his feet, grabbed an empty plastic ice bucket from the bedroom and thrust it into her lap. She opened her eyes and thanked him with real gratitude. After a minute or so of tense silence, she sighed and leaned tiredly against the wall. "Maybe I'm not. Going to be sick, I mean."

Gas fumes were beginning to seep out into the corridor. Justin knelt beside her. "Courtney, do you know where the gas leak's coming from?"

Her eyes were still unfocused. "I knocked it under the bed."

He couldn't imagine what she meant, but she looked so

pale he didn't want to pester her more than necessary. "Back
in a minute," he said.

Justin gulped a lungful of air before venturing into their
room. He dampened a hand towel in the bathroom, then covered his nose and mouth and made his way over to the two
beds. He could hear a hissing sound coming from beneath
the bed nearest the window. Gagging even behind the protection of the towel, he knelt on the floor and lifted the cover.

A small gas cylinder of the type used for outdoor grills
and barbecues lay on its side, steadily squirting out its poison.
Justin pulled the cylinder up onto the bed and switched off
the valve. His head was already swimming alarmingly. He
staggered out of the bedroom and slumped down in the hallway next to Courtney.

"Want the ice bucket?" she asked, with a ghost of a smile.

"Thanks, but no thanks."

They sat in silence until Justin felt a bit more confident he
wouldn't throw up. "What happened?" he asked finally.

Her hands tightened around the ice bucket. "He was here,
waiting for me when I came into the room. I tried to find
something to hit him with, but he sprayed mace into my face
and I couldn't see. I was choking, doubled over with cough-
ing, and he grabbed me from behind. Then he threw me on
the bed and tied my hands to the headboard. I thought he
was going to rape me."

"But he didn't?"

"No." Her voice shook just a little. "Fortunately I don't
seem to turn him on, except to murder."

Justin put his arm around her, his seething anger fueled
partly by guilt. "I should never have left you alone."

"How could we possibly guess he'd find us?"

"More to the point, how *did* he follow us here? He wasn't
on the plane. We both checked."

"Unless he's a master of disguise."

He was about to reject the suggestion as ridiculous, until

he remembered the "woman" at the reception desk. "I suppose it's just possible," he conceded. "But how did he know which city we were coming to? For heaven's sake, there are hundreds of flights out of Stapleton each day. If the police couldn't catch us, how did he have the resources to know we'd pick that particular plane?"

Courtney shrugged helplessly. "I don't know."

Justin sighed. "Let's worry about the questions we can find answers to. Why was the gas cylinder under the bed, and how did you get into the bathroom if he tied you to the bed?"

"At first he put the cylinder on the mattress right next to me. I buried my face in the pillow to try to stop the fumes getting to me. I suppose the gas must have bothered him, too, because after a very short time, he checked to see if I was conscious. I pretended not to be. Just let myself go really limp and floppy. Then he started untying my hands. I guess he wanted it to look like I'd committed suicide."

"There was no hope of that," Justin commented harshly. "I'd never have let the police accept that."

Courtney suddenly buried her face in Justin's chest. "Oh, God, I was so frightened. I didn't want to die."

"I'm here now, sweetheart. You're safe, I promise you." He scarcely noticed the endearment, it slipped out so naturally.

"Hold me, Justin. I'm cold."

He wrapped his arms around her waist, holding her tight against his body. He didn't give a second glance to the maid who walked along the corridor, staring at them intently. He held Courtney, rocking her gently until the storm of weeping ended.

"You were unbelievably brave," he said softly, taking a corner of the damp towel and gently wiping away the last of her tears.

"No," she said. "I was a sniveling coward."

"Inside, perhaps, where it doesn't count. But you hung on to your common sense and tricked him by playing dead. You saved your own life, Courtney."

She leaned back, managing to produce a watery smile. "Well, at least I held on long enough for the cavalry to come galloping to the rescue."

Justin felt his gut squeeze tight. He brushed his thumb over her mouth. "Ready to tell me what happened next?"

She nodded. "Except the rest of it isn't too clear. He must have left the room, and I tried to turn off the gas, but I was so groggy by then I just knocked the canister onto the floor. I can't have been thinking rationally at that point. Instead of running like hell out of the room, I remember groping around under the bed for quite a while, trying to find the cylinder. Finally it dawned on me I was about to pass out. I tried to crawl to the door, but by then I was so woozy I couldn't tell one door from another. That must be why you found me in the bathroom."

"Fortunately the ventilation system seems to have kept the bathroom relatively free of fumes or..."

He allowed his sentence to trail away, but Courtney finished for him. "Or I'd be dead."

She was wretchedly pale and her huge violet eyes were shadowed with weariness and fear, but Justin thought she looked beautiful. Her face had the sort of high-cheeked bone structure that aged well and photographed ravishingly. At this moment the likeness between Courtney Long and Ferne Hilton was strong enough to be disconcerting.

Justin got to his feet, aware that they didn't have time to linger in the hallway. "You rest here awhile longer," he said. "There's no point in both of us making ourselves feel sick. I'll pack our bags."

"How are you going to explain to the hotel people that we need another room?"

"I'm not." Justin broke off as a suave, dark-suited man

walked swiftly along the hallway and stopped by their door. "Damn!" he muttered under his breath.

"Good evening, sir." The man's voice was scrupulously polite, but his gaze scanned first them and then their room with razor-sharp attentiveness. "Is there some problem with your room? I'm the assistant manager on duty tonight, and one of the maids reported that she smelled an overwhelming odor of gas." His gaze traveled over Courtney, taking every detail of her pallor, her crumpled clothes and her disheveled hair. "At first I thought the maid must be mistaken," the manager added. "We have no gas outlets in any of our rooms."

Justin gave what he hoped was a hearty chuckle. "We could certainly have used your help twenty minutes ago, but I think everything's taken care of now except for the dreadful smell. My wife had a little problem with a piece of our camping equipment."

"Camping equipment, sir? In the middle of Manhattan?"

"We're from Colorado," Justin said, as if that explained everything. "My wife accidentally opened the valve on our gas cooking cylinder, and then it stuck and she couldn't get it shut again."

"I'm absolutely hopeless with anything mechanical," Courtney contributed breathlessly.

"She's not used to dealing with camping equipment," Justin elaborated.

"Fortunately, here at the Grand Hyatt, few of our guests find any need for camp-fire cooking. In fact, the use of gas appliances in the room is strictly against our regulations."

"Oh, we weren't cooking," Courtney hastened to assure him.

"I'm sure you weren't." His voice smooth as silk, the manager turned to Justin. "I'll send up a bellboy with a key to a new room, sir."

"Thank you very much." Justin was afraid his heartiness

sounded about as genuine as the average game-show host's. "We're grateful for the chance to change rooms. We couldn't possibly stay here. The smell of gas is too strong."

"It certainly is. It's a pity we can't open the windows. We have them welded shut to ensure the heating and air-conditioning works effectively. And to prevent suicides, of course."

"Of course." This time Justin didn't bother to sound friendly. He deliberately turned his back on the manager as he spoke to Courtney. "The gas fumes aren't quite so bad now, honey. If you feel able to help me pack the cases, we can move to the new room that much sooner."

"Yes, of course. I feel fine."

As soon as the manger left, Justin started pulling T-shirts and underwear out of the drawers and stuffing them into his case. "Pack your things as quickly as you can," he said, going into the bathroom and denuding his side of the counter with a couple of quick sweeps.

Courtney obediently stripped her two skirts, two blouses and two jackets from their hangers, although she didn't understand the need for so much haste. "If we're not ready when the bellboy comes, surely he'll wait?"

"I don't want us to be here when the bellboy comes." Justin tossed a final sweater into his case and snapped it shut. "Don't talk, just pack your underwear and stuff from the drawers. I'll explain when we're out of here."

Her expanded wardrobe was still pretty basic by most standards, and Courtney took less than five minutes to transfer everything she possessed into her new suitcase. "The signs for the fire exit point left," Justin said, taking a suitcase in each hand. "Come on."

"Are we leaving without paying the bill?"

"They have my credit-card number. Don't worry, they'll charge me. Courtney, for heaven's sake, will you *move it*? We can't be here when the assistant manager gets back."

Courtney was still too woozy to walk down thirteen flights of stairs and talk at the same time. When they reached the steel door that marked the entrance to the main floor, Justin set the cases down. "I'll check and see if I can spot the assistant manager. If the coast seems clear, follow me across the lobby. Walk fast, but don't run, and try not to look guilty. The hotel's internal-security people will be on the watch for anybody acting furtively."

She lifted her chin stubbornly. "I'd like to know why we're skipping out like this."

"First, because the murderer knows we're here, and that doesn't strike me as a real healthy situation. Second, because I'd bet a substantial sum of money that the assistant manager went straight from talking to us to calling the police, or at least his own chief of internal security. We want to be well away from here before the police start feeding my name into their computers. It might already be linked to yours."

She started to laugh and then couldn't stop until Justin pulled her into his arms and shook her sharply. "What is it, Courtney?"

Her laughter shuddered to a stop. "Until Aunt Amelia died, I'd never even gotten a parking ticket. Now I'm wanted by the police in two states. I think I'd be a better criminal if I'd sort of worked up to it more slowly."

"You're not a criminal," he said, his voice hard. "You're a victim, and you owe it to yourself to fight back." He leaned his shoulder against the heavy steel fire door and it opened a crack.

"I don't see the manager," he said, closing the door. "I spotted a security guy over by the registration desk, but the lobby's still quite crowded. Try to attach yourself to a group as we head for the exit."

By the time she reached the glass doors fronting Forty-second Street, Courtney could have sworn the lobby was a mile wide and illuminated by thousand-watt strobe lights. If she'd been able to see, she would have suspected every little old lady crossing her path of being a cop in disguise. Fortunately she was blinded by fright. She didn't register anything except Justin's hand supporting her elbow until she was out on the sidewalk and Justin was opening the door of a cab. Heart pounding, palms sweating, she lay back against the seat.

"Drive through the park for a while," Justin ordered the cabbie. "We'll give you directions later."

The man shrugged and set his meter ticking. He'd been driving cabs for twenty years, and he no longer wasted his breath asking stupid questions. He edged out into the endless stream of Manhattan traffic, dividing his attention equally between the traffic and the horse-racing schedule printed in his newspaper.

"Living with Aunt Amelia doesn't train you well for a life of crime," Courtney murmured. "I'm still having palpitations."

"Palpitations?" She could see Justin's smile in the darkness. "I didn't know people had palpitations after Queen Victoria died."

She saw him glance out of the rear window, and she twisted around until she, too, could see out of the murky glass. "Is there anybody following us?" she asked in a low voice.

"I don't think so, but that's why we're driving through the park."

Courtney stared at the traffic to their rear. No one vehicle seemed to stay behind them for very long. A delivery truck followed them for two blocks, then turned on Fifth. Several cabs switched from lane to lane, obviously more interested in making the lights than pursuing anything ahead of them. Nevertheless, Justin waited until they were clear across the west side before he tapped on the the glass and gave the cabbie new directions.

"The Roosevelt Hotel, please."

The cabbie grunted. Twenty years ago he'd have pointed out that the Roosevelt was only two blocks from where they'd just come from. Nowadays he was too smart to waste his breath. If this couple wanted to cruise around the city, that was their privilege, provided they paid the tab.

He found the place where he could turn and swung around. Moonlight Dancer was thirty-to-one because there'd been reports she had a strained fetlock. One of the boys at the stables had told him that was all horseshit. A rumor started to keep the odds attractive. Hell, he felt in the mood to punt some real money.

He stopped at a traffic light and glanced into his rearview mirror. His eyes narrowed. That was damned odd. There was a white-haired priest in the cab behind him who looked like the old geezer who'd gotten into the cab right behind him at the Grand Hyatt. But if this was the same priest, he wasn't in the same cab. That one had been Yellow. This one was Checker.

The lights changed. The cabbie let out his clutch. Hell, it wasn't none of his business. He was gonna call his bookie and stick three hundred on Moonlight Dancer, right on the nose.

He turned onto Vanderbilt. The Checker cab followed him. He looked at the couple in back. Hell, if twenty years driving a cab had taught him anything, it had taught him to keep his nose out of other people's business.

"This is the Roosevelt," he said.

Chapter Fourteen

The dream started as it always did, smothering Courtney in fear. But tonight the fear was more alive, more urgent than she could ever remember. It prowled at the edges of her consciousness, a beast waiting to consume her.

Part of her knew it was only a dream, and she rebelled against it, determined not to succumb. The screams coming from her parents' bedroom crashed against her ears, but she willed herself not to hear them.

"Didi, don't let him catch you! Run, poppet, run!"

It was her father's voice, and it pulled her inexorably into the heart of the nightmare. Cowering in her bed, the covers pulled high over her head, Didi heard two muffled explosions. The screams stopped abruptly, horribly, and the silence was more terrifying than all the preceding noise. Sobbing, she ran out into the garden, pushing and shoving her way through the bushes until she got to her secret place, the place where she always hid from Janey. Tonight she wished Janey was here. She liked Janey, and she didn't like the Voice.

"Didi! Where are you?" The Voice was calling her. She covered her ears and screwed her eyes up tight so that she wouldn't have to see him. She couldn't believe it when she suddenly felt herself stand up and wave to the man searching on the other side of the driveway.

"I'm here," she called out. "Over here, Uncle!"

The tiny part of Courtney that knew she was dreaming screamed a warning, but it was too late. She had broken the lifelong pattern of her dream, and now Didi would be killed.

The little girl moved out from her hiding place behind the bushes, still waving and calling. She even smiled. "Here I am, Uncle! You can come and get me!"

Away in the distance, the man straightened and the moon shone full on his face. Courtney could see that his eyes were a brilliant, hypnotic shade of blue. Their utter coldness made her gasp.

The man she had once known as Justin Tanner stretched his mouth into a smile. "Why, Didi, you naughty little puss, you've told me where you are at last. Why did you keep me waiting so many years?"

"I didn't mean to hide from you, Uncle. Why is there blood on your shirt?"

"Because your mommy is naughty and I had to kill her. You've been naughty, too, Didi."

"No, I'm a good girl. I'm not naughty."

"But you'll talk to people, Didi. When you grow up, you'll write letters, trying to find out how your mommy and daddy died. And then, one day, you'll remember all about me."

"No, I won't! I won't think about you, I promise. Not even when I grow up."

"I'm sorry, Didi, but I don't believe you. I've seen your letters, so I know you're lying."

"*Uncle Nick,* please don't kill me!" The scream tore from her throat. "For God's sake, don't kill me! Uncle Nick, don't you see I'm only a baby?"

"I'm sorry, but you've seen too much and one day you'll remember it all. Don't worry, Didi, this won't hurt."

He produced a gas cylinder from out of thin air, spraying the fumes straight into her face. His hands reached for her neck, and she struggled wildly, lashing out with all the puny force of her childish arms and legs. Poor Didi, Courtney thought, biting viciously at the man's arms. Poor me. We're too little to die.

"Courtney, for God's sake, wake up! *Stop fighting me, honey!* Courtney, you're safe. I'm here, sweetheart. You're safe."

The reassuring litany drummed in her head. Panting, crying, sweating, Courtney woke up to find herself pinned to the bed by Justin's body, her legs trapped beneath the weight of his thighs, her arms spread-eagled above her head, her wrists clasped by his hands.

For a second or so, the fear remained so real that she felt no embarrassment, only relief that Justin was holding her, keeping the nightmare at bay. Then the tentacles of her dream gradually relaxed their grip. She realized that the bedclothes were all on the floor, and her panicky struggles had bunched her T-shirt beneath her breasts, leaving her stomach bare and her hips covered—if that was the correct word—by no more than a minuscule, lace-trimmed bikini.

In the instant of release from her dream, her body became aware of Justin in an entirely new way. His torso was bare, and through the cotton knit of her shirt she felt the roughness of his body hair rubbing against her nipples. He shifted his hips, and the denim of his cutoffs moved with pleasant abrasion against the sensitive skin of her inner thighs. Desire raced along her veins, leaving a tingling ache of longing in its wake.

He must have sensed some subtle change in her, for he sat up abruptly, releasing his hold on her wrists, and half turned away. "Are you awake now?" he asked, his voice unnaturally hoarse.

"Yes, I'm awake." If his voice was hoarse, hers was little more than a high-pitched squeak.

He cleared his throat. "I'm sorry I took so long to realize you were dreaming. I should have woken you before the nightmare took hold. Was it the same dream you always have?''

''Not quite. This time I didn't stay safely hidden in the bushes. I came out when the murderer called me.''

''You saw his face?''

She nodded. Even talking about the dream brought back all her feelings of terror and helplessness.

When she didn't speak, he prodded her gently. ''You recognized the man?''

Courtney drew in a deep breath. ''It was the man who impersonated you. The man who tried to…tried to kill me tonight.'' She shuddered. ''I'm sorry. I'm overreacting, but it's ages since the dream has been so vivid.''

Justin squeezed her hand. ''After all that's happened in the last couple of days, it would be amazing if you didn't have nightmares. Maybe it's better for your psyche that the dream finally has an ending.''

She grimaced. ''It didn't feel better. It felt rotten.''

His grip on her hand tightened. ''Once we run this murderer to ground, the nightmares will stop, you'll see.''

''I hope you're right.'' Courtney's voice was shaky, and Justin tousled her hair reassuringly before standing up. He would have liked to take her into his arms, but he didn't trust himself to keep the embrace platonic. Those last few minutes struggling on the bed had precipitated some very intimate physical contact, and his body was having a hard time accepting the fact that all those exciting tussles hadn't been leading up to an even more exciting grand finale. He kept his back carefully turned toward Courtney.

''Try to sleep,'' he said. He knew he sounded crass and foolishly cheerful. ''And remember, I'll be right here in the next bed if you need me.''

''I need you now, Justin.'' Her voice little more than a whisper, she added, ''I need you to hold me.''

She must have stretched out her hand. His back was just

within her reach and he tensed, unable to conceal his response to her touch. The tips of her fingers felt cool and tantalizing against the heat of his skin. He wanted to seize her hand and guide it to the hot, throbbing ache in his loins. He wanted to feel her slender legs grip him in passion instead of fear. He wanted—too many things.

He spoke without looking at her. "What are you asking me to give you, Courtney. Security? Comfort?"

"No."

The single syllable hung in the air between them, heavy with tension. Justin closed his eyes, fighting the desire that had been building relentlessly inside him for the past four days. Courtney had been through months of mental torment, and her life was in danger. Any man who took advantage of her tonight would be little better than a brute. He couldn't even gloss over the true nature of his actions by pretending that he loved her. This burning sexual attraction he felt wouldn't be anything more than the natural outcome of twelve long months of celibacy. And Courtney deserved better than to be used as an outlet for his sexual frustrations.

Justin gritted his teeth, wondering how the devil he was going to turn around and talk to her without revealing his all-too-obvious state of arousal. He heard the rustle of bedclothes and swung around just in time to see Courtney burying herself from the neck down in sheets and blankets.

"I'm sorry to have embarrassed you," she said in a dignified little voice, speaking to the air somewhere above his left shoulder. "You've never given me the slightest reason to think you wanted to make lo—to have sex with me." Her voice wavered, but she recovered quickly. "Please go to bed, Justin. We have a long day waiting for us tomorrow, and we both need the sleep."

"You think I don't want to make love to you?" Justin laughed harshly. "I've been thinking about damn little else ever since the first night we shared a bed."

"Then why haven't you..." She flushed and fell silent.

"Because any man with the conscience of a rat could see that you're vulnerable right now. Too vulnerable to act in your own best interests."

"I see," she murmured. The sheet she had been clutching somehow slipped through her fingers. "Do you have the conscience of a rat, Justin?"

"I thought I did." He breathed deeply, trying not to stare at the satiny soft skin of her shoulders and the tantalizing curve of her breasts, all too visible through the thin cotton T-shirt.

"Consciences can sometimes be very boring," she said softly. She reached up and linked her hands behind his neck, pulling his head slowly down toward her mouth. Her lips were only a breath away, and Justin remembered how sweet they tasted. His eyelids grew heavy, slumberous with the desire that had been mounting for much too long.

"I want you," he heard himself murmur. "I want to touch you all over, kiss you, possess you. Make you mine."

Her lips brushed his shyly, and he responded with a hunger that surprised him. He kissed her fiercely, tilting her head back and thrusting his tongue into her mouth with an urgency he'd imagined lost to him forever.

Courtney's world tilted on its axis. She clung to Justin as if he were the only stable point in her universe, drinking in all the heat and passion of his kiss. His lips were firm but not aggressive, his tongue seductive as he coaxed her lips apart to taste the softness of her mouth. She shivered as his teeth bit gently down the arc of her throat, surrendering to almost unbearable pleasure as he stripped away the sheet and laid her back against the pillows.

He kissed and caressed the swell of her breast, the slender curve of her waist, the athletic flare of her hips, the long, slim strength of her legs. "I can imagine how perfect you must look when you ski down a mountain,'' he said huskily. ''You're beautiful, Courtney.''

''So are you.''

He smiled. ''Men aren't beautiful.'' He suppressed the unexpected pleasure her words gave him. He wanted their lovemaking to be satisfying for both of them, but he didn't expect either of them to rocket to the stars when they hit their climax. He was old enough to realize that truly spectacular sex needed love as well as desire to fan the flames, and—of course—he and Courtney weren't in love. She was too confused to be in love with anybody at this point in her life. And he wasn't ready to give of himself.

Courtney raised herself on one elbow, touching his cheek in the lightest caress. ''You look...sad,'' she said.

He was upset with her perception. He didn't want to share his emotions with any woman yet, but especially not with Courtney. He knew that would be dangerous, although he didn't quite understand why.

He silenced her by taking her forcefully, sending his tongue deep into her mouth and propelling her back onto the pillows once again. When her hips started to arch up against him, he slipped his hand down between her thighs, experiencing a primitive, masculine satisfaction that he had been able to arouse her so swiftly and so completely.

When Justin's fingers touched her throbbing warmth, Courtney cried out, although she had sworn to herself that she would control her responses. She didn't want to humiliate herself or embarrass Justin by allowing her emotions to intrude too openly into their lovemaking. She knew he desired her body, there was no possible doubt about that, but she could feel the pulse of discontent simmering beneath his desire, and she was afraid she understood the cause of that emotion all too well. He resented the fact that he wanted her...loved her, even.

Still, she made no protest when Justin placed her hand on

the zipper of his jeans and guided it downward, and she trembled with pleasure when she felt him thrust demandingly against her body. In a couple of seconds, he'd removed his jeans. It took no more than the caress of his lips against her breasts to turn her entire body taut as a bowstring once again, no more than the renewed touch of his hand between her thighs to ready her for their union.

Again and again he brought her to the brink of climax. She clung to him, taking a fierce delight in the fact that his breath was shuddering in his lungs and that his expert caresses had long since changed from hungry to ravenous. Love might be missing on his part, but at least the two of them were equal partners in desire.

His penetration was swift and deep and hard. Courtney opened herself to him, able at last to express her true feelings for Justin. And he responded in kind. Heat gathered in the pit of her stomach, coiling, intensifying, waiting to burst into flame. With every thrust of Justin's body, the heat intensified, until it exploded in a conflagration that carried them both soaring over the edge of passion into the blinding darkness of ecstasy.

COURTNEY WOKE TO the sounds of Justin taking a shower. She buried deeper under the covers as searing images of the previous night flashed into her mind. In the cold light of morning, her common sense was working again. Even so, she couldn't regret what had happened.

Her body was still languorous, her mind still cloudy with sleep, when a vivid memory popped into the forefront of her thoughts. She sat bolt upright in the bed, the last wisps of sleep disappearing in a rush of adrenaline.

Uncle Nick! she exclaimed silently. *In my dream I called him Uncle Nick!*

She wrapped herself in a sheet, tumbled out of bed and banged on the bathroom door. "Justin," she shouted, forgetting her shyness in a surge of excitement. "I remembered something really important!"

The shower stopped and he opened the door, water dripping off his hair and down his face. Courtney had to clench her fists to keep from touching him.

She burst into incoherent speech. At this moment, talking seemed safer than feeling. "Justin, when I woke up I remembered! The Voice—he didn't just have a face, he had a name!"

Justin caught on quickly. "The man in your nightmare?"

"Yes. Last night, when I was dreaming, I called his name. I remember now. I waved to let him know where I was, and I called him Uncle Nick."

Justin's face broke into a delighted grin. He reached behind him for a towel and slung it carelessly around his hips. "Great going, Courtney!" he said as he came out of the bathroom. "And if you knew him well enough to call him *Uncle*, then surely Mrs. Grislechy is going to be able to give us a last name for him."

She tried to clamp down on her excitement. "We shouldn't count too much on Mrs. Grislechy. The nursing home said her mind often wanders."

"True, but they also said she has days of total lucidity, and maybe today will be one of those days. Luck has to be on our side some of the time."

"Perhaps it already is. Remember I told you in the cab last night about the list of names Pauline Powers gave me?"

Justin sat down on the bed. Her bed. The one they had shared last night. "I remember. And I also remember one of the people Pauline listed was an actor called Nick Harris."

"You're stealing my thunder." She sat on the other bed, as far away from him as she could without being too obvious. "What do you think? Could Nick Harris be the man we're looking for? The ages would be right, wouldn't they? A young actor in his early twenties when my parents were making *Snow Flight*. A man in his midforties now.''

Justin thrust impatient fingers through his wet hair. ''Geoff didn't mention any Nick Harris to me last night,'' he muttered. ''The guy must have had a really small part.''

''Does having a small part mean he couldn't be a murderer?''

''Of course not, but I guess I'm wondering why a bit player was closely enough involved with your parents to want them dead.''

''From what Pauline Powers said, I gather my parents were very democratic in their choice of lovers. Handsome bit players were just as welcome as major movie stars.''

She tried to speak casually, but she must have betrayed her uncertain feelings about her parents' behavior, because Justin looked at her searchingly. ''In their own exotic way they loved each other, Courtney. And everybody agrees they adored you.''

''I know.'' She bit her lip. ''It's just that after twenty-odd years living with Aunt Amelia, I suppose I'm almost as straitlaced as she was.''

Justin switched beds, his eyes gleaming with sudden laughter. ''Speaking personally, Ms Long, I'd say that straitlaced is a very inaccurate way to describe you. If Aunt Amelia was trying to turn you into a prude, she failed.''

Courtney blushed, and his teasing smile vanished. He tilted her face upward, then ran his hand lightly over her hot cheeks. ''Hey, what's this? Courtney, I didn't mean to embarrass you. I thought that what we shared last night was very…enjoyable. For both of us. Please don't tell me you regret what happened.''

For her, what they had shared last night hadn't been enjoyable, it had been earthshaking. She lowered her lashes, hesitating over her reply. ''I don't regret making love to you,'' she said finally.

"I'm glad of that. Very glad." His gaze was tender as he looked down at her, and for an instant, Courtney hoped he might say that he had found their lovemaking more than just a pleasant romp in the sack. But he dropped his hand rather suddenly, his manner becoming brisk and businesslike once again.

"Last night you said Nick Harris's name sounded familiar. Do you think you may have written to him back in March?"

Courtney gave a frustrated sigh. "I *think* I remember writing to him. I have this vivid picture of sitting in my aunt's living room and typing out his address. I even have a vague memory he lived in Manhattan. Somewhere in the East Eighties, maybe?"

"It's possible he's in the phone book." Justin leaned across to pull open a drawer in the nightstand. His shoulder accidentally grazed against Courtney's arm, and they both jumped back with exaggerated politeness.

"Sorry," Justin said. His voice was casual, but Courtney noticed that he avoided meeting her eyes.

"That's okay." She managed to sound even more casual than Justin. If he was determined to treat their lovemaking as a one-night aberration, she wasn't going to lay her pride on the line by disputing him. She held out the telephone directory. "Is this what you wanted?"

"Yes. Thanks." Justin thumbed quickly through the pages. "There's hundreds of Harrises listed here, and six Nicks, but none of them in the East Eighties. Damn! It would take us weeks to check all these out."

"And we don't even know our Nick Harris has a listed number." Courtney scowled. "There's some warning signal flashing at the back of my mind, but I can't grasp hold of it. The detective made a note next to Nick Harris's name, I'm sure of it. I have this gut feeling it was something important, and I can't for the life of me remember what it was."

"Don't fret about it. That'll only drive it farther away."

He reached out to give her a friendly pat on the back, then jerked back, dropping his arm to his side. He smiled at her, his manner a touch overhearty. "It's indecent to do all this heavy-duty thinking before we've had coffee. Let's order breakfast from room service and in the meantime, we can call Twin Oaks and confirm that appointment with your Mrs. Grislechy. Geoff Buck mentioned last night that Doug Mordern lives in Bayside, which is the town right next to the nursing home. Maybe we can fit in a visit to him as well as to Twin Oaks before lunch."

"Who's Doug Mordern?"

"The producer of *Search for Love*. Linda's soap."

"He certainly ought to be able to give you an accurate list of all her contacts on the show. Can you rent a car from here? That's easier than trying to take cabs."

"No problem, I imagine."

"Then why don't you make the calls, and I'll shower."

Courtney took herself off to the bathroom without waiting for a reply, then slumped dispiritedly against the closed door. That was the trouble with having brilliant insights first thing in the morning, she reflected gloomily. By remembering Nick Harris's name, she'd given Justin a perfect excuse to avoid discussing what had happened between them the night before. And, apart from a gentlemanlike reassurance that he'd "enjoyed" their lovemaking, he'd positively leaped at the chance to remain silent.

Courtney adjusted the water until it ran very hot, then stepped into the shower. First things first. Right now they had a murderer to track down. But later...well, later, when the murderer was behind bars and the police were no longer chasing her, Justin would find that things were different. Enjoyable be damned! She would have him crawling into her bed, *begging* to make love to her. Courtney smiled slyly. She seemed to have more of Ferne Hilton and Robert Danvers in her makeup than she'd ever suspected. Aunt Amelia would be horrified, but Courtney decided she was rather glad.

A WATERY SUN broke through the midmorning clouds as they arrived at Twin Oaks. A plaque on the entrance gate informed them the nursing home had once been the summer residence of a railway tycoon, and though the building itself was solidly ugly, the spacious grounds retained all their turn-of-the-century splendor.

A plump, middle-aged nurse greeted Courtney and Justin with a slightly harassed smile. "You've come to see Mrs. Grislechy, haven't you? Oh, dear! I know you've flown in from out of state, and I'm afraid this isn't one of her good days."

"I'm sorry," Justin said politely. "Isn't she feeling well?"

"She tires easily, that's all. She had a heart attack six months ago, but really she's doing great for her age. Eighty-five next birthday, you know. But sometimes she gets so stubborn! She's taken this bee into her bonnet that she'll see only you, Ms Long. She's had this tiff with her son-in-law, and she seems to be off men. She simply refuses point-blank to meet with you, Mr. Tanner."

"Don't worry about it. Why don't you go ahead, Courtney? I'm sure I can find a magazine to read while I wait for you."

Courtney thought rapidly. "Why don't you go and see Doug Mordern while I talk to Mrs. Grislechy? He's only ten minutes' drive from here. You told me so yourself."

"I'll wait," he said.

"Come on, Justin. I'm safe as Fort Knox in here."

He glanced toward the nurse, then spoke obliquely. "We thought that a couple of times before."

"This is different. I'm on my guard now. We both are."

"I'll go, if you promise not to leave here until I come and pick you up. Not for any reason."

She cocked her head teasingly. "Not even if I get a note telling me to meet you at midnight in a deserted warehouse?"

He didn't smile. "Courtney, you have two excellent reasons for knowing this isn't a joking matter."

She sobered. "You're right. I'm sorry. I promise I'll wait for you here, even if you take all afternoon."

The nurse was beginning to look at them both rather oddly, and Justin treated her to one of his most reassuring smiles. He seemed to have a way with middle-aged ladies, Courtney reflected, as the nurse visibly melted.

"Courtney got lost in Manhattan yesterday and had a rather nasty experience," he explained.

"How horrid," the nurse sympathized. "You're not safe on city streets these days."

Justin took both Courtney's hands in his, pulling her forward until he could drop a quick kiss on the end of her nose. "I'll probably be back before you've finished with Mrs. Grislechy. Bye, darling." His endearment was as casual as his kiss. "I love you, so please take great care of yourself." He shoved his hands into his pockets and strode toward the exit, jingling his car keys.

Her mouth hanging open, Courtney watched his departure. Damn him! How dare he make such an outrageous statement and then walk off? Whistling no less! She was strongly tempted to run after him and demand an explanation, but the nurse said, "Please follow me, Ms Long. Mrs. Grislechy's inclined to become anxious."

They walked along a brightly painted corridor with a cheerful, Mexican-tiled floor. The nurse knocked on a door signposted with Jane Grislechy's name and gestured for Courtney to follow her inside.

An elderly woman, back rigidly erect, was seated in an armchair, gazing out of the window. She turned as they entered the room, her initial frown instantly replaced by a smile of wonder. "Ferne!" she exclaimed. "Whatever are you doing in this part of the world? It's been years since I saw you. Oh, I'm so glad you came!''

The frown returned, and Jane Grislechy shook her head. ''You can't be Ferne. Ferne died years ago, and so did Robert. Most handsome couple I ever saw, those two.'' Sudden suspicion shadowed her eyes. ''They told me somebody was coming to see me today. Not Ferne. Courtney. I don't know anybody called Courtney. Who are you, and why do you want to see me?''

Tears ran unchecked down Courtney's cheeks. She hurried across the room and knelt down, taking the old lady's frail hands into her own. ''I'm Didi, Janey. Ferne's daughter. I didn't know where you were living or I'd have come to see you a long time ago. Do you remember me? I remember you very well. You still have the rosiest cheeks of anyone I know.''

''Didi. Little Didi Danvers, all grown up.'' Jane Grislechy breathed the name on a note of awe. She reached out and touched Courtney's hair. ''What happened to all those pretty blond curls I used to spend so much time brushing?''

Courtney laughed. ''The curl's still there, sort of. I dyed my hair brown for…for a part I was playing.''

''Humph, they'd have done better to have left you blond. Beautiful color, your hair was.'' Having delivered this gruff pronouncement, Jane Grislechy looked across at the nurse, who remained discreetly silent in a corner of the room. ''I know how busy you are, Nell,'' she said. ''We don't want to keep you when you have so much to do.''

The nurse looked dubiously at Courtney. ''I have time to stay if you'd like me here, Mrs. Grislechy.''

''No, I'll be fine. This young lady is one of the children I used to look after a long time ago. We have a lot to talk about. Maybe you could come back later with some of that herb tea you make everybody drink instead of coffee?''

Reassured, the nurse turned to leave, promising to return

with the tea. "It's mint flavored, Ms Long, and I'm sure you'll find it delicious."

"You're the living image of your mother," Jane Grislechy commented, as soon as the nurse had closed the door. "Although you look a mite more sensible than she ever was."

"I don't remember her at all, except from photographs, of course. I wish you could tell me something about my parents, Janey. I haven't met many people who knew them in the old days."

The old lady cast a shrewd eye over Courtney's tear-streaked face. "I'm not senile yet, you know, whatever those nurses may have told you. I'm like anybody else my age. Sometimes I can remember things that happened a long time ago better than I can remember boring things like where I put my clean stockings or what I ate for breakfast yesterday."

"The nurse said you were very healthy, Janey."

"That I am. And lively enough in my wits to remember that you're supposed to be dead. The hospital let me see you only once after your parents were killed—and then I could barely recognize you under the oxygen masks and the tubes going in and out of your arms. The next thing I knew, the hospital announced you were allergic to penicillin, and your aunt was arranging a funeral service for you. It's a pity you couldn't have been there," the old lady added tartly. "There wasn't a dry eye in the house."

Courtney grinned. "Well, I'm glad I was missed at any rate."

"I never *quite* believed you were dead," Jane remarked abruptly. "You see, I'd given you medication when you had an ear infection, and I knew you weren't allergic to penicillin. I even went to the hospital and tried to ask some questions, but nobody there was saying anything. What happened to you, Didi, all these years?"

"My aunt took me to live with her. She brought me up under an assumed name."

"Amelia brought you up? Now that surprises me. She wasn't the motherly type. Did she talk to you much about your parents?"

"She never mentioned them at all," Courtney replied. She looked up and met the sharp-eyed gaze of her former nanny. "What happened when my parents died? Were you with them that night, Janey?"

Silence filled the room. "I was there when they first got home," the old lady replied at last.

"Is it true they were…they were fighting?"

"It's true enough, as far as it goes." Jane's eyes lost their sharp focus on Courtney's face as she retreated into her memories of the past. "The police claimed that Ferne and Robert were fighting like cat and dog when they left the set of *Snow Flight* that night. There were a dozen people ready to swear that Robert had threatened to kill his wife."

"In one of the accounts of the murder, I read he pulled an ice ax from a box of props on the set of the movie," Courtney whispered.

"Well, maybe Robert threatened to kill her on the set, but I was there when they got home, and by that time I can tell you they weren't fighting for real anymore. Robert wasn't even pretending to be angry. Ferne was still shouting and storming about the place, but we all knew it was an act. When I came into the living room to let them know I was leaving—it was a Wednesday and my regular night off— Ferne was in the act of throwing a vase at Robert. Taking care to miss him, of course. Your dad winked at me, then put his arm around your mom and whispered something in her ear. I can see her now, pretending to be too mad to listen, but the color running up into her cheeks and your dad laughing down at her. She stormed upstairs and slammed the door of their bedroom, but Robert and I both knew she was waiting for him to come after her."

"And did he go?"

"He went into your room to say good-night to you first, but you were asleep."

"Asleep! How could any child sleep through all that?"

Jane laughed. "You were used to the way the pair of them carried on. That household was never quiet, always some grand drama or other going on. In a way I wish you *had* woken up, because then I'd have stayed and they'd never have been killed, that's for sure."

Courtney clasped the old woman's shaking hands. "There was no way you could have known what would happen," she said softly.

"No, there wasn't, and that's what I told myself over and over. They'd stopped fighting by the time I left, and that I'll swear to. Besides, they both loved you to distraction, and your dad would no more have killed your mother, knowing that you were in the house, than he would have flown over the moon. And that's why I'll never forgive Amelia for what she said at the inquest."

Courtney was shocked by Jane's vehemence. "Amelia? You mean my mother's sister? What did she say?"

"She claimed your mother always had a violent, ungovernable temper, and that Robert was often provoked by her to the point where he didn't know what he was doing. She said she always expected one of their fights to end in a tragedy, and from the arguments she'd heard, it was a miracle they hadn't ended up killing each other sooner. Of course, I said different and so did some other witnesses, but the judge chose to believe Amelia's story. After all, she was Ferne's sister, and she supposedly knew Ferne better than anybody else."

Courtney wrinkled her brow in bewilderment. "But what interest would she have in claiming my father killed my mother if she didn't believe it?"

"I never could figure that out, or I'd have said something. But to my mind, Amelia was flat-out jealous. Once she fell in love with that dreadful young man, she wasn't rational anymore. She was nearly forty, you know, and I don't think she'd ever been in love before. She was obsessed. And, of course, she was terrified she'd lose him to Ferne.''

Courtney's heart missed a beat. Aunt Amelia? Aunt Amelia of the Victorian morals and total disdain for men had been obsessively in love with a ''dreadful young man?''

''I don't understand,'' she said slowly. ''Do you mean that my aunt and my mother were both in love with the same man?''

''Your mother wasn't in love with anybody except her husband,'' Jane insisted. ''But Amelia couldn't see two inches beyond her own infatuation. She thought the sun rose and set on that horrible man, so it never occurred to her your mother hadn't the faintest interest in him. Mind you, I'm not saying *he* didn't fancy your mother. He was a young man with his eye to the main chance, that one was, and he'd have enjoyed having one of the world's greatest movie stars in love with him. Everybody else on that film set was so busy watching Pauline Powers and Robert Danvers they never noticed how Nick Harris was trying to insinuate himself with Ferne Hilton. Actors can be so self-absorbed, it's unbelievable what they miss.''

''Nick Harris!'' Courtney jumped up from her seat as a dozen pieces of the puzzle fell into place. ''You mean Aunt Amelia was in love with an actor called *Nick Harris*? And Nick Harris was in love with my mother?''

Jane seemed taken aback. ''Amelia came out to Aspen to stay with your parents, and she fell in love with Nick almost at first sight. Of course, he was wonderful to look at, I'll grant you that much. Handsome as the devil, with startling blue eyes and thick dark hair, but I never did trust him. I've had his sort as children. They're the ones who never get caught with their hands in the cookie jar, but you know they're the ones who've actually been there.''

Holding her breath, Courtney asked her next question. "Do you think my mother gave Nick any reason to suppose she was attracted to him?"

"Of course not," Jane said quickly. Too quickly.

"Somebody told me that tension on the *Snow Flight* set was running pretty high. My father and Pauline Powers were having an affair. Don't you think my mother may have decided to take her revenge?"

"Ferne was hurt by Robert's philandering," Jane said quietly. "Pauline Powers was young and beautiful and talented. I guess it's possible Ferne may have turned to Nick. Lord knows, I'm sure he was willing to make himself available. But if she slept with him at all, it was only once. She would never have hurt Amelia by having a full-blown affair with Nick. He just wasn't important enough to her. Robert was her life."

A tap at the door heralded the return of the nurse with a pot of herb tea and a plate of oatmeal cookies. Realizing that Janey looked tired, Courtney deliberately directed their conversation into less exhausting topics. She listened as Jane talked about her grandchildren; in exchange, she told her briefly about her own career as a professional skier.

The old lady was visibly tiring when the nurse came in to remove the tea tray. The nurse threw a conspirator's glance in Courtney's direction. "Mr. Tanner has come back, Ms Long. He's waiting for you in the visitors' lounge whenever you're ready to leave."

"Thanks." Courtney nodded her understanding, then turned back. "Janey, I've so much enjoyed visiting with you, but I guess it's time for me to go. I hope I didn't bore you talking about old times."

Jane Grislechy smiled. "My dear, when you're my age, talking about the good old days is about the only pleasure a body has left. Please come and see me again, and we'll talk some more."

"I will." Courtney kissed the old lady's cheek. "Janey, I've one more quick question. Do you by any chance know what happened to Nick Harris after the filming on *Snow Flight* stopped? Is he still acting?"

"I seem to remember hearing that he'd finished with acting and started producing," Jane commented slowly. "Somebody told me he was much better behind the camera than he was in front of it, for all he was so good-looking."

"He produced movies? In Hollywood?"

Jane wrinkled her brow worriedly. "I can't remember, it was all so long ago. Drat getting old! Didn't somebody tell me he was in New York, working for television?"

Courtney swallowed hard. "What do you think, Janey? Is there any chance he worked on one of the daytime soaps?"

"A soap?" The old lady sighed in relief. "Yes, that's what they told me. He directs one of those soaps about doctors and lawyers working in a city hospital. I never watch it myself, but I know it's very popular."

Courtney squeezed the old lady's hands very tight. "Janey, *Thank you*. I can't tell you how much help you've been to me."

"I wish I could remember the name of his show."

"I believe it's called *Search for Love*, and thank you again, Janey."

"My pleasure, Didi, you know it was. You'd better run along now, dear. You don't want to keep your young man waiting. Men are always so impatient."

The nurse apologized as soon as they were in the hallway. "I'm afraid I told a little untruth, Ms Long. Your friend isn't here yet, but Mrs. Grislechy tires so easily these days, and I didn't want to overtax her strength."

Courtney managed to murmur something polite. She would burst if she couldn't soon tell Justin that Nick Harris was probably the director on Linda's soap. Surely, with all the nformation they had now, they ought to be able to track the nan down in a matter of minutes?

"Why don't you step outside?" the nurse suggested. "The un's quite warm, and we really are proud of our fall flowers. need to persuade Mrs. Grislechy to take a nap, but if you tick close to the path, Mr. Tanner is sure to see you as he walks up from the parking lot."

Courtney strolled outside. The front gardens were pretty out nowhere near as extensive as the grounds at the rear, and he seemed to have the place to herself. Absently admiring he display of bronze and gold chrysanthemums, she mulled over the information Janey had given her. It was strange that Justin hadn't recognized Nick's name, she thought. Linda nust have mentioned her director's name a dozen times in he ordinary course of conversation. How could Justin have forgotten it?

Unless, of course, Nick Harris was no longer calling himelf Nick Harris. Maybe he'd changed names when he changed careers. He seemed to like pseudonyms.

Courtney sat down on a bench close to the side flagstone oath, screwing her eyes shut against the sun. Unbidden, the ist the detective had prepared for her sprang into her mind with crystal clarity. Nick Harris's name stood out, almost as f it was in boldface. And there next to it the elusive note. "*Nick Harris,*" the detective had written. "*Actor and later successful TV producer. Legally changed his name to Harvey Nicholson twenty years ago.*"

Harvey Nicholson. The name had an elegant, *Great Gatsby* sort of ring to it. Suddenly it seemed imperative to be in touch with Justin. She'd go back to the lobby and call him, if she could find Doug Mordern's phone number.

She jumped up from the bench and ran full tilt into the arms of an elderly, white-haired priest. Something cold, hard and round pressed against her waist. Her body stiffened seconds before her mind recognized the truth.

"Harvey!" she exclaimed in a hoarse whisper. "Oh, my God! How did you follow us here?"

Chapter Fifteen

"So you discovered who I am," he remarked conversationally. "I always knew you'd find out eventually. Start walking, Didi, and don't stop until we reach the parking lot."

The sun shone with friendly warmth, flowers nodded in the autumn breeze, and a bird chirped in a nearby tree. The scene was idyllic, but for the gun shoved hard against her waist. Desperate, Courtney strove to reason with him.

"Uncle Nick, there are people all over the gardens, and one of them could come by at any minute. You can't kill me here; you'll be arrested."

"Nobody will come. They're all going inside for lunch. Naturally I checked to make sure we were alone."

"Uncle Nick, for God's sake, you don't need to kill me!"

"Of course I must kill you." He sounded offended by her lack of understanding. "I didn't want to, but you've left me no choice. Everything would have been fine if you'd only stayed in Walnut Park."

"But if you hadn't approached me that day in Aspen, none of this would have happened. I'd never have realized you had anything to do with my parents' murder!"

"You wrote all those inquisitive letters, Didi. Once I discovered you were alive, I couldn't afford to take any risks. You saw me that night, you know."

"But I didn't! I didn't see you!"

"You saw the gun in my hand and you saw Robert hur
himself toward me. And you were a very precocious child.'

Courtney pressed her hand to her mouth. "Yes," she whispered, horrific memories crushing in upon her. "My father
was struggling with you in the bedroom. My mother was
hiding behind him. That's when my father shouted at me to
run away—just before you fired the gun."

"You see, you're remembering everything." Harvey
shook his head more in sorrow than in anger. "Please keep
walking, Didi, we're taking far longer than we should to
reach the parking lot."

A dreadful sense of unreality slowed her steps. She needed
to think.... It was lunchtime, but surely *somebody* had to be
in the front gardens. "Why did you kill my parents?" she
asked.

"Move, Didi. I know what you're doing!" The words
burst out, revealing a fine edge of hysteria. "You hope if I
keep talking, somebody will come and save you. But they
won't. I told you—I made sure nobody was around."

"You're a very intelligent man," Courtney said, trying to
restore his calm. "Anybody can see how smart you are.
That's why I want you to tell me what happened the night
my parents died. You can explain it to me so it makes sense.
After all, it doesn't matter what you tell me. Nobody else
will ever know."

"Maybe it *is* time somebody knew the truth about Ferne
and Robert." Harvey's voice became contemplative. "They
deserved to die, you know. They were cruel and heartless
people. Ferne used me when she wanted to make Robert
jealous and then she discarded me. Tossed me aside as if I
had no feelings at all."

"Perhaps she wanted to be loyal to her husband."

"He didn't deserve her. He was a mindless jock." Anger
laced Harvey's voice. "I was the man who could have
changed Ferne into the woman she was meant to be. But she

wouldn't listen. She never gave us the chance to be alone together. When she and Robert fought that night on the set, I thought she'd finally turn to me for help. Amelia kept nagging me to stay home with her, but I went to Ferne's chalet anyway, and waited for that interfering nurse to leave. I climbed in through the kitchen window and went upstairs. Ferne was struggling on the bed, trying to get away from Robert. I tried to rescue her, but Robert laughed at me, and Ferne suggested I should trot on home to Amelia. Trot home.'' His lips curled over the bitter words. ''As if I were a tame donkey or something. Couldn't she see I was more of a man than Robert? I was the best-looking man on the set; everybody said so.'' Satisfaction crept into his voice. ''They stopped laughing when I pulled the gun from the dresser. They'd forgotten it was there, but I hadn't. Amelia told me about it once and I never forget anything I'm told.''

''You killed my parents because they *laughed* at you?''

''Ferne was a whore. She deserved to die. When she ended our affair, she tried to put the blame on me, saying I should be loyal to her sister. But Amelia knew I was years younger than she was. Amelia had no right to expect me to be faithful.''

Courtney's stomach churned nauseatingly, but she realized the pressure of the gun against her waist had lessened while Uncle Nick spoke. Not Uncle Nick, she corrected herself mentally. Harvey. Harvey Nicholson. Did she have a chance of escape? Could she manage to twist around and knock the gun out of his hand before he fired, or was he too close? She could attempt to reason with him again, to point out that Justin Tanner was certain to finger him as the murderer. But she wasn't sure Harvey would respond to such logical arguments.

He led her into the tree-shaded parking lot, and the pressure of the gun against her waist increased once again. Time was running out, Courtney realized. She needed to think of something—fast.

Harvey nodded toward a royal-blue Buick Regal. "That's our car by the maple tree. I'm going to drive somewhere deserted, and then I'm going to shoot you. I'm sorry I'll have to squash your body into the trunk, but you'll be dead so it won't hurt. That's modern cars for you. None of them have a decent-sized trunk. I put plastic in there, too, so your blood won't make a mess on the rug."

"The car-rental company will be glad of that."

Harvey jabbed her angrily with the gun, and she clenched her teeth together in an effort to contain her rising panic. Threatening Harvey with the danger of discovery was clearly a waste of time. A man who could sound more apologetic about the size of his car trunk than the fact that he'd murdered your parents was past the point of caring about being found out and punished for his crimes. However remote her prospects of escape, escape was what she'd have to try for.

With icy calm, fully aware that she wasn't likely to succeed, she planned her moves. Breathing deeply, she listened to the rhythmic crunch of their footsteps on the gravel. The sun felt warm and life-giving on her back. How frustrating it would be if she died before she had the chance to tell Justin she loved him. At this moment the pride that had kept her silent over the past twenty-four hours seemed totally ridiculous.

The gun pressed with bruising force against her ribs. Harvey reached for the car door handle. *Now!* Courtney thought, and dropped to the ground, kicking out at Harvey's groin as she fell. She tried to roll under the car, but he smashed his foot onto her arm, grinding it into the gravel.

The wail of a rapidly approaching police siren drowned out her cry. The pressure of Harvey's foot slackened as a car roared into the parking lot, making the turn from the driveway on two wheels. It slammed to a halt in a squeal of tires and smell of burning rubber. The door burst open, and Justin came toward them at a run. Almost simultaneously a police car turned into the parking lot and screeched to a halt behind the Buick.

Justin ignored the young policeman exiting from the squad car. In a flying tackle aimed at Harvey's knees, he sent him crashing to the ground. Harvey's gun went off, exploding with shocking force into the branches of a nearby maple.

The acrid smell of burning gunpowder released Courtney's momentary paralysis. She crawled over to the fighting men and wrenched the gun from Harvey's hand before he had a chance to take aim.

"We make a great team," Justin said, panting. "But in future could we stick to easier routines?" He got to his feet, dragging Harvey with him and thrusting him against the side of the Buick. He ripped off Harvey's white-haired wig.

"You are Nicholson!" he muttered. "So Doug Mordern was right. Damn it all, I saw you in the lobby of the Hyatt last night and still didn't put two and two together."

Harvey shook his head dazedly, then clutched at his collar.

"It's going to take a hell of a lot more than a clerical collar to save you now," Justin said grimly. "My God, I'd like to kill you myself."

Harvey found the energy to curse foully, despite the fact that his nose was pouring blood and two of his front teeth were hanging only by shreds of skin. Courtney reached into her pocket for some tissues. Her hands were shaking so badly she could hardly hold the tissues.

"Here," she said to Justin. "He's dripping onto your jacket."

The young policeman jerked himself out of his trance and interposed himself between Justin and Harvey. "Er...thank you, miss, I'll take those." He wadded the tissues under Harvey's nose. "Here you are...um...Reverend, and I'll take that gun now, miss, if you don't mind."

He looked every day of nineteen years old and Courtney, feeling vaguely light-headed, had to repress the urge to pat him reassuringly. She obediently handed him the gun, which he tucked into his belt before turning to face Justin. His Adam's apple bobbed nervously.

"You, sir, are under arrest for failing to obey a police order to halt, and for traveling at seventy-nine miles per hour in a fifty-five-mile-per-hour zone. Let me see your driver's license, please."

"You can't arrest Justin for speeding!" Courtney cried. "He was saving me from being murdered."

Her words brought home the awful reality of what had nearly happened, and she crumpled against the side of the squad car, dry sobs racking her body.

Justin didn't even spare a glance for the poor policeman. He skirted the bloody-nosed Harvey and gathered Courtney tight in his arms. "Hush now, sweetheart. It's all over, everything. The mental hospital, the running, the police, the nightmares, it's all finished. You can put your past behind you, where it belongs. For the rest of your life, there'll be no more mysterious shadows."

Courtney hiccuped through her final few sobs. "I thought he was going to kill me before I ever told you I loved you—"

She stopped short, appalled at what she had admitted. Without the imminent threat of death hanging over her, pride reasserted all of its old power.

Justin cupped her face in his hands and looked down at her tenderly. "After what we shared last night, I guess I'd figured that out for myself. But it makes me feel great to hear you say it."

Still holding her, Justin spoke over his shoulder to the bewildered police officer. "This young lady is Courtney Long. The man with the bleeding nose is Harvey Nicholson, and this is the third time he's tried to kill her. He also murdered Courtney's parents twenty-two years ago. She was an eyewitness to that crime.''

"She's a whore!" Harvey screamed, taking them all by surprise. "She's a whore and it's my duty to kill her!" He lunged toward Courtney, his fingers curled into claws, biting the arm that Justin threw out to protect her.

The cop sprang into action. "That's enough, Mr. Nicholson," he said sharply, but it took several seconds before he and Justin could restrain Harvey's wild struggles.

A nurse came running into the parking lot. "We heard the siren," she said, staring goggle-eyed at the bleeding Harvey. "Has there been an accident?"

"Everything's under control," the policeman replied bravely. He mopped his sweating forehead with a handkerchief. Looking younger and more uncertain by the minute, he slipped a pair of handcuffs onto Harvey's wrists and attempted to caution him.

Harvey tossed his head, little flecks of spittle foaming at the corners of his mouth. Instinctively the nurse stepped forward and was pushed roughly away by Harvey's shoulder. She would have fallen if Justin hadn't moved swiftly to catch her. Harvey's voice rose to a violent shriek. "Ferne Hilton was a creature of the Devil, I tell you, and she's come back to live in Didi's body! Why won't you let me go? It's my duty to rid the world of women like Didi. My *duty*, do you understand? My duty!"

The nurse recoiled, and the policeman cast a harried glance toward the radio transmitter in his car. Handing out speeding tickets was usually easier than this. He mopped his brow for the second time and drew in a deep breath.

"I think you'd all better come with me," he said.

THE WEATHER IN New Hampshire was far colder than it had been in New York, although that was nothing unusual. Staring out of the parlor window, Courtney could see hints of

approaching winter in the scudding gray clouds and leafless
tree branches. This far north, fall was well and truly over.

The phone rang and she hurtled toward it, hoping it might
be Justin. It wasn't, of course. For the past four days, ever
since they'd parted at New York's La Guardia airport, it had
never been Justin.

Detective Sergeant somebody or other from the Bayside
Police Department introduced himself. She tried to listen at-
tentively as he informed her that Harvey Nicholson's brother,
Geoffrey Harris, had been arrested in California.

"Geoffrey's admitted to playing the roles of doctor and
judge for his brother, Miss Long, so now we have the evidence to tie in with another part of your story. We're pro-
gressing real fast on tying up all the loose ends."

"I'm glad."

"The captain asked me to inquire how things are going
with your own situation."

"Everything's working out really well." *Except Justin's
disappeared into the wilds of Colorado,* she amended silently. *I'll be in touch soon,* he'd said. But when was soon?
And how would he be in touch? With a quick message
scrawled on a card at Christmas?

Doing her best to sound cheerful, Courtney added, "My
lawyer called this morning and said the official paperwork
has already gone through, confirming my release from Walnut Park."

The detective chuckled. "They'd probably agree to hand
carry the papers to you, they're so darn relieved you're not
planning to sue them. But don't tell anybody I said so."

"I won't," she promised.

"To get back to the subject of Geoffrey." The detective
sounded formal again. "He insists he had no idea of the true
purpose behind the impersonations, and we're inclined to believe him. He's an alcoholic, and he was off the wagon when
his brother approached him. People who know him all agree

that when Geoffrey's on a binge, he'd believe any story his brother cared to feed him. In fact, he seems to remember only the barest details of what actually went on.''

"Will he be prosecuted?"

"Drunk or not, it's an offense to impersonate a judge or a member of the medical profession, but we may let him off the hook if he agrees to give evidence against his brother. That's up to the D.A.'s office. At the moment it looks as if Mr. Nicholson may be declared mentally incapable of standing trial.''

"Well, thanks for letting me know Geoffrey's been found. I really appreciate your department's keeping me informed.''

"My pleasure. To tell you the truth, this is the most interesting case I've had in years. I've seen your mother on television, on the late-night movies, and she was a wonderful actress. It's an honor to help set the record straight about her murder.''

"Thank you," Courtney said, and hung up the phone. All the detectives kept telling her how interesting this case was. From their point of view, that might be true, but from her perspective it had been eight months of a waking nightmare.

She looked around the cozy, old-fashioned parlor of her aunt's home, knotting her hands into a white-knuckled ball to prevent herself from reaching out and smashing all the neat little china ornaments so carefully set out on neat little cherry-wood tables. She had always loved this room and its antique knickknacks. Now she hated it. It represented everything phony in the life she and her aunt had led together.

In some ways the bitterest part of finding out the truth about her parents' murder had been the realization that her aunt—that monument to New England virtue—had built their relationship on a foundation of self-serving lies.

Courtney stared into the empty fire grate, wondering if she had enough energy to bring wood in from the back porch and light a fire. She decided she hadn't. These past few days, she didn't have energy for much. If only Justin hadn't left her with no more than a brief word about taking care of some urgent business....

She cut off the thought and rubbed her arms, trying to dispel the chill. It was painful to accept that the woman who had instilled in Courtney rigid precepts of honor, truth and personal dignity had been a woman weak enough to lie to save the life of the man she loved. It was Amelia's testimony that had condemned Robert as his wife's murderer, just as it was Amelia's testimony that had shielded Harvey Nicholson from suspicion.

Her thoughts were beginning to chase the same narrowing circle they had already chased far too many times before, and Courtney gave an impatient glance at her watch. Four-thirty. She hadn't eaten lunch yet. For the umpteenth time she considered the possibility of picking up the phone and calling Justin. She rejected it again until it dawned on her how foolish she was being. With Harvey's gun at her back, she'd realized how crazy it was to let pride get in the way of things that were truly important. How many times did she need to be taught the same lesson?

Her decision made, Courtney hurried to the phone and dialed Justin's number with shaking fingers.

From the very first ring, she knew the house was empty. Perversely she let the phone ring on and on, unwilling to break the connection, however tenuous. Suddenly it seemed incomprehensible that she'd let four whole days go by without attempting to speak to him. What in the world had she been trying to prove, she wondered.

The buzz of the doorbell interrupted her. She frowned and ignored it. The buzz came again, louder and more insistent.

Courtney slammed the phone into the cradle and marched to the door. She whipped it open. "Yes?"

Justin grinned, his gray eyes warm, his smile heart-stopping. "I'm glad to see you, too, sweetheart. You look great. That pink color suits you."

"Where've you been?" Courtney demanded. "Why didn't you call me? I've been worried out of my mind." She closed her eyes. That hadn't been what she meant to say at all. She'd meant to say, *Justin, thank God you're here. Don't ever leave me again and, please let's go to bed right away.*

Her questions didn't seem to annoy him. His eyes gleamed with laughter as he stepped into the narrow entrance hall, bringing the crisp tang of winter with him. He closed the door and looked around appreciatively, stashing his luggage in a corner, next to the coatrack.

He dropped a casual kiss on one of her cheeks. "Hey," he said softly, "you sound hot and bothered. I figured we could have lots of fun living in sin, but if you're going to nag anyway, I guess we may as well get married."

"M-married?"

He framed her face with his hands. "What do you say? Are you willing to take on a slightly battle-scarred computer jock who often forgets what day of the week it is when he's working on one of his pet problems?"

She swallowed over the huge lump in her throat. "Is that what happened? You went home to work on a computer problem?"

"No," he said. "I went to Aspen to put my house on the market. I decided it had too many memories for both of us, and we needed to start somewhere fresh. Besides, I wanted to give you time to get yourself together again. I meant to stay away for a month. By last night I'd decided to hell with honor. Right now I'm into coercion and taking advantage of you when you're vulnerable."

Her heart was pounding with happiness. "You want to take advantage of me?" she murmured. "How do you plan to do that?"

He bent his head toward her mouth. "I hoped I might be

able to blow your mind with my lovemaking,'' he said huskily. ''That's what you do to me, and I thought it might work both ways. According to my master plan, around the third time we make love you'll be too far gone to protest when I tell you we're getting married next Friday.''

''Next Friday?'' she repeated with studied casualness.

''It seemed like a good day for a wedding. And my parents are free that weekend.''

''I see.'' Courtney cast down her eyes demurely. She removed herself from his grasp, and as if directing visitors on a house tour, pointed primly toward the stairs. ''My bedroom is the first door on the left, but I have only a single bed.''

Justin pulled her into his arms, kissing her with an intensity that shook them both. It was a very long time before he raised his head, and his gaze was unashamedly hungry. ''If we run,'' he said, ''we just may make it to your room before I tear your clothes off.''

They ran.

''DON'T MOVE,'' Courtney ordered sleepily. ''I'm too comfortable.''

''The fire will go out.'' Justin stroked her breast lightly, laughing softly when her nipple responded instantly to his touch. He closed the lapels of her robe. ''You'll get cold. We should have stayed in bed.''

''I can think of a way you could keep me warm.''

His mouth twisted. ''Honey, right now I'd say you're asking the impossible.''

She feigned dismay. ''A couple of little seduction scenes and you're exhausted, huh? That doesn't bode well for our married life.''

''At least you know the worst before you say *I do*.''

''I guess.'' With an exaggerated sigh, Courtney eased herself out of Justin's arms and leaned against the sofa. ''Go ahead, then, and build up the fire. I've made the supreme sacrifice of moving.''

Justin got lithely to his feet, belying any trace of exhaustion. Drowsy, senses replete with love, Courtney watched the firelight flicker over his features as he bent down to add two hefty logs to the flames. For the first time in her life, she knew what was meant by total contentment.

"More coffee?" she asked, when he came to sit down.

"Mmm. The way you make it could be addictive. Each cup tastes better than the last. I'm surprised Aunt Amelia kept Irish whiskey in the house.''

Courtney laughed. "She kept it especially for me. She said that I was entitled to one small indulgence so long as I didn't—'' Her voice broke. "Oh, God, she was such a damned hypocrite, and I loved her so much!''

Justin took the half-poured cup of coffee and set it on the table. "Courtney, you're being unfair to your aunt and cruel to yourself. Don't keep doubting her motives.''

"Why not?" she asked bitterly. "Amelia had a passionate affair with the man who murdered my parents. She lied through her teeth to protect him and then raised me to believe that it was a mortal sin if I fibbed about the tiniest thing. Every rule she drummed into me, she'd broken. Isn't that hypocrisy? Isn't it fair to despise her?''

"Sometimes we have to break a rule before we understand why it's important. Maybe that happened with your aunt.''

Courtney's mouth set in a stubborn line. "She could have told me the truth. She *owed* me the truth.''

"When you were four years old?" Justin asked. "You're being a little unrealistic, aren't you? And once she'd started telling the lies, how could she stop? I'd guess the murder of your parents totally changed her view of the world. The life she created for you here wasn't a lie, Courtney. It was the life she genuinely wanted to lead once she realized how disastrous her infatuation with Harvey Nicholson had been. If she kept urging caution and moderation and all the old New England virtues, it was because she'd seen what terrible consequences unbridled passion could have.''

Courtney stared into the fire for a long time before turning. "It's going to take me a while to straighten out all of my feelings about the past. Are you sure you're willing to bear with me while I work my problems through?''

"I'm sure," Justin said quietly. "I'm very sure. We'll just take it one day at a time, that's all.''

"You make it sound easy.''

"It is easy when you love somebody.''

There was the faintest hint of a question in his voice. She turned to him quickly. "Justin, I love you. That's one feeling I already have totally straightened out.''

"Good," he said. "So that's what we'll build on. We'll spend twenty-three hours a day strengthening our love. That leaves you one hour a day for the rest of your problems. The balance seems about right.''

"You haven't left any hours for sleep.''

"Excellent planning on my part. We have so many more productive ways of spending our time. Think what interesting children we're going to produce. They can all be mathematical prodigies during the week and ski champions on the weekend.''

She sat up very straight. "When did we discuss having children? Especially children in the plural.''

"Two seconds ago," he said placidly, hauling her against him. "And you told me it was a terrific idea.''

"I didn't hear me saying that.''

"Shockingly short memory you must have. We'll have to squeeze a few minutes out of each day to work on your problem." He leaned over and slowly untied the belt of her robe. "Mmm, did I ever mention to you that you have the world's sexiest nipples?''

She squirmed pleasurably against him. "Not that I recall.''

He pushed her robe open, his hand cupping her breast. "'Fraid that proves it, my darling. You have a terrible memory. I'll have to give you a quick refresher course in the delights of your body."

She wriggled away from the exquisite torment of his fingers, then leaned back against the pillows. She trailed her hand slowly down his rib cage, across the flat plane of his stomach, then stopped. He sucked in his breath, his entire body taut with anticipation.

Courtney looked up at him, her violet eyes sparkling with laughter. "I think I've forgotten what to do next."

He expelled his breath. "Witch. Don't worry. I'll show you what we have to do."

His mouth blazed against hers, lighting her body with the fire of his love. Laughter faded as passion mounted, drawing them closer and closer. She gave to him without restraint and demanded from him confidently, soaring to the ultimate heights, knowing that together they were finally free to walk out of the shadows of the past and into their future.

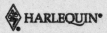

If you enjoyed what you just read,
then we've got an offer you can't resist!

Take 2 bestselling
love stories FREE!
Plus get a FREE surprise gift!

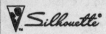

INTIMATE MOMENTS™

A mugging leaves attorney
Alexandra Spencer with a head
injury—and no recollection of her
recent divorce. Dylan Parker's
investigation into the not-so-random
attack is nothing compared to
the passion he feels for the woman
who once broke his heart. Can he
find answers before losing himself
to Alex—again?

MEMORIES
AFTER
MIDNIGHT

BY LINDA RANDALL WISDOM

Silhouette Intimate Moments #1409

DON'T MISS THIS THRILLING STORY,
AVAILABLE MARCH 2006 WHEREVER
SILHOUETTE BOOKS ARE SOLD.

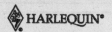